Shaw's left hand lay on the bar top, his fingertips near the wad of cloth, which was rolled and ready to stick into his ear, should this talk turn into a shoot-out. His right elbow lay propped on the bar edge, but his right hand hung loosely down toward his holstered Colt as if drawn there by instinct or predestination. "About your men . . . ," Shaw reminded him.

"Yeah," said Lowe, "I just want to hear it from you, make sure you or my man here ain't either one jerking my reins. He says you fired first."

"I never fired a shot," Shaw said in a quiet, restrained voice. "Did you check his gun?"

"Sure did," Earl Hardine cut in. "It was empty, still smoking. I even smelled it for good measure."

This was the opening Shaw wanted. His right hand streaked upward, his Colt leveled at Lowe's heart. The move came so fast, no one had caught it until it was too late. Then Shaw cocked his gun with a flick of his thumb and flipped it around sideways in his hand, the barrel pointing away from Lowe.

"Want to smell mine?" he said.

GUN COUNTRY

Ralph Cotton

A SIGNET BOOK

SIGNET
Published by New American Library, a division of
Penguin Group (USA) Inc., 375 Hudson Street,
New York, New York 10014, USA
Penguin Group (Canada), 90 Eglinton Avenue East, Suite 700, Toronto,
Ontario M4P 2Y3, Canada (a division of Pearson Penguin Canada Inc.)
Penguin Books Ltd., 80 Strand, London WC2R 0RL, England
Penguin Ireland, 25 St. Stephen's Green, Dublin 2,
Ireland (a division of Penguin Books Ltd.)
Penguin Group (Australia), 250 Camberwell Road, Camberwell, Victoria 3124,
Australia (a division of Pearson Australia Group Pty. Ltd.)
Penguin Books India Pvt. Ltd., 11 Community Centre, Panchsheel Park,
New Delhi - 110 017, India
Penguin Group (NZ), 67 Apollo Drive, Rosedale, North Shore 0632,
New Zealand (a division of Pearson New Zealand Ltd.)
Penguin Books (South Africa) (Pty.) Ltd., 24 Sturdee Avenue,
Rosebank, Johannesburg 2196, South Africa

Penguin Books Ltd., Registered Offices:
80 Strand, London WC2R 0RL, England

First published by Signet, an imprint of New American Library,
a division of Penguin Group (USA) Inc.

First Printing, March 2010
10 9 8 7 6 5 4 3 2 1

To Mary Lynn . . . of course.
And to James Earl Coots,
in appreciation of the Old West,
of rocky trails and a time gone by. . . .

Prologue

Three men—Madden Corio, his right-hand man, Bert Jordan, and a younger gunman named Willard Dance—sat atop their horses, gazing out across the Rio Grande. In the grainy dawn light a low wisp of fog skimmed the river's low, rocky banks. A tall heron stood, one thin leg raised beneath itself, seemingly as translucent as a ghost in the silver-gray swirl.

"This low water will be just about perfect for us," Corio remarked, noting the shallow river as it drifted along lazily in its bed. Behind them, the rest of the men stood saddling their horses, checking their shooting gear. A few men still lingered near a low, glowing fire. They finished their coffee and tossed back whatever whiskey and mescal they had leftover from the night before.

On the other side of the river, less than fifty yards away, a young boy watched them as his donkey stood in the water, drinking and swishing its ragged tail. The three horsemen stared back at the boy until he ducked his face, jerked on the lead rope and pulled the donkey back from the water's edge.

"Easy crossing for us is easy crossing for anybody on our trail," said Jordan.

"You mean the two border lawmen," Corio said bluntly.

"Yeah, that's who I mean," said Jordan, watching the boy turn the donkey and poke its rump with a short stick to get it moving.

"They've got lots of hombres like us spooked along both sides of the border," Dance commented.

"Not hombres like us, Willard," said Corio. "Hombres like us don't spook." He turned a stiff gaze toward the young gunman.

"I didn't mean it like that," Dance offered in a less confident tone.

"He knows how you meant it, Willard," Jordan cut in, sounding a little impatient with him. "Why don't you go help everybody get ready to move out?"

"Sure thing, Mr. Jordan," said Dance. He pulled his reins around quickly and rode away.

Jordan caught a gaze from Corio and said on Dance's behalf, "He's a good man, Madden. I just need to set a fire under his ass now and then—keeps him on his best game."

Corio gazed back out across the river, putting the matter aside. Now that they were alone, he said in a lowered voice, "I figured how we best deal with the soldiers once we cut the train away from them."

Jordan grinned. "I knew you would."

Corio said, "I've also solved the problem of moving

all that hardware across the hill country without losing it back to the Union cavalry, or the *federales*."

"The hill country?" said Jordan. "So we're not even crossing the river near here?"

"No," Corio said under his breath, "that was all said for Dance's benefit. He doesn't need to hear my real plan—not yet anyway. But you do. We're crossing the badlands, through the hill country and across the desert flats."

Jordan gave a thin smile. "If Easy John Lupo can move a wagon of gold across the hills and desert the way he did, I suppose we're up to moving stolen guns the same way," he said.

"Don't forget, Easy John had the American lawmen helping him," offered Corio. "I expect once they hear we've taken all those guns and ammunition, they'll be all over us. But we're not going that deep into Old Mex. We won't have to. We've got something Bocanero wants so bad he'll come to us to get it."

"Yeah? What's that?" Jordan asked.

"You'll see when we get there," said Corio. "But it's the latest in military armament."

"You amaze the hell out of me, the way you come up with jobs like this," Jordan said. "Are we still meeting my brothers in Nozzito after this gun deal?"

"Absolutely," said Corio. "This gun deal just gives us the money we need to set up some bigger jobs. Both your brothers are in as far as I'm concerned. We need fast guns like you Jordan brothers." He paused and added thoughtfully, "Provided you can keep them under control, that is."

Jordan gave a proud smile. "Between the two of them, Grayson and Tolan have killed more men than small-pox. But they're as loyal to me as hounds. Nobody messes with the Jordans."

"Good enough for me," said Corio. "Now form the men up and move them out. We'll rendezvous in a week up at Hueco Pass. I'm riding on into Old Mex to make sure our buyer is ready and eager to take delivery."

As Corio turned his horse, Jordan asked, "I expect you don't want to say why we're hitting the army train all the way up in the badlands?"

"You'll see why when the time comes," Corio said with a tight-lipped smile. "I think you'll like seeing how it's going to happen." He finished turning his horse and rode south along the shallow river's edge.

As soon as Corio had ridden out of sight, Jordan smiled to himself. He turned his horse and rode back a few yards to where Willard Dance stood putting out the smoldering campfire with his boot. The rest of the men stood beside their readied horses. They looked on expectantly as Jordan reined his horse down.

"I never seen a bunch of men run out of whiskey as quick as this," a red-faced Kansas gunman named Irish Tommie Wade said under his breath. He wore a bat-tered derby hat and fingerless black jersey gloves. "I hope I haven't mistakenly taken up with a consortium of drunkards and malingerers." He gave a slight tip of his hat.

"It's likely you may have . . . but I'm speaking only for myself," a former James-Younger Gang member named Robert Hooks replied in the same lowered voice. He gave a tip of his battered hat in return. Muffled laughter rippled across the men, then settled.

"All right, everybody listen up," said Jordan, settling the men even more. "We're riding up to Hueco Pass. That's where we'll make our play. I hope you enjoyed your drinking. There'll be no more of it until we've completed our job."

"Mind telling us why we're riding all the way to Hueco Pass?" Tommie Wade asked.

"You'll see why when the time comes," said Jordan, repeating Corio's words. "From here on, none of yas separate yourselves from this group any longer than it takes to relieve yourself. If you do you've broken our oath of secrecy. It'll be the responsibility of everybody here to shoot you dead." He looked solemnly at each of the twelve men, then added, "Is that clearly understood?"

Tommie Wade leveled his battered derby hat and asked bluntly, "Do you and Corio treat all your regular men this way, or is this just aimed at us newcomers?"

Jordan turned a glance toward a gunman named Harvey Lemate. "Harve . . . ?" he said.

Lemate took a step away from his horse, his reins still in hand, and said loud enough for all the men to hear him, "I've been riding with Corio's Black River Guerrillas since right after the war, when he got started. It's always been this way before a big job."

"I'm only making sure I get the gist of things, laddie," Irish Tommie said with a curt nod. "There's no offense intended."

"Nor has any offense been taken ... *yet*," Jordan said in a cool, even voice.

Tommie Wade touched a fingerless jersey-gloved hand to his frayed hat brim.

Jordan's eyes stayed riveted on Irish Tommie Wade a moment longer, then moved across the rest of the men. "All of you came into this knowing it's not going to be a quick cash-in-hand job. When this job is over you're going to have enough money to keep yourselves flush for a long time. But until it's over, you do as you're told, stick close together and account for your time. We've got lawmen riding both sides of the border now, hunting down men like us. We play our cards close to our vests."

Willard Dance stepped into his saddle. He turned his horse and nudged it closer to Jordan. Lemate did the same. The rest of the men followed suit. "All right," said Robert Hooks, repeating a line he always said to himself before riding off to commit a robbery, "go make yourself rich. . . ."

As Hooks stepped into his saddle and turned his horse toward the forming column of men, Tommie Wade sidled his horse closer to him and said in a quiet voice, "What about these lawmen he's talking about? Do you know who they are?"

Hooks eyed him skeptically. "Where have you been lately?"

"Nowhere near here," said Tommie. "I've been laid up at the Red Wall the past year, keeping my neck away from a noose. Haven't kept much track of what's gone on along the border." The two rode on at the end of the column of riders.

"Up at Hole-in-the-wall, eh?" said Hooks, still eying him. "How's ole Denver Hale getting along? It's been over two years since I last saw him."

"Two years—no kidding?" said Tommie. "Bet he didn't have much to say two years ago, did he?"

"Why's that?" Hooks said coolly.

"Because he's been dead almost *three* years," said Tommie.

Hooks gave a sly grin. "Can't blame a man for being too careful these days, can you?"

"I expect not," said Tommie. The two relaxed a little as they rode on. "Now, what about the two lawmen everybody's so damn worried about? Should my soul quake with trepidation?"

"You'll have to decide that," said Hooks. He looked him up and down and added as they rode along, "The Mexican government and the U.S. have lawmen working together, trying to put some of us folks out of business."

"Mexican lawmen don't bother me much, unless they're standing upwind," Tommie said with a wry grin.

"There's a U.S. marshal by the name of Dawson . . . Crayton Dawson," said Hooks. "He's comes out of Texas. Ever heard of him?"

"Texas, huh . . . ? I believe I may have," Tommie said, considering the name. "But notice that I'm still not quaking."

"Duly noted." Hooks went on. "Dawson rides with a deputy named Jedson Caldwell. They call Caldwell *the Undertaker*." His grin widened a bit. "Frightened now?"

"I'm holding out fairly well," said Tommie.

"I believe Caldwell really was an undertaker before he started walking behind a badge," said Hooks. "So don't make more of it than that."

"Good advice," said Tommie. "I won't let it concern me." As he spoke, he reached his fingerless jersey gloves inside his coat and eased out a small battered whiskey flask. After looking around warily, he passed the flask over to Hooks, unseen. "Here, you look like a man who enjoys a little eye-opener."

"I hope you're not about to get us both a harsh scolding," Hooks said in a mock tone. He held his hat down to conceal his hand and face as he drank from the flask.

"I allow we've both lived through harsh scolding before," Tommie offered. He took back the flask. "Here's to us," he said guardedly. He took a sip, capped it and buried it back inside his coat. "Now then, is that the whole of it, this marshal and this undertaker?"

"No, there's a third one," said Hooks. "He rides with them only now and then."

"Oh dear," Tommie said in a mock tone, "yet another one to keep me all upset? And who might this third tough hombre be?"

Hooks replied quietly, staring straight ahead, "Third one's name is Shaw . . . Lawrence Shaw."

Tommie almost stopped his horse before catching

himself. "*Fast* Larry Shaw . . . ?" he said, keeping himself from sounding too stricken by the name. "The fastest gun alive . . . ?"

"Yep," Hooks said, hearing the difference in Tommie's voice. "I figured you'd heard of that one."

"Jesus . . ." Tommie fell silent.

After a moment Hooks asked him sidelong, "What's wrong, Irish Tommie? Cat got your tongue?"

"Damn . . . ," Tommie said under his breath.

PART 1

Chapter 1

———

Badlands, New Mexico

In the cold, wind-stirred desert night, his senses had abandoned him for a time; it was as if he'd vanished into the swirling emptiness around him. He might have fallen asleep in his saddle for all he knew. During the missing time the pain inside his head had disappeared into a warm, furry blackness. But with the first dark silvery streak of dawn, his senses had returned, and with them the insistent pain.

He rode on, his aching head bowed and turned against a moaning wind.

He knew who he was, he reminded himself. He knew his name, his age, flashes of details and particulars of his life. Oh yes, he knew. . . . But he'd had to grapple with it for a time in order to get the information back clearly into his mind. For a time when his memory had come and gone, he'd almost hoped he might lose it altogether. But that was not to be the case, he told himself.

At daylight Lawrence Shaw, aka Fast Larry, aka the Fastest Gun Alive, rode upward into Colinas Secas from the southwest, off the dusty badlands floor. He wore a battered stovepipe hat and a long, ragged swallow-tailed coat. A broad, faded red bandanna mantled the bridge of his nose and had shielded most of his face against the sharp wind-driven sand. Behind him the cold desert breeze still moaned in the grainy light like a field of lost souls.

At the edge of town Shaw stopped his speckled barb and jerked the bandanna down below his chin, stirring a rise of dust on his chest. Beneath him the barb chuffed and shook itself off. "Easy, boy," he murmured to the dust-coated animal. "We'll get you fed and stalled first thing."

He patted a gloved hand to the barb's withers. Dust billowed. At a hitch rail in front of a dimly lit saloon, Shaw eyed three horses huddled together with their heads lowered against the cold wind. He saw shadows looming in the saloon's dusty front window. With pain throbbing in his head, he veered the barb away from the saloon and rode on at a walk. He had no idea who the men inside the saloon were, but he had no doubt they were the sort of men who could lead him where he needed to be.

Inside the saloon, three gunmen stood sharing a bottle of rye whiskey. Seeing the stranger turn his horse away, one of the gunman, an Arkansan named Thurman Thornton, said proudly, "Well, well, it appears this drifter doesn't desire our company." He wiped his wrist across his lips and passed the bottle sidelong to the other two.

"I suspect he might be faint of heart," a gunman named Bell Mason replied, "if just the sight of our horses scares him."

"Suppose we ought to wake up Dex and tell him? See what he wants us to do?" Thornton asked.

"Naw, Dex is passed out with the whore," replied a third gunman named Roland Stobble. He took the bottle, threw back a drink and passed it on.

Beside him Bell Mason took the bottle and said, "Hell, he'll just tell us to run this scarecrow out of town. It looks like we already done that." He gave a dark grin. "We didn't even need permission," he added with sarcasm, and threw back a drink.

"Yeah," said Stobble, eyeing Thornton with a sour expression, "do you ask Dex's permission to go to the jake, or do you figure that out on your own?"

Thornton ignored the remark. Still looking out the dusty window, he said, "I can send any scarecrow hightailing. I don't need no help or permission."

The three watched the ragged dust-covered stranger appraise a seedy hotel from his saddle as he rode on past the saloon and turned the speckled barb toward the livery barn at a tired walk.

"Ah, look, he's going to attend to his horse," said Stobble in a mocking tone. "Ain't that commendable? You got to always admire a man who puts his horse's needs ahead of his own." He chuckled, grabbed the bottle back from Mason and took a drink.

"I'll tend his horse," Thornton threatened, staring out toward the livery barn as Shaw and the speckled barb walked out of sight. He adjusted his coat and started to stroll toward the front door.

"Whoa, hang on," said Stobble, blocking his way with a raised arm. "What's your hurry? It's raw and cold out there. Listen to that wind."

"So?" said Thornton, stopping abruptly.

"So let's let him come to us, if he gets his nerve up." Stobble shrugged.

"What if he doesn't?" said Thornton. "What if he goes someplace else?"

"Where the hell else is he going to go?" Mason cut in, sounding agitated by Thornton's slow-wittedness.

"What's wrong with you, Thurman?" Stobble asked Thornton with a goading smile. "Are you still floating around on them cactus buttons?"

"Never mind what I am or ain't floating on," said Thornton. He settled back into place and let his coat fall open again. "When he does get here, I'll send him hightailing out of town—you watch."

"Oh, we'll watch, sure enough," said Stobble. "You can bet on that."

"Send him hightailing?" said Mason. "Hell, that ain't nothing. My poor old grandma could send him hightailing. I thought we might get a chance to see some fireworks."

"I can do that too," said Thornton, confidently. "It makes me no difference."

"You mean you don't mind killing a man before breakfast?" Stobble goaded.

"Before breakfast, after supper, during dinner, I don't care," Thornton said. "Dex said not to let any strangers into town. Far as I'm concerned, I'll drop this saddle tramp when he walks through the door."

"All right, that's more like it," said Stobble. "To hell with sending a man *hightailing*." He gave Mason a knowing grin. "Show us some action."

Inside the livery barn, Shaw slapped his hands up and down his coat sleeves; the speckled barb shook itself off again, chuffed and blew as dust swirled about them.

From inside a stall a man grumbled and coughed and stood up from a blanket spread on a pile of fresh hay. He held a flickering lantern up against the morning gloom. "Damn it," he said, "drag yourself and that dirty cayuse out back and dust him down! I've swallowed too much of this blasted desert as it is."

Shaw turned and faced him, his swallow-tailed coat hanging open down his chest, his big bone-handled Colt standing tall and clean in its holster. He stared at the liveryman without saying a word.

Uh-oh . . . With an appraising look, noting both the gun and the stranger's cool, confident presence, the liveryman said in an apologetic voice, "Pay me no mind, Mister." He chastised himself out loud. "Damn it, Radler. I expect swallowing a little dirt is better than having a bunch of it shoveled into my face."

"Is that your name—*Radler*?" Shaw asked the old man quietly. As he spoke he opened his coat enough to reach into a vest pocket and pull out a gold coin.

"Yes, sir, it is," said the old man. "Caywood Radler,

if you want to know the whole of it. You can call me Radler. Most folks do." He caught himself and added nervously, "That is, unless you prefer calling me something else. I'm not what you call a stickler on formality. I go along with most anything."

Shaw flipped him the gold coin. "This is for me and the horse. I want a stall big enough for both of us while I'm here."

Radler caught the coin with his free hand and gave him a puzzled look. "Mister, we've got a hotel in Colinas Secas, a saloon and brothel too. A man ain't held to sleeping in a stable." He looked Shaw over in the thin glow of the lantern.

"I saw the hotel on my way here," Shaw said in a flat tone. "I'll take the livery."

"I do pride myself on running a good, clean livery barn," the old man said as he stepped away and hung the lantern on a post. He hefted a wooden water bucket, carried it to the barb and set it down before the horse's probing muzzle. He slipped the horse's bit from its mouth, lifted its bridle and let it draw thirstily from the bucket. "But I don't want you to feel like I said anything against the hotel."

Shaw only stared at him.

"A fellow has to be careful what he says these days in Colinas Secas . . . or Dry Hills if you prefer not to call the town by its Mex name," he continued. "Either name you want to call it is all right by me. I just don't want you to get the wrong idea—"

"What's got you strung so tight, hostler?" Shaw asked, cutting him off.

"I don't want no trouble, is all, sir," the liveryman said. "I saw what happens to anybody who gets in you boys' way—"

"*Us boys . . . ?*" Shaw asked, again cutting the frightened man short. "What *boys* is that?"

"Why, Dexter Lowe's boys, of course," said the old man. He blinked in surprise. "Who else's boys would I mean?"

"Let's stop asking each other the same question," said Shaw. He began to get the picture. "I'm not one of Dexter Lowe's men." He studied the old man's nervous watery eyes. "Is Lowe and his men holding up here in Colinas Secas?" Dexter Lowe and his gang were one of the countless gangs that Shaw, U.S. marshal Crayton Dawson and Deputy Jedson Caldwell had been sent to break up along the border badlands.

Radler looked stunned, but he refused to offer a reply. "Look, Mister, I'm an old man. I've got no business meddling where I don't belong. Lowe told us all what would happen if we said anything about him and his boys being here . . . so I *ain't* saying nothing. For all I know you might be here to see if I can keep my mouth shut, like I was told."

"I understand," said Shaw, the sound of his own voice making his head throb deeper in pain. He thought about the battered U.S. deputy marshal badge he carried in his pocket. "Now, what about that stall?" As he spoke he loosened the barb's saddle cinch, lifted the saddle from the horse's back and slung it over a rack while the barb continued drinking. He knew he could reach into his pocket to pull out his badge and ease his mind, but he wasn't going to do that, he told himself.

Showing Radler he was a lawman would settle the old liveryman's fear, but keeping the fact a secret seemed to always work to his advantage, he reminded himself, turning and pulling his ragged dust-coated bedroll down from behind his saddle.

"This one here is freshly cleaned," Radler said, gesturing toward the closest stall standing with its door open, its floor partly covered with clean straw.

"I'll take it," Shaw said. He could feel Radler's curious eyes on him as he beat the rolled blanket against a support post, then unrolled it and stepped inside the stall.

"Yes, sir," said the old man. "A fellow wants to sleep in the barn, who am I to wonder about another man's peculiarities?" He stood watching until the barb raised its dripping muzzle from the empty water bucket. Giving the horse a nudge on its rump, he followed it inside the stall, where Shaw stood fashioning his sleeping blanket into a hammock.

"Now I've seen it all," he said, watching as Shaw tied the gathered blanket ends along the stall rail. "Mister, you must be a man who has slept his share of nights with heathen animals."

Shaw turned around, sat down in the drooping hammock and leaned against the wall planks. "You don't know the half of it," he said tiredly. He took off the battered stovepipe hat carefully and pegged it on a post atop the rail. The liveryman winced at the sight of a bloodstained bandage covering the top of Shaw's head.

"Lord God . . . !" the old man said. "Was you scalped?"

"Scalping would have been a treat," Shaw said. He touched his fingertips gently to the bandage. The fabric was wrapped around Shaw's head nearly down to his ears, but beneath the hat brim the otherwise white gauze wrapping had turned brown under a coating of trail dust.

"Somebody shot you?" the old man ventured. "You was shot in the head and *lived*? My God, man! You must hurt something fierce!"

"Only when I talk about it," Shaw said, giving him an irritated glare.

"I understand, say no more." Radler dropped his inquiry, growing less fearful now that Shaw was off his feet and making himself at home in the barn. "I'll get this cayuse rubbed down right away," he said. He couldn't keep himself from staring at the bloodstained bandage.

"Not yet," said Shaw, stopping Radler from reaching down and picking up a handful of clean straw from the floor. "He likes to stand for a few minutes first, collect his thoughts."

"Really . . . ?" Radler eyed him, wondering whether or not he was joking. "Then he's one hell of a horse."

"Yes, he is." Shaw fished another coin from his pocket and flipped it to the old liveryman. "Before you rub him down and grain him, suppose you go to that saloon and bring me back a bottle of rye." He winced at the pain in his head.

"Oh, you need whiskey for all the torment you must be in," said the old man.

Instead of replying, Shaw said, "Stand it on the post for me while I catch some shut-eye."

"Want me to wake you up soon as I return with it?" Radler asked.

"That wouldn't be a good idea," Shaw said firmly. Turning lengthwise and slinging a dusty leg up onto the hammock, he sank down, folding his hands and carefully tucking them behind his head.

Chapter 2

Inside the saloon, the three gunmen stood waiting expectantly. They'd seen the figure emerge from out of the grainy morning light and limp quickly toward them. But upon recognizing the old liveryman, they eased down and watched him step up onto the plank boardwalk. "Hell, it's only Radler," said Stobble, seeing the front door swing open in a gush of dust and cold desert wind.

"The hell are you doing, Caywood?" Thornton asked as the old liveryman limped to the bar and laid the coin down on it.

Ignoring the gunman, Radler said to the sleepy-eyed bartender behind the counter, "I'm getting a bottle for a stranger who just rode in from the badlands."

"The hell you say," Stobble called out to Radler. "Is he too timid to come get his own bottle?"

Radler ignored him.

The three gunmen looked at one another. As the bartender rose from his stool where he'd sat dozing rather than leave his saloon at the three gunmen's mercy, Stobble called out to Radler, "You best look at me when I'm talking to you, Caywood. Who is this stranger? What's he doing here in Dry Hills?"

Radler turned a cold stare toward the three men. "If I knew who he is, he wouldn't be a stranger," he said acidly.

"It's time I give this old gimp a serious backhanding," said Stobble.

Knowing he'd pushed the three too hard, Radler said quickly, "Which do you want me to answer first, Mr. Stobble, who he is or what he's doing here?" He barely managed to mask his contempt for the three.

But his prickly attitude had already drawn him trouble. Stobble gave him an icy stare as the three men walked slowly across the floor from the dusty window. "Damn it, Caywood," the bartender warned under his breath, "couldn't you see they're all three barking drunk?"

"He—he didn't introduce himself," Radler said quickly to Stobble, hoping it would stop the gunmen from coming closer. It didn't. "He never said why he's here neither," he hurriedly added. "All I can tell you is he's asleep right this minute, in his horse's stall. His head's hurting him."

"Ah, now, that's too bad, he's got a headache," Mason said mockingly.

"Sleeping in his horse's stall . . ." Stobble chuckled. "He must've heard about the hotel here."

"You didn't even ask this fool's name?" Stobble said menacingly. "Shame on you, Caywood."

"I—I figured he's one of you," Radler said, sounding more nervous as the men gathered around him. "I never like to meddle. I was warned against it by Dexter Lowe himself."

"One of us?" said Thornton. "You thought that sorry slab of buzzard bait is here to ride with Dex and us? I ought to seat you on the woodstove, Caywood."

"Easy, Thurman," Mason chuckled. "I have to admit, at first glance I thought that ragged drifter might have been some kin of yours, say, a cousin or something?"

Stobble stifled a laugh; Thornton only stared fiercely in dark reply and said, "Did you, now?" His hand clenched his holstered gun butt.

"Come on, take it easy, Thurman," said Mason. "I never seen you with so much bark on this early in the morning."

"There's something about this man riding at this hour of the morning that strikes me the wrong way," said Thornton. "I see nothing funny about this." He turned his harsh stare to the old liveryman. As the bartender set the bottle of whiskey on the bar, Thornton snatched it before the liveryman could get his hand around it. "How funny is it going to be when I send you back to the barn without his bottle under your arm?"

The liveryman summoned up the courage to say, "I wouldn't do that if I was you, Mr. Thornton."

"Yeah, why not?" Stobble cut in.

"I don't believe this is a man you want to tangle with," Radler ventured.

"I thought you didn't know anything about him?" Mason asked, the three gunmen drawing into a tight knot around him.

"I don't," said Radler. "I only know what I see, and what I see is a man intolerant of abuse."

"*Intolerant of abuse . . . ,*" Stobble said mockingly. He and Mason chuckled. "That's enough to send me the opposite direction."

Thornton shook the bottle in his hand. "I believe I'll just deliver his whiskey myself. Any objections?"

"Not from me," said Radler. "But you might get a sharp rise out of him. He warned me not to wake him when I return."

"Warned you, did he?" said Thornton. He looked at the other two and added, "Now, we can't have strangers riding in here issuing warnings to our liveryman . . . maybe speaking rudely or in some harsh manner."

"No," said Radler, "he wasn't rude! He was polite as any man could be. I don't want him thinking I came here and accused him of anything! He is not the sort of man I want getting cross with me!" He snatched for the bottle, but Thornton shoved him away and turned toward the door. Stobble and Mason followed close behind him.

"Don't fret yourself about it, Caywood," Mason said over his shoulder. "This saddle tramp ain't going to be around long enough to get cross with anybody."

"J.W., I believe I might have just gotten somebody killed," Radler said to the bartender as Mason stalked out behind the others with a ringing of spurs and pulled the door shut against the cold moaning wind.

"I wouldn't worry about it, Radler," said the bartender, J. W. Quince, who was too tired to care. "You don't owe that drifter nothing. Like as not, he's no better than this bunch of trash."

Radler looked at him. "Who says I was talking about the drifter?"

When the three gunmen stepped out of the cold wind and eased the livery barn door closed behind them, they looked around in the thin glow of the flickering lantern hanging on the post. They saw the tall battered stovepipe hat sitting atop a stall post and the dusty swallow-tailed coat hanging over the rail beside it. With their guns already drawn, Stobble whispered sidelong to the other two, "Radler ain't lying. This sonsabitch sleeps with his horse."

"It's unnatural," Stobble whispered.

"We're doing this fool a favor, killing him," Mason whispered in turn.

Without a word, Thronton eased over to the stall door and unhooked it. Standing to the side of the stall, the speckled barb tossed him a glance and chuffed under its breath. "Easy, now . . . ," Thornton whispered, Shaw's bottle of whiskey in his left hand, his Remington cocked and poised in his right. To the two men behind him, he said in a hushed voice, "He's not in here."

"What the hell . . . ?" said Stobble, moving closer to Thornton's side and peeping over at the drooping hammock hanging along the stall wall. Mason moved in and stood beside him.

"This fool must think he's a sailor," Mason said, eying the empty hammock.

Thornton straightened from a tense crouch, unhooked the stall door and stepped inside. "He's no sailor," he said, lifting Shaw's dusty swallow-tailed coat on the tip of his gun barrel and inspecting it closely.

"Maybe he thinks he's one of them British chimney sweepers," said Mason.

The three eyed the hat and coat in the glow of the lantern. "Whatever he thinks he is, he must've heard us coming and had sense enough to cut out before we got here," said Thornton.

"He left without his horse?" said Stobble.

"Naw, I don't think so," said Mason, looking the speckled barb up and down. "Maybe he went out back to the jake."

"I'll go see," said Thornton.

"Hold on, Thurman, damn it," said Stobble. "We'll all go together."

But Thornton only shook his head and walked away. "I think I can handle this saddle tramp by myself," he said over his shoulder.

"Let him go," Mason said to Stobble. He wagged the bottle in his hand and pulled the cork. "We'll have ourselves a little drink while he's—"

Mason's words stopped short at the sound of loud metallic twanging as Thornton stepped through the rear door into the morning gloom.

"What the hell was that?" Stobble said, ignoring the bottle and clasping his hand tighter around his gun butt. He moved to the open rear door in a crouch and called out in a whisper, "Thornton? Are you all right—?" His words were cut short beneath the same twanging sound as he flew back onto the dirt floor, his nose flattened and pumping a stream of blood.

At the sight of Stobble lying knocked cold, Mason tensed like a coiled rattler. But he remained back away from the open door, the bottle of whiskey in hand, his gun cocked and ready. "All right, you son of a bitch!" he called out through the whir of wind. "Your game's over! Step into sight with your hands high and I won't kill you!"

When no reply came from the open door, he took a step backward and called out, "If this is the way you want to play, it's straight-up fine with me! You won't be the first two-bit saddle tramp I ever had to—" His words also stopped short as the wind gusted and slammed the rear door shut.

The suddenness of the slamming door caused him to drop the bottle on the dirt floor with a loud yelp and run backward, firing shot after shot into the thick plank door. When his gun hammer fell on an empty chamber, he turned and bolted out the front door into the glooming morning light. But his flight stopped when he tripped across Shaw's outthrust boot and lunged face forward into the dirt.

Shaw swung a long-handled shovel low and sidelong, smacking the gunman full in the back of his head just as he raised himself from the ground. The loud twang resounded again, sending another strong vibration up Shaw's arms into his already throbbing head. *Damn. . . .*

He pitched the shovel aside and walked into the barn, cupping a hand to the side of his head. He picked up his hat and the bottle of rye and walked out the rear door. He walked toward the dimly lit saloon, staying off the main street, which had begun to come alive with voices and raised lantern light.

In front of the hotel, Dexter Lowe stood shirtless, hastily strapping on his gun belt and shoving his hair back out of his face. Three of his men ran up beside him, buttoning their trousers and checking their guns. "The shots came from the livery barn," said a young wild-haired gunman named Sonny Lloyd Sheer. He held his Colt poised in his right hand; his gun belt hung from his shoulder.

"Who'd you leave on guard tonight?" Lowe asked in a demanding tone, his voice gruff from sleep, alcohol and cocaine.

"Mason, Thornton and Stobble," Sonny Lloyd said, the whole group moving forward as one along the dirt street toward the barn.

"Damn . . . ," Lowe said under his breath, "that could be the whole problem right there."

As they drew closer to the barn, a fleshy young whore named Tuesday Bonhart came running from the hotel wearing nothing but Lowe's long wool shirt and battered broad-brimmed Stetson. "Wait up, Dexter!" she called out loud enough to get the men's attention.

"What the hell?" said Lowe, looking back over his shoulder. "Get the hell out of here, Tuesday, before you get your ass shot off."

"I brought you your hat and shirt," said the young

whore. Running up and hurrying along barefoot at his side, she pulled the Stetson from atop her head and offered it to Lowe.

"Yeah . . . ?" Lowe looked her up and down, snatched the hat and shoved it down onto his head. "And what does that leave you wearing back to the hotel?"

"Oh, I hadn't thought of that," said the young woman with a giggle. She jerked the shirt closed across her large breasts, but she didn't bother trying to button it.

"Dumb whore," Lowe whispered to himself. In a louder voice he said to her, "Stay back out of the way!"

"You said I could ride with you and your boys to Mexico," Tuesday said, pouting.

"Does this look like us riding to Mexico to you?" asked Lowe.

Before she could reply, a figure came staggering toward them from the direction of the livery barn. "Dex, it's Thornton!" said Sonny Lloyd.

Thornton staggered in place, then slumped and sank to his knees in the street as the men ran to him. Lowe propped the bloody gunman's head onto his knee. Seeing the gaping wound in Thornton's chest, Lowe asked quickly, "Who did this to you, Thurman?"

"Is it lawmen, detectives?" Sonny Lloyd asked, leaning in close, his gun still poised for action. He cut a guarded glance toward the livery barn.

Thornton choked on his blood and only managed to raise a trembling bloody finger toward the livery barn. "Mason . . . and Stobble . . . dead."

"Who shot them, Thornton?" Lowe demanded of the dying man.

Lowe pointed toward the dimly lit saloon. But when he struggled to speak, Lowe realized that no more words were going to come from his lips. "Damn it." Lowe dropped his head to the dirt and said to the men who stood staring toward the saloon in grave anticipation, "All right, spread out. We don't know how many there might be in there!" To a short, stocky gunman named Earl Hardine he said, "Earl, find Mason and Stobble, and see if they're still alive. The rest of yas follow me."

Chapter 3

––––––––

At the saloon, Shaw stood with his head bowed, his hat off and lying atop the bar. A full shot glass and the bottle of whiskey stood before him. The old liveryman stood looking out the dusty window toward the livery barn where the gunmen had gathered in the silvery-gray morning light.

A few townsfolk looked on through cracks in ragged curtains and from partly opened doors. Behind the bar the bartender said to Shaw in a quiet voice, "I expect that must hurt something fierce."

"That's what everybody says," Shaw replied. He sipped the whiskey without raising his head.

A moment of tense silence passed, and then the bartender ventured, "Well . . . does it?"

Shaw just looked at him without raising his head. He sipped more whiskey.

The bartender asked, "Do you mind saying who it was shot you?"

"I have no idea," Shaw said, not wanting to get into

the particulars of the incident. He had, in fact, a real good idea who had shot him, but it wasn't the sort of information he wanted to share with anyone, especially a bartender.

"An ambush, huh?" the bartender pressed.

"Let it go, Mister . . . ," Shaw said in a low menacing tone.

"Damn, J.W.," said Radler, turning from the dusty window and looking over at the bar. "Can't you see my friend here is in pain, and doesn't want to jaw about how it happened, who done it or nothing else?"

"I was only trying to make conversation," said the bartender.

"Well, you're going to have plenty of time to make conversation soon as Dexter Lowe and his gun-monkeys get here," said the liveryman. He looked at Shaw as he walked over and stood beside him at the bar. "I except you will too, pard," he said in a softer tone, realizing Shaw's pain. "Is there anything I can do for you before they come barging in?"

"Naw," Shaw said, his head still lowered. "You might want to get out of here. Things could get dangerous here any minute."

The bartender rolled his eyes upward a bit, as if realizing that Lowe and his men were going to make short work of this wounded stranger.

"I ain't worried about it," said Radler. He gave a short devilish grin. "This town has been bullied around by these gunmen long enough. It's time somebody stood up to them."

Shaw gave him a pointed look.

"What I mean is, somebody who's as tough as they are, which I'm betting you are, Mister . . . ?" He let his words trail, hoping for an introduction. But none came.

"One man against Lowe and his killers?" said the bartender. Again he rolled his eyes slightly at the improbably of it.

Raising his head enough to look across the bar at the bartender, Shaw asked, "Do you have a clean bar towel I can cut a couple strips out of?"

"You mean for a fresh bandage?" the bartender asked, eyeing the dirt- and bloodstained wrapping on Shaw's head. Even as he asked he reached under the bar and produced a clean, neatly folded bar towel.

"No," Shaw said grudgingly, not wanting to talk and further encourage the pain inside his wounded head. He bit down on an edge of the towel and ripped a strip off as the two men watched.

"I get it," said Radler, watching Shaw rip the strips in half, then into the two smaller strips that he rolled into tight little balls. "Loud noise makes your head hurt worse, does it?"

"That's right, Radler," said Shaw. He stuck one cloth ball into his right ear and laid the other on the bar near his left hand. He slid the bar towel back to the bartender. "Obliged," he said.

"Obliged . . . ?" The bartender just looked at the ragged-edged towel. "Hell, you've ruined it."

"Dang it, J.W.," said Radler, "Why do I have to keep reminding you how bad my pard here is hurting?"

"Yeah, but still," said the bartender, fingering the now worthless towel, "towels don't come free to me."

"I'll pay you for it," Shaw said quietly. He reached into his vest pocket for a coin.

But J.W., who had been studying Shaw's face, finally found a spark of recognition. "Did I ever see you in Somos Santos, Texas, Mister?"

"It's possible," said Shaw, laying a coin on the bar top. "I'm from there."

"Oh, *Jesus!*" said the bartender, realizing who he'd been talking to these past few minutes. He backed away, snatched a derby hat from a wall peg and jammed it down onto his head on his way out from behind the bar.

"Here's for the towel," said Shaw, gesturing toward the coin.

"Never mind, it's on the house!" said the bartender, sounding shaken by his recognition of Shaw. "So's everything else right now. I'm closing!" He hurried toward the rear door, snatching his coat from a wall peg on his way.

"*Closing . . .* ?" Radler called out. "What the hell's got into you, J.W.? There's fixing to be a gunfight here."

"Nothing's got into me," said J.W. "I'm skedaddling out of here before the trouble starts! If you've got any sense, Radler, so will you!" he added. Without slowing down to wait for the old liveryman, he swung open the rear door, stepped out and slammed the door behind himself.

"What the hell got him so rattled?" Radler asked, dumbfounded. "I know he's seen his share of fighting in here, guns, knives or bare knuckles."

Shaw nodded toward the rear door. "Why don't you go too?" he said softly but with finality.

"Huh?" Radler looked surprised. "What if you need some help? J.W. keeps a short-barreled twelve under the bar. I can get it and see to it everything—"

Shaw raised a hand, cutting him off. "You want to help? There'll be a couple of lawmen coming before long. Tell them you saw me." He didn't want to reveal any more than he had to to get a message to Dawson and Caldwell.

"You mean you want me to sic the law on you?" Radler asked, looking puzzled. "I mean, that is, if you still, you know . . ."

"Alive?" Shaw said, finishing his words for him. "Yeah, sic them on me."

"I'd rather you let me get that scattergun and tar the walls with their—"

"Obliged, but I'll be all right," Shaw said with quiet confidence, cutting him off again. He gave a stiff gesture toward the rear door. "Go on, get out of here."

When Dexter Lowe and his men reached the street in front of the saloon, the morning gray had begun to lift beneath the first rays of sunlight. The wind from the desert had died down to a lower whir as it moved off across the dusty sand basin like some large retreating beast. Earl Hardine stayed at the livery barn, looking around.

"Hey, in the saloon, lawdogs, bounty hunters, whatever you are!" Lowe shouted, flanked by Sonny Lloyd and New York Joe Toledo. "Are you going to come out or are we going to come in and get you?" Off to their right a serious-looking gunman named Dan Sax stood with a rifle poised and ready. Behind Lowe stood the half-naked young whore.

"There's only one of me in here," Shaw called out from inside the otherwise empty saloon. "I'm not coming out. If you want me, come on in."

"By hell we will come in there," said Lowe. "It makes us no difference. You don't shoot three of my men and expect not to pay the reaper for it."

"I didn't shoot any of your men," Shaw called out, his own voice accelerating his pain. "I only swatted their lights out with a shovel."

"Swatted them . . . ?" Lowe said to Sonny Lloyd standing beside him.

On his other side, New York Joe Toledo said in his deep, growling voice, "We all heard the shots, Dex. Besides, I've never seen a swat from a shovel leave a man spitting up his busted lungs." He raised his voice toward the saloon. "This man is a lying no-good sonsabitch. He shot these three! Now you've got to answer for it. You hear me in there?"

"I hear you," said Shaw, "but you're dead wrong. I didn't shoot those men."

Lowe shouted, "Then who the hell did?"

Shaw didn't answer. Instead he grimaced in pain and kneaded his temples with both hands. "What the hell do I care?" he said under his breath.

"All right, let's get ready to rush him," Lowe said to the others.

Back in the direction of the livery barn, Earl Hardine called out, "Dex, wait! I've got Mason here! He ain't shot. He's just been knocked cold!"

"What the hell's this?" Lowe said to no one in particular. He watched Hardine help Mason stagger along the middle of the street toward him.

When the two stopped in front of him, Earl Hardine said, "He's got a knot the size of a melon the back of his head. His gun was lying in the dirt empty. It was still smoking some when I got there."

"What about Stobble? Did you see him anywhere?" Lowe asked.

"Yeah, I saw him. He's dead," said Hardine. "Shot all to hell . . . got a chest full of splinters too. His gun was fully loaded."

"Splinters?" Lowe asked.

"Yep," said Hardine. "It looked like he was shot through the rear barn door. It's full of bullet holes too."

"You're saying Mason here was the one doing the shooting?" Lowe asked pointedly, looking Mason up and down curiously.

"It sure looks that way," said Hardine, Mason standing half knocked out, his arm looped around his shoulder. "I haven't gotten much sense out of this knocked-out sonsabitch yet." He shook the dazed gunman a little as he spoke. "See what I mean?"

Mason's head wagged limply; he mumbled incoherently at Hardine's side.

"Yeah, I see," Lowe said skeptically. "Hey, Mason, wake up!" he shouted, roughly slapping the groggy gunman's face back and forth. A long string of drool swung down from his lips to his chin. "Tell us what the hell happened back there. Did you get spooked and shoot Thornton and Stobble?"

Mason's lowered head bobbed a little. "He can't hear you, Dex," said Hardine with sarcasm.

"I can fix that," said Lowe. He jammed his pistol barrel up under Mason's chin and cocked the hammer. "Here's how it goes, Bell. You either straighten up right now, or I'm sending you on the longest journey of your worthless life."

"Don't shoot him, Dex, please!" said the half-naked young whore. She stood cringing behind him with her hands over her ears.

"Wait—wait a minute, Dex," said Mason as if through a foggy veil. "I'm coming around some. I'm just having trouble staying awake and talking."

Hearing the grogginess in Mason's voice, Dex gritted his teeth and said, "Adios, Bell, I've got no time for the weak and afflicted." He jammed the barrel tighter as if to pull the trigger.

"No, please, Dex!" Mason said in a frightened but more coherent voice. "I'm all right, look!" He opened his eyes wide above his swollen crooked nose. "I was just knocked out for a while is all!"

"Look, Earl, we're seeing a miracle here," said Lowe with a bitter twist to his voice. He gave Mason a rough shake. "You better tell me what the hell happened back there and make it quick."

"It all went crazy, Dex, I swear to God," said Mason in a frightened whimper. "This man had already done something to Stopple and Thornton, I just didn't know what! For all I knew he'd slit their throats. I was alone. He slammed the door! I started shooting. But I never shot Thornton or Stobble, I'm damned positive!"

"Positive, huh?" Lowe queried.

"Damn positive," said Mason. "What else could I do but start shooting?"

"You could've held your fire and kept the yellow from running down your leg," New York Joe Toledo put in, standing a few feet away listening.

"There was three of us," said Mason. "He had already put the other two out of action. Damn it, Joe! I'd already seen that Thornton and Stopple couldn't do nothing against him." He paused, then lied, "I heard shooting. Shooting back was the only natural thing to do!"

"Son of a bitch . . . ," Lowe growled. He stared away from Mason and Toledo, toward the saloon, as early sunlight peeped over the distant horizon. "You in there," he demanded, after a moment of serious consideration. "Get on out here. We've got some talking to do."

Shaw made no reply.

Realizing that whoever was in the saloon wasn't about to take any orders from him, Lowe let out a breath and said, "All right, stay where you are. We're coming in. But we're not coming in shooting." As he spoke he holstered his Colt and drew his hands up chest high. "I want to talk." He paused, then asked, "All right? After all, I've got two of my men dead and one knocked half senseless."

There was a moment of tense silence as Lowe and his men looked back and forth at one another.

"Suit yourself," Shaw finally called out, his pain increasing with every word he spoke.

"All right now," Lowe said quietly to those around him. "Everybody be ready for a signal from me once I see who this is, and what we need to do about him. Like as not I'm still going to kill him."

Chapter 4

Shaw raised his lowered eyes just enough to acknowledge Lowe and his men as they filed in slowly and spread out in a half circle around him. They had holstered their pistols, but Shaw paid their gesture little regard. Guns sprang up quick in his world.

"There, you see?" said Lowe, standing in front of him, his hands chest high, his right glove off and stuck down behind his gun belt. "I'm not here for killing, unless it comes down to that."

Shaw looked at him, then let his eyes drift past him to the fleshy young whore who'd slipped inside and eased over behind Lowe. Seeing Shaw's eyes go past him, Lowe said over his shoulder without looking around, "Tuesday? Damn it, girl. You've got no business in here." He gave Shaw an almost apologetic look. "Whores, huh? What can you do with them, right, Mister . . . ?" His words trailed as his eyes went to the bandage atop Shaw's head.

Shaw didn't respond. Instead he said, "You came here to talk. Talk."

Lowe looked taken aback at his bluntness. "All right," he said, "Let's talk, *whoever you are*." He looked Shaw up and down, but his eyes couldn't stay away from the white bloodstained head bandage, the dusty brown edges of it circling his skull above Shaw's ears. "Jesus, what happened to you?"

Shaw looked at him. He'd heard of Dexter Lowe, aka *Dangerous Dexter*. From the tales he'd heard, this young gunman was hickory tough, ready to kill at the drop of a hat, the turn of a card or the cock of a hammer. Yet, in person, Lowe didn't measure up to much more than a dirty grin and a dark promise of trouble. Shaw breathed in and said dismissively, "I took a gunshot to the head. Now, you want to know what happened to your men out there?"

"Yeah, that's right, I do," said Lowe. "What happened to them?" But his eyes only flicked down to Shaw's for a second, then went back to the bandage. Before Shaw could reply, Lowe cut in and asked, "You took a bullet to the head and you're still—"

"*Alive . . . ?*" Shaw said, cutting him off and finishing his sentence for him.

Lowe leveled his gaze on Shaw's eyes again.

"You're not the first person who's asked me," Shaw said, leaning back a little onto the edge of the bar.

"I bet I'm not," said Lowe, not knowing what else to say, realizing his men were standing, watching, listening, waiting behind him.

A tense silence ensued. Lowe had let his hands

lower slowly from chest high, closer to his holstered Colt, close enough for drawing if he decided to take things in that direction. But he took note that this drifter didn't seem concerned one way or the other with where his hands were.

Shaw's left hand lay on the bar top, his fingertips near the wad of cloth, which was rolled and ready to stick into his ear, should this talk turn into a shoot-out. His right elbow lay propped on the bar edge, but his right hand hung loosely down toward his holstered Colt as if drawn there by instinct or predestination. "About your men . . . ," Shaw reminded him.

"Yeah," said Lowe, seeming to lose interest in what happened to Thornton and Stobble, but having to sound menacing for the sake of his gunmen. "I think I've already got an idea what took place." He thumbed over his shoulder toward Bell Mason. "I just want to hear it from you, make sure you or my man here ain't either one jerking my reins. He says you fired first."

"I never fired a shot," Shaw said in a quiet, restrained voice. "Did you check his gun?"

"Sure did," Earl Hardine cut in. "It was empty, still smoking. I even smelled it for good measure."

This was the opening Shaw wanted. His right hand streaked upward, his Colt leveled at Lowe's heart. The move had come so fast, no one had caught it until it was too late. Then Shaw cocked it with a flick of his thumb and flipped it around sideways in his hand, the barrel pointing away from Lowe. "Want to smell mine?" he said.

Shaw's eyes riveted into Lowe's for a second, long enough to let Lowe understand that he could just as easily have killed him. "Holster it," Lowe said in a tight voice, now that the gun was aimed away from him. His hand had managed to get around his Colt's butt, but the move would not have come soon enough to save his life. "My men get itchy when a gun is drawn in their presence."

Shaw uncocked and holstered the Colt almost as fast as he'd drawn it. His eyes held the same confident message as he went on to say, "Feel the back of your man's head, there's a whelp the size of your fist. I turned a shovel blade loose on him." He eyed Mason as he spoke. "I did the same on the other two. I smacked them open-faced. Killing them wasn't my intent."

"How do I know that?" said Lowe stiffly, needing to save face among his men.

Shaw looked from face to face among the men, at the young whore too, as if establishing himself with everyone in the salon. Then he said, "If a little shovel smacking killed them, I expect you're better off losing them now instead of down the trail"—he stopped his words as he went back to Lowe's eyes with a knowing look—"when you need men less prone to fall victim to farm implements."

Lowe stared stone-faced, calculating his best response. The man standing before him wasn't going to back down or compromise. The men behind him were looking at how he handled this. He had two men dead, but now it appeared that his own man, not this bandaged-headed drifter, had been the one who killed them. But he needed something to ease the tension, get him off the spot.

Behind Lowe, New York Joe Toledo muffled a dark chuckle in response to Shaw's reference to farm implements. That was all Lowe needed. He allowed himself a grudging grin. Then he let the grin turn into a dark chuckle of his own. Over his shoulder he asked in a dry but joking manner, "Is there anybody else here prone to fall victim to *farm implements*?"

Behind him on his other side, Sonny Floyd said, "If there was, do you think they'd admit it?"

Lowe let himself ease down even more. He nodded with a short laugh, then asked Shaw, "You said killing them wasn't your intent. Just what was your intent?"

"I saw those three when I rode in," said Shaw. "I even recognized Roland Stobble. I'd heard he rode with you. I figured we'd get around to meeting each other soon enough. I wanted to see what the game is and see if there was room for another player."

"There is now . . . ," Joe Toledo said quietly to Lowe from behind.

Shaw went on. "I didn't like it when they came sneaking around like coyotes—this is *wolf* country we're in." He turned a frown toward Bell Mason, who stood scowling at him with a reddened face.

A gunman named Jimmy Bardell, standing back in the middle of the floor, cut in, saying, "It's not *shovel* country either, Mister. It's *gun* country. We saw how fast you can skin one. How sharp can you make one shoot?"

Instead of answering Bardell, Shaw asked Lowe, "What do you want shot?" As he asked he picked up the wadded strip of cloth and stuck it into his left ear, his right already plugged.

Without hesitation Lowe jerked his head toward Bell Mason and said, "Shoot him."

Almost before his words were out of his mouth, Shaw's big Colt streaked up from his holster, cocked and leveled. But Lowe quickly shouted, "Whoa! Hold on! I didn't mean that!"

Shaw only heard him enough to stop and jerk the plug from his ear. "What?" he asked, his cocked Colt still pointed at Bell Mason's chest. Mason stood staring wide-eyed with fear.

"I said stop," Lowe said with a dark grin turned toward Mason. "I'm short enough on men as it is." He looked from Mason to Shaw. "Let's call that a little test."

"A test . . ." Shaw lowered the Colt, uncocked it and slipped it back into his holster in one sleek move. "Good, I hate wasting bullets," he said, his eyes going back to Mason.

A short, tight laugh rippled across the men. "Hear that, Bell?" said Lowe. "He figured you're not worth the cost of lead and powder." He looked at Shaw. "So, you are a man who makes a living with a gun."

"Just as much as I can," said Shaw. "Have you got work for me, being short on men like you said?"

"Yeah, you're on," said Lowe. He had things back in hand now, and he knew it. "Let me ask you something, though. Should I be hiring you or the man who put the bullet in your head?"

Shaw gave a trace of a grin. "What makes you think he's for hire?"

Lowe tried not to look impressed. "You managed to kill him?"

Shaw considered his words before turning them loose. "To be honest with you, I don't *know* who did it."

"Damn!" said Lowe. "Then I guess you're most eager to find out?"

"It might make me sleep better," Shaw said. He eased back against the bar again, picked up his shot glass and sipped his whiskey. "But I can be a patient man when I need to."

Lowe stepped back and looked around at the men, gauging whether or not they were satisfied with how he'd handled things. He was relieved to see their expressions said they agreed with him. The drifter's story sounded believable. Nobody liked being set upon in their sleep, especially a man who already had a bullet wound in his head, Lowe told himself. It made sense to him.

"It's sunup," he said. "I don't know about the rest of yas, but I'm ready for some breakfast." He looked at Shaw, and asked, "What about you? Are you ready for some breakfast?"

"I'm just finishing up breakfast." Shaw threw back his shot of whiskey in a gulp. He looked around, seeing the men's eyes on him, expecting him to accept Lowe's breakfast invitation as his entrance into their group. "But I will have some coffee," he added, catching himself. He jerked the cloth plug from his other ear and stuck both plugs in his vest pocket.

While the men surrounded Shaw and accompanied him to a small restaurant farther down the dirt street, Dexter Lowe and Tuesday stopped off at their hotel room. Lowe reclaimed his shirt from her and stood watching as she pulled on her dress, a pair of lace-up shoes and reached for her frayed wool coat. Suddenly a flash of recognition came to the young woman.

"Oh my God!" she gasped, stopping cold with only one sleeve of her coat on. "I know who he is!"

"Who *who* is?" Lowe asked, reaching out and directing her other arm into the empty coat sleeve.

"Him, the drifter!" said Tuesday, wide-eyed in her discovery. She slid into the empty sleeve, hiked the coat and gripped Lowe's forearm. "I saw him last year, in Wooten, when I worked at Bentley's Pleasure Palace."

"Jesus, you worked at Bentley's?" Lowe asked. "Is there anywhere you haven't whored this side of the Mississippi?"

Ignoring him, she said, awestruck, "He's Fast Larry Shaw."

"What?" Her words recaptured Lowe's attention. "Him? This head-shot gunman is Fast Larry Shaw?" He considered it for only a second, then let out a short chuckle of disbelief. "You've got to be crazy, woman. Fast Larry Shaw, here, with a bullet in his head?"

"I'm telling you, Dex, it's him for a fact," Tuesday insisted. "I did—" She caught herself and said, "That is, I knew a whore who *did* him while he was there."

Lowe gave her a suspicious look. "You started to say *you* did him, didn't you?"

"No, I didn't," said Tuesday, but her words didn't sound convincing. "Besides, what if I *did* do him? That's my job—it was then anyway."

"It's not now," Dexter said, pulling her roughly to

him. "It better never be again. You belong to me now. Don't forget it. I get riled hearing about all the men you did. Sometimes it sounds like you've done every sonsabitch who pulls on britches."

"I'm a young woman in high demand," Tuesday reminded him. "Don't worry, I didn't use it all up. You've got plenty left to keep you busy." She gave a lewd grin and squirmed away from him.

But Lowe grabbed her by her frayed coat sleeve and menacingly raised a finger near her face for emphasis. "But you're not interested in *doing* anybody else, ever again, right?" he asked for reassurance.

"Yeah, right, whatever," Tuesday said in a dismissing manner. She wiggled herself loose again. "But back to Fast Larry Shaw. That is him, I damn well promise you it is."

"All right, then, it is," said Lowe. "So what?" He gave a shrug, not wanting to appear rattled by the news that he'd just looked down the pointed barrel of the fastest gun alive.

"*So what?*" Tuesday mocked. She hiked a hand onto a fleshy hip. "So, what are you going to do about it? From what I heard he turned lawman."

Without taking on alarm, Lowe said calmly, "Yep, I heard that myself."

"You're not concerned?" Tuesday asked.

Lowe let down his cavalier facade. "If it is him, I expect the best thing I can do is not let him know that I'm onto him. I'm going to keep a close watch on him. If things start to look wrong to me, I'll have the boys shut his eyes for him, fast gun or not."

"Is this going to mess anything up?" Tuesday asked. "I mean for you and your gang riding for Corio on that big job you told me about."

"Naw, don't worry about it," said Lowe. "Everything is going right. I'll see to it it stays that way. After all, I need good gunmen. Whoever this drifter is, he's slick at handling a gun."

"All right," said Tuesday, "but don't forget you've promised me diamonds and rubies, remember? I'm still expecting them."

"You'll get them," said Lowe. "No head-shot gunman is going to change anything." He swung open the hotel door, ushered her out into the hall and down the stairs to the street.

From the boardwalk out in front of the restaurant, Shaw and two of the men stood watching as Lowe and the young woman came walking toward them from the hotel. Under his breath, Dan Sax said to Jimmy Bardell, "Damn, I love a fleshy young whore like her."

"Get it out of your mind," Bardell warned him in a lowered voice. "She's Dex's now."

"Ha!" said Sax. "I've never seen a whore turn down a little extra gold or silver, I don't care who she claims to belong to."

"That's the kind of talk that can get a man killed," said Bardell. "Lucky for you I'm the only one who heard it." They both looked over at Shaw.

Without taking his eyes off Lowe and the young woman, Shaw said, "I didn't hear a word." After a silent pause he added, "Let me ask you this. Am I wasting my time, looking to make any real money with you fellows?"

The two chuckled among themselves. After a moment, Sax said quietly, "Drifter, you're fixing to make more money than you've seen in your life."

"That's all I needed to hear," Shaw said. He continued staring out at Lowe and the woman, and said silently, *All right, Dawson, I'm here where you want me. Ready when you are. . . .*

PART 2

Chapter 5

Wooten, Texas

Jane Crowley sat out of the scalding sunlight, on the edge of a boardwalk in the shade of a saloon overhang. She stared out through the wavering heat at the same low cloud of dust she'd been observing for the past half hour. Squinting, she watched a collection of black dots bounce steadily closer until they began to turn into thin vertical lines. She shut her eyes for a moment and when she reopened them she took in as much as she could before the harsh sunlight again overpowered her vision.

"Riders coming . . . ," she murmured instinctively to herself, her voice still a bit slurred from a weeklong whiskey binge. She cut a glance back and forth with hangover contempt and said to the empty street in general, "As if any of you square-heads even gives a damn. . . ."

Beside her, a black cat had stood up and arched its

back, and in its movements had knocked over an almost empty whiskey bottle she'd stood there. The sound of the corked bottle against the plank boardwalk resounded like a gunshot inside her jittery brain.

"Lord A'mighty!" she said, jerking sidelong with her hands thrown up as if to protect herself. Catching herself, seeing the bottle roll back and forth and settle, she snatched it up, clutched it to her fringed doeskin bosom and shoed the cat away with a shaky hand. "Get out of here, you yellow-eyed son of a bitch. I've got all the bad luck I ever prayed for!"

As the cat leaped down and shot away along the edge of the boardwalk, Jane jerked the cork from the bottle and stared at the half inch of amber rye whiskey as she swirled it around. "What the hell?" she said submissively to the amber liquid. "All you ever did was try to help." Out of habit she wiped the tip of the bottle on her sleeve, raised it to her lips and drained it.

"There was too much working against you," she added, dropping the empty bottle to the dirt between her boots and staring down at it in contemplation.

Twenty minutes later when the black wavering lines took the form of two riders leading a three-horse string, Jane looked up from her dark musings and batted her red tearful eyes. "Oh, hell, Dawson and the Undertaker." Even as she spoke she eased up and tried to turn away before they spotted her. But she was too late.

"Jane . . . Jane Crowley, wait up," Dawson called out to her before she could duck around the corner of the saloon and disappear into an alley.

Damn it. . . . She stopped, turned and tried to look surprised. "Who's there?" she called out, as if not immediately recognizing the two lawmen. "Oh, Dawson!" she said, feigning surprise. "Caldwell!" She gave a bemused but stilted smile. "How the hell are you, pards?" She staggered a bit in place.

Caldwell and Dawson shot each other a glance, each of them seeing through her feigned behavior. "Jane, didn't you see us ride in?" Caldwell asked, looking concerned. "Are you all right?"

"Well, hellfire, yes, Undertaker, I'm all right." Even as she spoke to Caldwell, she nodded at the sweaty three-horse string he led behind him, each horse carrying the remains of its former owner tied down over its back. "I'm a hell of a lot better than some I'm seeing today." She reformed her crooked smile and offered one that appeared more authentic. "Who've you got tied down there?" She walked toward them and stopped at the edge of the boardwalk for a better look at the bodies.

"The Higginses," said Caldwell, "Brady, Earthen and Lars. Do you know them?"

"Hell yes, I know them," Jane said, craning her neck for a profile look at the grim faces. "I know their cousins, Mose and Shorthand Higgins, too. I'd count on them being along any time if I was you."

"We are," said Caldwell. "The Higginses were all riding with a bunch we chased across the border two weeks ago—caught up to them this morning early. There's a five-hundred-dollar bounty on each of these three. Maybe more on Mose and Shorthand."

"Oh . . . ? You've taking up bounty hunting now?" Jane asked, standing unsteadily and having to take hold of a post for safety.

"No, we're not bounty hunting," Caldwell said with patience. "But we'd like to get you to—"

"You're wasting your breath asking her, Jed—she's drunk," Dawson said flatly, cutting him off. He looked at the empty bottle lying in the dirt. Then he looked Jane over, her disheveled condition, her red and watery eyes.

"Well, thank you very much, Marshal," she replied sharply. "We'll take that into consideration before ever voting me into office."

The two lawmen stepped down from their saddles and led the horses the last few feet to the iron hitch rail. Jane stepped down and leaned with both hands on it. "Is that what brings you here? You come to announce my drunkenness to the white Christian public?"

"No," said Dawson, spinning his horse's reins onto the rail. "We heard you and Shaw were here." He looked around. "Where is he?"

Without answering, Jane said, "For your information, Marshal, I'm not drunk. But I do have a steam boiler running in my head. So it would be best for all three of us if we tried to speak kindly to one another."

"Fair enough," said Dawson. "You go first."

"Obliged," said Jane. She steadied herself and asked in a civil tone, "What were you telling Undertaker he's wasting his breath asking me about?"

"We thought we'd get you to witness who these three are, since you said you know them. We're going to need the bounty money for supplies. Who's the sheriff here?"

"Oscar Watts," said Jane. "He's old, half-blind and can't hear worth a shit. You would not want to leave him to face Mose and Shorthand alone."

"We won't," said Caldwell. The two lawmen turned a searching glance out along the trail they'd ridden in on.

"Where will we find Sheriff Watts?" Dawson asked.

"A wild guess?" Jane answered with sarcasm. "At his office, unless he's wandered off again." She squinted off along the dirt street, then looked back up at them. "*Expenses*, eh? Doesn't the U.S. federal government pay your expenses?" Jane asked. "What kind of miserly bunch are you working for?"

Dawson looked embarrassed. "We don't have time to wait around for expense money," he said. "We've got too many outlaws on the run. As soon as we deal with Mose and Shorthand, we're pushing on across the border." He looked all around again and asked, "What has Shaw found out for us?"

"Yeah, where is he anyway?" Caldwell asked.

"He's not here," Jane said, growing tight-lipped at the mention of Shaw's name. "Why? Would you rather have *him* witness the Higgins brothers for you?"

"No," said Dawson, "your witness will do. Where'd Shaw go?"

"No place that I'd want to be," Jane said. "He left me in the middle of the night, like every other no-good son of a bitch I've ever given my heart to." Her words ended in an emotional tremor.

Dawson and Caldwell looked at each other. To keep her from breaking down in front of them, Dawson asked, "Is he drinking?"

"Oh yeah, he started drinking again," Jane said. "No sooner than we got to this pig-rut of a town, we both went on a wild drinking spree. I'm still trying to sober up enough to find my ass with both hands." She nodded toward a dingy sheriff's office down the street. "Sheriff Watts is the man with the star here. He'll take the Higginses off your hands, and he can tell you what happened to Shaw. I can't bear to speak of it."

"What are you talking about, Jane?" Dawson asked in a firm but level voice. "What's happened to Shaw?"

Her eyes welled with tears. "I just told you I can't bear talking about it," she sobbed.

Caldwell stepped forward. "Where are you staying, Jane?"

Crying into her hands, she gestured toward the boardwalk where she'd been sitting. "Right there is my home from now on," she sobbed. "I'm never moving from this spot."

"Where's your horse, Jane?" Dawson asked.

"He left me too," said Jane, sniffling and wiping her eyes, trying to take control of herself.

"You sold your horse?" said Caldwell.

"What if I did?" Jane said in defiance. "It was mine to sell."

"Where's your gun?" Dawson asked, noting the empty holster on her hip.

"I threw it away," Jane said.

"Threw it away?" asked Caldwell.

"Yeah," she replied, "I threw it away . . . or lost it, or sold it. Hell, I don't know! Do I look like somebody who ought to be carrying a loaded firearm?"

"Shaw was sent ahead to scout out Madden Corio's gang," said Dawson. "Did he do any good?"

"None that I know of," Jane said. "But the way we were drinking and fighting, I suspect he wouldn't have confided in me anyway."

Dawson looked at Caldwell with a grimace and said quietly between them, "This is what I'm always afraid of with Shaw." Then he asked Jane, "Which direction did Shaw go in?"

"How the hell would I know?" Jane retorted. "Most likely he crawled off into the badlands along the border. Ain't that generally where he goes to shut himself off from everybody?" She paused in dark reflection, then added, "And to lick his wounds?"

The two turned their eyes back to her. "Lick his wounds?" Dawson asked. "Is he wounded?"

Jane hesitated, but finally said, "Yeah, he's wounded. Somebody shot him in the head."

"My God," said Caldwell.

"How bad?" asked Dawson.

"I don't know." Jane flung her arms, as if tossing off any knowledge or responsibility on the matter. "I ain't a doctor and I ain't God. I can't answer neither of your questions."

"Who shot him?" Dawson asked.

"Was he in a gunfight?" asked Caldwell.

"Hell no, it wasn't a *gunfight*, Undertaker," Jane said to Caldwell mockingly. "There's nobody alive could take Shaw in a *gunfight*." She looked at Dawson. "I don't know who shot him. I found him shot in his bed. Luckily he was still alive. . . . I went and got the doctor—"

"In his bed?" Dawson asked, cutting her off. "He was shot in bed?"

"What did I say, Marshal?" Jane snapped. "Yes, he was shot in his bed—in his sleep." She tossed her hands again, taking a step back as if feeling crowded and put upon. "I don't know who shot him, or how, or why. I only know he was shot. He nearly died. Now he's left me." Her eyes welled again. "I don't know where he went. He could be wandering around out there like some mindless idiot for all I know."

"Jesus. . . ." Caldwell stood staring at her with a stunned look on his round, bearded face.

Dawson stepped in closer and laid a hand on Jane's trembling shoulder. "Listen to me, Janie," he said quietly, almost in a whisper. "Did you get drunk and shoot Lawrence Shaw?"

"What? Are you crazy?" Jane shouted. "I love the son of a bitch! How could I do something like that?" She tried to jerk out from under his hand. But Dawson held on to her firmly. "I would have done anything for him," she cried. "I still would! He left me, I didn't leave him!" She thumbed herself on the chest.

"Jane, it's all right," said Dawson, "you're starting to sober up. Things always look their worst when the whiskey starts turning you loose." In the same quiet calm, almost soothing voice he said; "You shot him, didn't you?"

"I—I don't know, Marshal," she said. "I swear I don't know." Her eyes looked cloudy and confused on the matter. "We was both so damned drunk, I can't remember what happened."

"So it's just as likely that you might have shot him?"

She stared at him, vexed, unsure. "Hell, I suppose I might have. I was the only one there."

Dawson fell silent, observing her, letting the events play across her mind. He saw something try to take shape and form itself from within her dark drunken memory. "We'd been arguing—" She paused. "I—I hit him." She shook her head. "He never even tried to hit me back. I—I left the room in a huff, went to the saloon and drank some more. When I came back . . . he was asleep, on the bed." As she spoke her eyes revealed more and more terror. She stopped with a gasp. "Oh my God!"

"Go on, Jane," Dawson coaxed. "Get it out."

"Oh my God, Marshal," she repeated, unable to contain herself any longer. "I—I might have shot him. I might have shot the only man I love." She flung herself against Dawson's dusty chest and sobbed.

"Might have, Jane?" Dawson inquired, keeping his eyes on hers.

"But if I did shoot him, I didn't mean to, Marshal," Jane said, racking her whiskey-soaked mind. "Things are so foggy." She trembled against him like a woman with a terrible fever.

"Take it easy, Jane," Dawson soothed. "We're here. We'll help you get sobered up and get back on your feet."

"Oh Lord, Marshal, what have I done?" she said, suddenly letting go. "What have I done?"

Holding Jane to his chest, Dawson looked along the empty street, seeing curious faces appear in doorways. "Take the bodies to the sheriff's office. I'll join you as soon as I get her off the streets." He looked all around and said, "Come on, Jane. Let's get you to the hotel, get you cleaned up and get some food in you."

Chapter 6

Dawson left Jane Crowley at a bathhouse behind the hotel, where a young Cajun woman named Raidy Bowe helped Jane undress and step over into a long hot tub full of water. "I expect you know what happened between Lawrence Shaw and me, how I screwed things up for the both of us."

"Shhh," said Raidy, soothingly. "You lie back and let me attend to you, Miss Janie."

When the young woman didn't give the kind of response she was looking for, Jane continued by saying, "I expect you and everybody else is judging me to be a damned drunken fool. Well, I don't blame you, Raidy. I am one."

"No, Jane, I do not judge you," said the young woman with a Louisiana backwater French accent. "I know you are not a drunken fool." She helped Jane settle into the tub, then leaned her back until only her head remained above the water.

Jane let out a short gasp before surrendering to the steaming water. "Lord, girl, this water is hot enough to scald chickens."

"*Oui*," Raidy said with an easy smile, "it is hot, but it is good for you. It sweats out the whiskey and its many poisons." She held a drinking gourd to Jane's lips. "Here, drink this. It will help to clear your mind. Whiskey makes one forget things of importance, both to ourselves and to others."

"There's a lot I'd just as soon not remember," Jane commented.

"Drink," said Raidy with persistence.

Jane made a face as she smelled the thick greenish liquid. "What is it, dog puke?"

"It is made from *mousse* and *champignons*, and the bark of a tree that grows in the swamplands of my people."

"Oh, mushrooms, swamp moss and tree bark, how charming," Jane said translating Raidy's words with sarcasm. "Just the things I've been most hankering for of late."

Raidy smiled and held the gourd against Jane's closed lips. "You must drink it."

"Well, since I *must*, here goes." Jane forced herself to part her lips and drink the concoction, her eyes turned upward to Raidy's for approval.

Raidy reached down with a free hand and brushed Jane's wet hair from her forehead. "I did not know that you speak French. Perhaps you learned some from me?"

Jane didn't answer. Instead she gasped as she finished the liquid. "Don't tell nobody," she said. "No of-

fense, but understanding French doesn't exactly make
me feel good about myself. Besides, I've found that
once folks start thinking you know a lot, they start re-
quiring more of you. As you can see, I'm a drunk. I
doubt that I'll ever be much more than that."

"Do not be so hard on yourself, Janie," Raidy said.
Laying the gourd aside, she soaped up a thick washcloth and began washing Jane, left arm, then right arm.
"Perhaps it is not your fault things didn't work out
between you and Lawrence Shaw."

"Oh . . . ?" Jane cut her an upward glance. "What
do you know about whose fault it was or wasn't?"

"I hate to pass along gossip," said Raidy, washing
her as she spoke. "But I have heard talk about Lawrence Shaw. The doves all say that he is a *difficult* man,
with a dark past that haunts him."

"All my men are *difficult*, and haunted by a *dark*
past," Jane said with a twist of irony in her voice. "I
seem to draw that kind of man like sugar draws flies."
She gave a sad smile and relaxed beneath the young
woman's skillful hands. "Maybe I should say like a
stinking carcass draws flies, the way my luck has been
running."

Raidy ran her forearm under the water and washed
Jane's breasts slowly, then her stomach, then lower.

Jane allowed herself to relax more. She closed her
eyes and said with a swoon, "This is the best I've felt
for a long time. I might take up mushrooms and moss
on a regular basis."

"It makes me happy that I am able to make you feel
good," Raidy said. "Relax . . . relax." Her voice and her

hands seemed to work in unison to a slow and soothing rhythm beneath the hot water.

Jane allowed herself to drift, her eyes closed, her
lips parted slightly. In a moment of dozing, she imag-
ined Shaw's lips on hers, and she let herself give in to
his long, deep kiss. *Lawrence . . . Lawrence, what have I
done . . . ?* But before the kiss had ended, she realized it
was not Shaw's lips on hers, stirring her passion; it was
Raidy Bowe's. *My God!*

"Jesus, Raidy!" she said, shoving the young woman
away and sitting upright in the long tub. "What the
hell are you doing?" She rubbed a wet hand vigorously
across her lips.

"I am kissing you, Janie," Raidy said, not a bit put
off by Jane's rejection of her. "Was I wrong? Do you not
like it?"

"God, no, I *did not* like it," Jane said, looking back
and forth for a towel to grab.

"You seemed to like it," said Raidy. She shrugged,
moving back in close to Jane, the soapy washcloth still
in hand, as if to continue her bathing chore with no
more thought to the kiss. "I only kiss you hoping to
make you feel good."

"I don't want to *feel good* if that's what it takes," Jane
said sharply. "Whatever made you think you could
pull such a stunt as that?"

Raidy only lowered her gaze and made no reply.

Jane waved a hand toward a folded towel lying on a
stand near the tub and said in a shaken voice, "Give
me that. I'm getting out of here." She stood straight up
in the tub.

Raidy picked up the folded towel, shook it out and stepped to the edge of the tub. She held it out to drape around Jane as she stepped out onto a braided rug on the wooden floor. But instead of letting the young woman wrap the towel around her, Jane took it from her and began drying herself off.

"I am sorry, Janie," Raidy said, watching her, reaching in and still trying to assist. "Please do not tell Perkins what I did. He will fire me, and I will end up back to the line."

Jane saw a tear form in the corner of the young woman's eye. "Ah, hell, forget it," she said, holding the towel against her flat stomach. "After all I've been through, I should feel flattered, a pretty thing like you kissing the likes of me." She gave a forgiving smile and cocked her head in curiosity. "But whatever made you think I'm that kind of gal?"

Raidy looked confused for a second, then embarrassed. "I—I have heard some things. The doves at the saloon say that in the past . . ." She let her words trail into suggestion.

Janie shook her head and held the towel loosely at her side. "For a gal who hates gossip, you sure are toting around a headful of it," she said, standing naked at the edge of the tub.

"Then it is not true, what I have heard about you?" Raidy asked.

Jane stared at her for a moment, as if choosing her words carefully. "Whether it's true or not, it was in the past, Raidy. There are things I've done in the past that I will never do again. I'm a drunkard—I have an excuse for every damned stupid thing I do. When I sober up I try not to do it again."

"Even if it is with someone you care for, and who cares for you?" the young woman asked, stepping closer to her again.

"That is hard to answer. . . ." Jane felt herself calmed and soothed by the concoction Raidy had given her. "My nature has been as unpredictable as a desert wind. I can't even speculate what I might or might not do, especially when it comes to affairs of the heart."

Raidy looked her up and down, then lowered her dark eyes and said, "I wish I had waited to kiss you. I think if I had, you would not have turned me away. Instead we would have become *close*, which is what I want more than anything. Do you think it would be so?"

"Good friends . . ." Jane stood in silent contemplation for a moment, looking her up and down in return. "I can't rule out that possibility," she said at length. "Stranger things have happened."

"Then perhaps we could start over?" Raidy asked quietly.

Jane gave the appearance of considering it before saying studiously, "Perhaps." She held out the towel for Raidy to take from her. "I still need to sweat this whiskey out of me . . . and I still need myself a good hot bath." She took Raidy's hand for support and stepped back over the edge of the tub.

Out in front of the sheriff's office, town sheriff Oscar Watts looked closely at the three bodies while a small gathering of townsfolk stood nearby. "These are the Higgins brothers, you say?" he asked the two lawmen loudly.

"Yes, that's them, Sheriff," said Dawson as he and Caldwell followed the ancient lawman back into his office and out of the harsh sunlight. "We have Jane Crowley coming to sign an affidavit, identifying them."

"Jane Crowley, hmmph...," he said loudly, compensating for his impaired hearing. Back inside the office, the old sheriff closed the door and walked to a pile of wanted posters on his battered oak desk. "She's been blind drunk so long I wouldn't expect she could recognize herself in a mirror."

"We've got her soaking and sobering right now, Sheriff," said Dawson, using the same raised voice to make himself heard.

"What about these men's cousins you were telling me about?" Watts asked, as he picked up the wanted posters and began leafing through them. He cut a glance at the Winchester rifles in both the lawmen's hands. "Are you expecting them?"

"Yep," said Dawson, glancing out the dusty window as he spoke, "Mose and Shorthand Higgins. They'll be coming along most any time. They'll be gunning for me and my deputy, but by the time they get here they'll have their bark on toward anybody wearing a badge."

"Dang it all," said Watts. "Where is Shaw when I need him? The one man who could help me is gone . . . with his head split open across the top like a ripe melon."

"We won't leave you to face the Higginses alone, Sheriff," said Dawson.

"I hope not," said Watts. "I've never seen any of them, but I've heard some ugly stories from as far away as Mexico City. It ain't just them, it's that whole gang of border trash they ride with." He looked Dawson and Caldwell both up and down appraisingly. "But I expect I can't tell you two anything you don't already know about border trash, eh?"

"We've run into our share, Sheriff, that's a fact," said Dawson.

"You're the two lawmen I've heard about, the ones sent to clean up on both sides of the border?" Watts asked in his loud voice.

"That's us," said Caldwell. "What can you tell us about Lawrence Shaw getting shot in the head?"

"Not much, I'm afraid," said the old sheriff. "He was dumb as a stump about it. Either he never knew who shot him, or he didn't want anybody else to know. He said he lay down to sleep—drunk, I'd wager. When he woke up his head was bandaged. He didn't even know why until Dr. Wheeler told him he'd been shot."

Caldwell asked, "Where will I find this Dr. Wheeler this time of day?"

"His office is at the end of the street. He ought to be in right now if you're wanting to talk to him. Lucky for Shaw that Doc Wheeler was here when it happened. Had he been off on some of his house calls, Shaw would have likely died."

From the doorway a voice interjected, "He might still die from it."

The old sheriff and the two lawmen turned toward a portly white-haired man wearing wire-rimmed spectacles. Watts said to Dawson and Caldwell, "Speaking of Doc Wheeler, here he is." To the doctor he said, "Doc, these two lawmen are inquiring about Lawrence Shaw. I was sending them to your office."

"I saw the dead out front," said Doc Wheeler. He looked the two lawmen up and down. "I came by just being nosy. I saw those fellows are beyond any help from my profession." He gave the lawmen a flat stare. "What can I tell you about Lawrence Shaw, except that it's a miracle he's alive—that is, *if* he's still alive."

"What do you mean *if* he's still alive, Doctor?" Dawson asked. "He must've been well enough to mount up and ride out of here. Was he in no shape to leave when he did?"

"He wasn't even close," said the doctor, "not with a head wound like that. He shouldn't be out there traveling these desert lands alone. He took a terrible impact to his brain. He needed to let it have time to heal. He could be lying somewhere dead out there, or else paralyzed, or without enough sense to know who he is."

"Just how deep did this bullet go into his head, Doctor?" Caldwell asked.

"It didn't," the doctor said gruffly. "That's the miracle of it. The shot was so close to his skull that the powder burned his hair off. But instead of entering his skull, the bullet skipped upward, ran along across the top of his head—split his scalp like a hatchet and came out on the other side." He reached inside his vest, produced a flattened .45-caliber lead slug and handed it to Caldwell.

"Good Lord," said Caldwell as he and Dawson examined the bullet.

"Imagine the jolt that must've been to his poor brain," said the doctor. "He can expect some aftereffects from this for a long time to come."

"Can I keep this, Doctor?" Dawson asked as Caldwell dumped the flattened slug from his palm into Dawson's.

"You're going to be seeing Shaw, if he's still among the living?" the doctor asked.

"Yes, we are," said Dawson. "When we catch up to him, I'll see that he gets it."

"Then yes, you keep it," said the doctor, "I have no use for it."

"Obliged," said Dawson, closing his hand around the bullet. "What sort of aftereffects are we talking about him having?"

"Oh, temporary blindness, paralysis, blackouts, loss of balance. Take your pick. Loss of memory, loss of time, loss of reasoning. Maybe all of these at some time or other until his brain is healed."

"How long before he's safely over it?" Caldwell asked.

"That's hard to say. We don't know enough about the human brain to say accurately everything it controls. But imagine how a massive bruise would affect your arm or leg, then think of what it can do to your brain." He added in a lowered tone of voice, "I saw the U.S. deputy badge he carries in his pocket. I take it he works with you two?"

"He has, some," said Dawson, not wanting to reveal too much about their work.

"Don't let him," the doctor said flatly, "at least not for the time being, not until you see that he's back in command of all his faculties. The trouble will be convincing him there's anything wrong. When the brain is not functioning properly, its owner can often be the last one to notice."

The two lawmen exchanged a troubled glance. Dawson started to speak, but Watts called out in his raised voice from the dusty window he'd turned and looked out, "Uh-oh, Marshals. It looks like the Higgins cousins have arrived."

Caldwell stepped over beside him and looked. "Looks like the Higginses had more local kin than we counted on," he said, watching five horses slide to a halt at the far end of the street.

Chapter 7

Atop their settling horses, Mose and Shorthand Higgins stared at the bodies of their cousins lying tied down across their saddles at the hitch rail in front of the sheriff's office. Upon hearing the horses' hooves and seeing the dust and commotion, a big yellow hound ran to the middle of the street. The excited animal bounced on its front paws, barking and baying furiously toward the five horsemen.

"These rotten lawdog sonsabitches! Look how they're treating our poor cousins!" Shorthand Higgins growled through clenched teeth. In the street the hound continued its insistent barking until a rifle bullet hit the ground near its front paw and spat dirt in its face.

Over his shoulder, Mose Higgins said to the three gunmen behind him as the yellow hound yelped and fled, "All right, hombres, get all set to make 'em bleed." He jerked a big Dance Brothers pistol from his belly holster and cocked it briskly. To Sandefur Reid he said,

"Sandy, get over to that mercantile store and gather up what we'll need."

"You got it, Mose," said the rough-faced gunman. He leaped from his saddle, hurried away across the dirt street and shoved the mercantile door open as the owners inside tried to close and lock it. A woman's voice shrieked above the sound of Sandefur rummaging merchandise and breaking glass.

Out in front of the sheriff's office, the gathered bystanders had already read trouble in the way the riders had raced into town. The rifle shot sent them running, disappearing into doorways and storefronts; the hound vanished into an alleyway.

From the dusty window of the sheriff's office, Dawson jacked a round into his Winchester and said to Caldwell beside him, "Look who's riding with them."

Caldwell had studied the gunmen closely as the dust around them settled. "Albert Colon, Dent Parker and Sandefur Reid. Where do you suppose the Higginses ran into them?"

"They were riding with them all the time. They were close by, we just didn't see them all," said Dawson. "We might be closer to Madden Corio and his gang than we thought."

"Too bad we're not full-time bounty hunters," said Caldwell, checking his rifle. "This bunch would've been a bonanza for us."

Across the office, the sheriff took a long double-barreled shotgun down from a gun rack and hurriedly loaded it. "Doc," he said in his loud voice, "it's best you skin on out the back door before these killers get situated and try pinning us in here."

"Nonsense, Sheriff," said Dr. Wheeler, grabbing a rifle from the rack and checking it. "Just because I'm sworn to save another man's life doesn't mean I'm not allowed to defend my own." He levered a round into the rifle chamber. "When I was a boy I kept our Pennsylvania farmhouse provided with rabbit and squirrel."

"These are not squirrels we're shooting, Doc," Sheriff Watts warned him.

"Right you are indeed, Sheriff," said the determined doctor. "Nor am I any longer a boy." He stepped over to a back window and opened it. "These saddle bums are in for a big surprise."

At the window hearing the conversation between the doctor and the sheriff, Caldwell and Dawson gave each other a knowing look. With no more thought on the matter, Dawson called out to the gunmen as they advanced on the small building, "Mose, Shorthand, my deputy and I are coming out, just the two of us. We'll settle this with you in the street."

"That's mighty obliging of you, Marshal," Shorthand called out in reply. "But we don't want you out here. We've already made other plans."

Sandefur came running from the mercantile with a tin of kerosene in hand and a bolt of cloth and a half dozen axe handles under his arm. "*Yee-hiii!*" he shouted. "Let the fun start!" He dumped the handles and cloth to the ground at Mose's and Shorthand's feet.

"They're going to try to burn us up," Caldwell said.

Watching through the window, he saw Shorthand hurry to a freight wagon parked along the street.

"Oh my," muttered the doctor, never having thought of the gunmen trying anything so dastardly.

Caldwell and Dawson watched Shorthand jump aboard the wagon, drive it halfway across the street, stop it and set the brake, providing themselves perfect cover.

"Don't you worry, Doc," Watts called out in his loud voice. "There'll be armed townsmen rallying to us as soon as they get over their surprise. We're going to shoot these snakes before they do such a thing—"

"Sheriff Watts, you two stay here until the townsmen show up," said Dawson, cutting the old lawman off. "Let's go, Deputy, before they finish getting their torches made up."

While Jane Crowley was soaking in the tub, she heard a rifle shot that made her eyes snap open. "Well, hell, it sounds like Mose and Shorthand have arrived just when this was getting interesting." She stood up in the tub even as the young woman's wet hands tried to stop her.

"No, no, lie back down," said Raidy Bowe. "This is their stupid man's play! Let them handle it themselves. Stay here with me. Please! Do not get yourself shot for *them*!"

"Sorry, little darling, much as I hate to, I've got to go," said Jane. She stepped out of the tub again, hurriedly snatched up her fringed doeskins from across a chair and began throwing them on. As she dressed, her eyes searched the room. "I don't suppose there's a gun lying around anywhere?"

In the street, Dent Parker and Albert Colon had spread out, Colon taking a position behind a stack of wooden farm implement crates straight across the street from the sheriff's office. Parker had run around to cover the rear door in case anyone tried to escape once they had successfully started their fire.

"Hurry up, Sandy!" Shorthand growled as the gunman finished making a torch, poured kerosene onto its cloth head and handed it to Mose.

Mose and Shorthand had kept a close watch on the front door of the sheriff's office from the cover of the freight wagon. Still, they were almost caught off guard by the fierceness of the lawmen when the front door seemed to explode open and the two came out firing.

"It's commenced for certain, Doc!" Watts called out loudly, stepping forward long enough to swing the front door shut. At the rear door, the doctor peeped out and saw Dent Parker running toward him in a crouch.

"Here's one!" said the excited doctor, throwing the rifle to his shoulder just as Parker fired. He took quick aim and pulled the trigger just as he felt Parker's shot hit him in his soft round stomach. He grunted, but only leaned sidelong against the door frame and watched Parker spin in a circle and fall limp onto the ground. "By gads, sir, I—I got him!" Dr. Wheeler said over his shoulder, sounding surprised at his gun prowess.

"Doc, are you okay?" shouted Watts, hurrying to the wounded man's side as he slumped down the door frame.

"I'm . . . all right, Sheriff," said the doctor. But Watts knew better. He'd seen as many of these kinds of wounds as the doctor himself had seen.

"Doggone it, Doc," Watts said with regret.

In the street, Caldwell and Dawson split up a few feet and rushed forward as bullets whistled around them. "Kill the sonsabitches!" Mose shouted, firing from around the rear corner of the freight wagon.

Shorthand shouted as he fired from the other corner of the wagon, "Forget the torches, Sandy, they've busted loose on us!"

But Sandefur Reid wasn't about to let all of his work go for nothing. He quickly set fire to two of the torches and ran from behind the cover of the wagon, waving the flaming axe handles with a rebel yell. Dawson and Caldwell, who had just found cover, one behind a water trough, one amid the clutter of a busted shipping crate, both turned their fire onto Sandefur.

As the outlaw hurled one torch high and let out another yell as it arched down atop the roof of the town barbershop, a shot from Caldwell's rifle hit him squarely in his chest and caused him to stagger in place. Sandefur managed to hurl the other torch blindly and scream out in rage, "You no-account lawdog sons-abit—"

A shot from Dawson cut his words short as the second torch he'd thrown came down onto the board-walk out in front of the Southwestern Stage Lines. The torch buried itself amid a pile of luggage, packages and mail pouches. Flames immediately began licking upward along the front of the weathered clapboard plank building.

From his well-covered position Albert Colon fired at Caldwell, forcing the lawman to dive facedown in the dirt before shots from Dawson's rifle provided him cover and sent Colon backing away from a spray of splinters and dust from the implement crates.

"To hell with this," said Shorthand, reloading while Mose fired steadily at the two lawmen. "Remember our cousins, and follow me!" He gestured toward the bodies lying across the nervous horses out in front of the sheriff's office.

"Here they come," Dawson called out to Caldwell. The two half stood from behind their cover, rifles in hand. But when they saw that Mose and Shorthand were coming out, walking forward down to the middle of the street to meet them face-to-face, Dawson reached over and leaned his rifle against a post.

Seeing the lawmen step out to meet them, Shorthand called out to Albert Colon, "Show yourself, Albert. These sonsabitches want a reckoning . . . so do we. Let's finish it up like the bold men we are."

"Yeah," said Mose with a look of pure hatred. He lowered and uncocked his Dance Brothers pistol, preparing himself for a face-to-face showdown. "Our poor cousins deserve no less."

Albert Colon watched from behind the protection of the shipping crates. Seeing Shorthand and Mose step forward, and seeing the two lawmen move sidelong slowly into the open, he shook his head. "This is a bad mistake," he said to himself, yet he lay his rifle aside, checked his Colt, then held it at his side and walked out from behind his cover. "However you want to do this, pards," he called out to Shorthand and Mose, "is A-okay with me."

Dawson and Caldwell looked at the two gunmen walking slowly toward them in one direction, and at Colon advancing slowly from the other.

"Well, well," Shorthand said with a dark chuckle, "I'm thinking it looks like you badge toters have gotten yourself amidst a little cross fire situation."

But the grin on his face turned flat when from a half block away Jane Crowley called out, "Think again, you shorthanded idiot. I'm packing a double load of nail heads and glass, and I'm still whiskey-bent enough to use them!"

"Jane Crowley, by God," said Mose, turning and looking toward her, seeing her advance along the dirt street with determination. "What's a low degenerate like you doing siding with the law?"

"Oh, did we all come out here to talk some?" Jane said in an acid tone. She stopped twenty feet from the two and held the old flintlock shotgun cocked and ready at her side. "I thought I was coming to gun-fight."

"Jane, back away, you're drunk," Caldwell called out from the other side of the two Higginses.

"She always is," Shorthand said, staring at Jane, his gun hand ready to swing up and fire his pistol. "But it doesn't matter." He gave a dark grin. "She's got no guts for killing, I heard."

"Like he said, you shorthanded pecker, I'm drunk," Jane called out. "I'll do most anything."

As the fighters had gathered, Sheriff Watts had slipped out the back door and joined several townsmen who had armed themselves and come looking for the old sheriff to lead them. Having seen Doc Wheeler sitting in a chair in a puddle of blood, his hands clasping his bleeding stomach, the townsmen had grown bold and vicious in their need to avenge him.

"Look at this," Dawson said quietly to Caldwell, seeing the townsmen and their sheriff line up along the street facing the Higginses.

Also seeing the townsmen lining up along the street, Mose Higgins cried out, "You people have no right siding with them! Look what they did to our poor cousins! What would you do in our place? These were fine, decent men who didn't deserve—"

Jane shouted out, "If their ma was smart she would have smothered them with a pillow the day they were born."

"Why, you filthy, woman-loving—" Shorthand growled through clenched teeth, swinging his pistol around level toward her.

"Oh, shit!" Mose shouted, seeing all of the guns pointed at him and Shorthand from three directions.

Caldwell and Dawson fired the same time hoping to stop Shorthand before he could kill Jane. At the same time the townsmen opened fire.

Shorthand's bullet hit the front stock of the double-barrel shotgun in Jane's hands and caused her to drop the weapon just as she pulled both triggers. The wild load of glass and nail heads missed both gunmen, but some of the glass sprayed the wagon horses' rumps and sent them into a whinnying frenzy. The team took off with the empty wagon even though its brake handle was firmly set. The locked wheels skidded back and forth wildly along the dirt street until the horses disappeared out of sight around a corner.

For a moment a merciless hail of gunfire held the Higginses up on their feet as bullets ripped and sliced through them. Blood spewed and poured in jetties from their twisting, jerking bodies.

While the two Higginses did a crazy death dance in the middle of the street, Albert Colon fired once at the two lawmen, then saw his chance to run and took it. But before he got fully turned, Caldwell swung around and fired. The bullet hit Colon in his right buttocks. He screamed, grabbed his bloody behind and fell to the ground into a crawl. As he tried to crawl toward an alley, Caldwell ran forward, wanting to take one of the gunmen alive for questioning.

Before Caldwell could get closer to Colon, a young boy ran out of nowhere with a small .22-caliber pistol, reached down and shot the crawling outlaw twice in his back.

"Hold it, kid!" shouted Caldwell, hearing the sharp snapping sound of the small loads.

The boy looked around with his mouth wide open at the lawman running toward him, a Colt in his hand.

"My pa said I could! He said I could!" the boy shouted, flinging the gun to the dirt and turning and racing away.

In the street behind Caldwell, the firing had died down beneath a thick cloud of burned gunpowder. Townsmen began to cough and fan their hats back and forth as Dawson trotted toward Caldwell, who had leaned down and turned Colon over onto his back. Watts came forward and ran with a brittle gait alongside him.

Colon gasped and batted his eyes and looked over the small gun smoking in the dirt. "Can you believe this?" he said mournfully. "I'm done in by a damned little rat killer." He looked up at Caldwell. "Shoot me with something bigger . . . before I go."

"Lie still, Albert," said Caldwell. "We want to know about Madden Corio and his gang's next move."

"I'm dying here," said Colon.

"You're not going to die, Albert," said Caldwell. "There's a doctor here. He'll save you."

"There is?" Colon asked with a look of hope coming to his frightened eyes.

"There was a doctor, a damn good one," Sheriff Watts cut in, stopping alongside Dawson and looking down at the wounded outlaw. "But one of you sonsabitches just killed him."

"See?" Colon said in disgust, turning his eyes back to Caldwell. "That's just my *damn* luck. . . ."

Chapter 8

Once a bucket brigade had extinguished the fires at the barbershop and out in front of the stage line office, Jane unhitched the wagon horses and looked them over good while both animals whinnied and chuffed and tried to shy away from her. "Sorry about that, fellows," she said, seeing the animals take frightened note of the ancient shotgun in her hand. "Seems like I shoot every damn thing except what I'm supposed to."

Jane leaned the shotgun against a post and continued to inspect the less anxious horses. Seeing that both animals were going to be all right, she led them to the livery barn and left them for the hostler to attend to. On her way back through the alley behind the sheriff's office, she saw a bloody smear leading across the dirt, and she followed it to the rear of a woodshed, where she heard a voice saying from inside, "Help . . . Somebody help me."

Her hand instinctively slapped against her empty

holster. "Damn it . . . ," she growled to herself. But then she said through the partly opened door of the woodshed, "Who's in there? How bad are you shot?"

"It's me, Dent Parker," the wounded outlaw said in a strained voice from within the darkness of the shed. "I'm bleeding . . . something awful."

"So you need some help, eh Dent?" said Jane, looking all around to see if there were any armed townsmen near enough for her to wave down.

"Yeah . . . ain't that what I told ya?" Parker managed to say with a cross edge to his weakened voice.

"Watch your smart mouth, Dent Parker," Jane warned him, "else we'll leave you in there to bleed out like a split pig."

"Is that . . . Jane Crowley I hear?" Parker asked, summoning up his waning strength.

"Yeah, Dent, it's me," said Jane. "Looks like I'm the one who found your bloody ass. I saw your white-faced roan wandering around in the street. I'm surprised that horse stuck with you this long."

"He's your horse now, Janie," said the pain-racked voice, "if you can . . . help me out here."

Jane let out a bothered breath. "All right. Throw out your guns. We'll see what we can do for you."

"Is there more than . . . one of yas out there?" Parker asked as if checking his odds first.

"What's the difference, Dent?" Jane said. "Are you wanting help or not?"

"Here—here they come," Parker said.

Jane watched a Remington pistol sail through the

partly opened door and land near her feet. She grinned to herself, reached down, picked it up and sized it up in her hand. She cocked it. "I managed to do that much right," she said proudly to herself.

"What's that? What'd you say?" Parker called out.

"Nothing," Jane replied in a raised voice. On a hunch she said, "Reach down, pull that pig sticker out of your boot and toss it out too. This is not a time to be holding out on us."

She heard him grumble and curse under his breath. Then a long knife arced out the doorway and fell to the dirt. "There, I'm all in," said Parker. "You all come ahead and get me. I promise not to . . . fight yas."

"See to it you don't," Jane said in a firm tone. Shoving the door open all the way, she watched sunlight fall in a wide strip upon Parker's bloody face, his chest and his raised hands. "Keep them bloody claws up where we can see them," Jane instructed, stepping inside.

"Hellfire, Janie!" Parker said. "You bluffed me. There ain't . . . but one of yas." He looked past her and saw no one else. He noted the empty holster on her slim right hip, and his own Remington pistol in her hand. "Unarmed at that . . . ," he added in disgust.

"What did you think it would take, an *army* to bring your lousy ass in?" Jane said. "You think much too highly of yourself." Seeing how badly he was wounded, she holstered the Remington and stooped down to help him up. "Besides, I thought you were wanting to give yourself up."

"Hell . . . I am giving up," said Parker, looping his arm over her shoulder as she struggled and stood up with him at her side. "But these old habits . . . die hard, don't they, Janie?"

"Don't ask me, Dent, I still got all mine," Jane replied, turning with him toward the shed door, "all the bad ones anyway."

"I haven't seen you . . . since Deadwood," Parker said, his voice growing weaker. "Are you . . . still going all moony-eyed over gunslingers?"

"Keep talking, Dent, like as not I'll finish you off myself," Jane cautioned him, helping him along the alleyway to the street.

On the street, Caldwell turned when he saw an angry townsman point and say, "Here comes another of the lousy sonsabitches, still alive!"

Hurrying over to Jane, Caldwell said, "It might've been best to leave this one where you found him. This is the maddest bunch I've seen for a while." He looked at Parker's bloody chest and asked in a lowered voice, "Are you the one who shot Dr. Wheeler?"

"I shot somebody back there . . . hell, I don't know who he was," said Parker. "He pointed a rifle . . . what do you expect?"

"Dent, you stupid turd," Jane said sidelong to the wounded outlaw. "You've shot the one man who might have saved your damned life."

"That doesn't . . . surprise me," Parker said, shaking his bowed head.

"You and Colon will be lucky if these folks don't lynch you both," said Caldwell, seeing the townsmen mill and stare behind Sheriff Watts. Beside Watts stood a big man with his arm around the shoulders of the boy who had shot Colon in the back. The man held the small gun in his big hand. He squeezed the small gun's handle as Jane and Caldwell led Parker closer.

"Albert . . . is alive too?" Parker asked.

"For now," said Caldwell. "Without a doctor I don't expect he'll be planning his future."

"Me neither," said Parker, "but I hate to hang . . . as close as I am to dying anyway."

Caldwell gave Jane a look, then said to Parker, "In that case you need to start telling everything you can about Corio's gang and what they're up to. Maybe we can keep a rope from circling your neck until you die peaceably."

"Mama always said . . . I'd hang someday," Parker reflected. "I've always done everything . . . to prove that old hag wrong."

"Then here's your last big chance to frost her over, Dent," Jane said. The three of them walked on through the angry, slow-parting group of townsmen to a board-walk, where Dawson had dragged Albert Colon out of the sun—hopefully out of the townsmen's reach.

"We've got another one here who wants to tell us about Corio to keep from getting rope burnt," Caldwell said to Dawson as the two stepped up and laid the wounded outlaw down beside his fellow gunman.

"Really?" said Dawson. He eyed Colon up and down. "That's too bad. Albert here doesn't want to hang either. He's told us nearly everything about Corio except his birthday."

"Trouble is," said Parker, "Albert here don't know shit." He turned his bloody face, looked at Colon and added, "No offense intended."

Colon either ignored him or didn't hear him. He stared straight ahead with a blank expression taking over his face and said to Dawson, "I can't . . . feel my toes. That snot-nosed kid . . . ruined me. . . ." Dawson, Jane and Caldwell watched his eyes glaze over. He let out a long, even breath and made no attempt at replacing it.

Dawson looked out into the street at the gathered townsmen, then said to Parker, "It's all you now, Dent. You better start telling us what Corio's up to. These men are starting to buzz like hornets."

Parker gave Jane a worried look, then said to Dawson, "Marshal, I wish I knew . . . something to tell you, but the fact is I don't. Whatever Madden Corio is up to, he's keeping it . . . all to himself."

"How many men is riding with him these days?" Dawson asked, trying to get some kind of an idea about the outlaw's plans.

"I've seen as many as fourteen lately," Parker said, speaking quickly, making nervous glances toward the crowd in the street. "That's not counting men like myself or Albert here. We come and go as the next job requires." Among the men stood the town blacksmith, Irvin Broward, busily looping a hangman's noose with a hemp rope.

"There's smaller gangs that Corio brings in to do his dirty work," said Parker, his eyes flickering across the angry townsmen as he spoke. "I've seen lots of them lately, enough to tell me there's something big in the works."

"Marshal," the blacksmith called out to Dawson from the middle of the street, "if you're through with those two, we're ready to send them to hell, where they belong."

"Yeah," said another townsman, "they'll lie to you all day long if it'll keep them from getting their necks stretched."

"One of them is already dead," Dawson offered. "This other one isn't far behind. Anything I can find out from him is worth knowing."

"That's bull!" said a townsman. "It was you two lawmen who led them here to begin with. If it hadn't been for you, Doc Wheeler would still be alive."

"Staley here is right, Marshal," said the big blacksmith. "You two brought them here. Now turn this one over to us. We're avenging our beloved doctor, whether you like it or not."

"There's not going to be a lynching," Dawson said, his Colt slipping from his holster and hanging loose but ready in his hand. "I'm advising every one of you to get off the street, let me and my deputy question this man and go on with our business."

"Yeah, Broward, you thickheaded son of a bitch!" Jane bellowed. "If I have to I'll kick you worthless balls up into your—"

"Jane, no!" said Caldwell, grabbing her and clamping a hand over her mouth. "Let the marshal handle this," he added closer to her ear. "All that kind of talk will do is make things worse."

Jane slung her head and grumbled under his hand until he finally released it from her mouth. "All right," she said. "I just couldn't stand here and listen to that big turd make his threats." She glared at the blacksmith.

On the boardwalk behind her, Dent Parker said in a failing voice, "Jane . . . come here."

Jane turned, bent over him and looked at him questioningly. "What is it, Dent?"

"Can you help me out, Janie?" he asked. "For the horse and the gun?"

"Damn it, Dent," Jane said under her breath, reading the dark pleading in his eyes, "that's a lot to ask for a horse and a gun."

Parker only stared at her through fading eyes, until finally Jane gave a determined look and said quietly, "All right, Dent, here goes, okay?"

She slipped the knife she'd taken from him out of her fringed shirtsleeve and slid it back down into his boot well. Dent watched her with a weak knowing smile. "Okay," he replied.

Straightening, turning back toward the crowd, Jane slipped the Remington from her holster and watched the blacksmith and the rest of the townsmen advance a step forward as one. Their rifles and pistols were poised and ready; so were Dawson and Caldwell's. Sheriff Watts stood off to the side, torn between his loyalty to the town he'd sworn to protect and the lawmen with whom his profession bonded him.

"Broward, stand down!" Watts finally called out to the big blacksmith, seeing that neither side was about to give an inch. "The marshal's right. There's not going to be a lynching here! I cared as much for Doc Wheeler as anybody here. But hanging a dying man ain't going to bring him back."

"We're all through talking, Sheriff," said the blacksmith. To the rest of the townsmen he said, "Come on, men, let's get this done."

Jane saw by the look on Dawson's and Caldwell's faces that the lawmen would be firing onto the townsmen at any second. She saw the blacksmith lead the townsmen forward and knew that at any second he would break into a run and charge the boardwalk. Watching, she cocked the Remington and took a deep breath, knowing every second counted. *Do it . . . ,* she told herself.

Just as it appeared that nothing would keep the fight from commencing, she spun around quickly toward Dent Parker as she shouted, "Watch out, Marshal! Behind you!"

Parker lay with his eyes closed. Jane had no idea if he was dead or alive. But she fired the Remington into his chest and watched his body jerk upward from the shot's impact. "There, you sneaking bastard!" she shouted, staring down at the sprawled body.

The townsmen and the lawmen stood frozen in place. A stunned silence loomed as Jane looked all around. Finally Caldwell said, "Janie, what have you done?"

"What have I done?" Jane appeared indignant about the matter. "Hell, he was going for a knife, Undertaker. Had you been watching him instead of studying what these fools were about to do, you would've seen it."

"A knife, your drunken lying ass, Jane," said Broward, hurrying forward and staring down at both Parker's and Colon's bodies. "You've denied this town our rightful vengeance."

"He was going for a knife," Jane insisted.

As she and Broward stood fuming at each other, Sheriff Watts stepped in, reached down and jerked the knife from Parker's boot well. "Looks like you owe her an apology, Broward," he said, pitching the weapon at the blacksmith's feet.

All eyes went to the knife, then to Jane. She stood glowering at Broward. "I don't want this metal-bending monkey's apology." She shoved the smoking Remington down into her holster and said to Dawson with a tone of sarcasm, "Ah, hell, Marshal, don't bother *thanking me* for saving your life."

Dawson replied to her under his breath, "Parker couldn't have raised a hand if he had to."

"Tell them that," Jane whispered back to him. "Maybe you can get another lynching started."

Dawson turned to Caldwell and said quietly, "Let's get our supplies and get out of here." He then studied Jane skeptically. "Are you sober enough to come along with us? I've got a feeling you've worn out your welcome around here."

"I'm sober enough to ride," she said. She reached down onto the boardwalk beside Albert Colon's body and picked up his battered hat and slapped it against her thigh to dust it. "I'm sober, I've got a gun and horse. What more does a gal like me need?"

Before she could put the floppy hat down onto her

head, Raidy ran in as if from out of nowhere, handed Jane a towel and said, "Here, dry your hair first."

"Obliged, ma'am," said Jane. She took the towel and rubbed it back and forth roughly on her head. "It's kind of you to think of me," she said.

Dawson and Caldwell gave each other a look, then turned to Sheriff Watts, who had stepped in closer now that the tension had begun to relinquish its hold on the townsmen. "I want you to know these are good people here, Marshal," he said to Dawson. "It's not every day they lose a man like Doc Wheeler."

"I understand, Sheriff," said Dawson. "This was thrown upon them too suddenly. They did the best they could with it." As he spoke he stared straight at Broward. The blacksmith lowered his head and backed away a step.

"Some of yas come with me," said Watts to the townsmen, taking charge. "Let's get Doc's body out of my office and ready to bury." He eyed the outlaws' corpses. "A couple of yas stay here and help drag these carcasses off the street and get them underground."

Dawson and Caldwell watched as Jane walked away to a hitch rail, where one of the townsmen had gathered the outlaws' horses and secured them. Raidy followed along close to her side, one step behind her.

"What's going on with these two?" Caldwell asked Dawson quietly.

"I don't even want to guess," said Dawson. "With Jane you never know what to expect. Don't worry, she's only with us until we catch up to Shaw. She's his problem then."

"I'm wondering how long that's going to take," said Caldwell. "There's no telling what Shaw is up to out there, if he's even still alive."

"That's what I'm determined to find out," Dawson replied. "Shaw's never let me down yet."

"But he's never had a bullet in his head," Dawson offered.

"The bullet's not in his head," Dawson said with the trace of a wry grin. "You heard the doctor—his head's just split open and badly bruised. His *brain* is badly bruised, the doctor says."

"Damn," said Caldwell, "what a shape for a gunman like Shaw to be in. For all we know, he's wandering around not knowing his own name."

"One more reason for us to find him as quick as we can," said Dawson.

Chapter 9

For three days Lawrence Shaw had ridden with Dexter Lowe and his men across the border into the badland hills of Mexico. He had been awake and aware, yet, in reflection, everything around him had seemed to come and go as if he were watching someone play out his life on a poorly lit stage. He thought about his condition as he gazed out across a line of jagged hilltops.

He realized that his thinking was not back to where it should be, not yet. But as long as he was the only one who knew it, he would be all right. He still had a job to do, he told himself, pulling his speckled barb back from the edge of a cliff and turning it toward the trail as the other riders filed past him.

"Hey, you," said Sonny Lloyd Sheer, pulling his horse over to Shaw. "What're you doing breaking ranks?"

Shaw stared at him, unable to put any words together quick enough to respond. *A bad sign . . .* , he thought.

"Well," said Sonny, "are you with us, or are you going to sit here and take in the scenery?"

Hearing Sonny, the other men reined down and sat watching. "Breaking ranks?" New York Joe Toledo said with a bemused look. "This ain't the army. What's got your bark on so tight, Sonny?" As he spoke he eased his horse a step nearer to Shaw and Sonny. "The man's carrying a head wound, for crying out loud." Beside Toledo, Tuesday Bonhart nodded in agreement.

"Stay out of this, Toledo," Sonny snapped. "My job is to keep everybody close together 'til Dex gets back from meeting with Corio. You want to face him this evening, tell him you don't know where everybody is?"

"No," Toledo replied, "but it ain't like anybody's rode away. The man's got a head wound, he stopped for a minute. It's nothing to get yourself riled over."

"I'm not riled," said Sheer. He grinned and stared at Shaw. "You would not want to see me riled, drifter. It wouldn't be a pretty sight."

Shaw made no response, but his senses had piqued at hearing Sonny's words regarding Madden Corio. Lowe had left sometime during the night without even taking the whore, Tuesday Bonhart, with him. So that was it—he'd gone off somewhere to meet with Corio. *Good.* . . . Things were in motion for the big job the men had spoken of. *Sit tight* . . . , he advised himself.

Dan Sax eased his horse over beside Toledo's and said under his breath, "Easy, Joe, this drifter can take care of himself. We've all seen that."

Toledo knew that Dan Sax was right. Without another word, he backed his horse a step and sat watching quietly while the young whore cut away from beside him and rode over closer to Shaw and Sheer. Shaw sat with a blank stare on his face as if he'd suddenly traveled a thousand miles away.

"Get away from here, Sonny, and stop talking tough just because Dex left you in charge."

"I don't get away from here until this one gets back in line like everybody else," Sheer said.

"Can't you see he's not feeling good, Sonny?" said Tuesday, reaching out and placing her hand flat on Shaw's bandaged-wrapped forehead. "What's wrong, Mister? Is your head hurting?" she asked with childlike sympathy.

Shaw only stared, wanting to speak but unable to get himself started.

"He's turned idiot on us, if you ask me," said Sheer, seeing nothing threatening in the ragged drifter's demeanor.

"Nobody is asking you," Tuesday said with frosty authority in her voice. "Now go away. Him and I will ride along behind the rest of yas."

"Who the hell are you, telling me what to do?" Sheer asked. "I'm the one who leads this outfit 'til Dex gets back!"

"Yeah . . . ?" Tuesday shot back at him. "And I'm the one who sleeps with him when he does get back. Do you want to see which one of us counts the most?" She didn't wait for Sheer to reply. "Now get moving. I'm looking after this one."

Watching Sheer jerk his horse around and ride away,

Joe Toledo said to Dan Sax, "Damn it, Dex told me to look after her. I expect I best go pull her away from there. He's known to get killing jealous of his women-folk."

"Naw, let it alone, Joe," Dan Sax said. "It might be interesting to see how jealous Dex gets with a man this fast with a gun." He gave Toledo a sly grin.

"Yeah, come to think of it, Dex has been awfully agreeable with this gunman. It might be fun seeing how worked up he gets over this little whore."

Sitting close to Shaw on her horse, Tuesday shook him by his forearm and said, "Hey, mystery man, can you hear me in there?"

Shaw heard her, but her voice sounded distant and halting. He saw her, but she came in and out of focus against a harsh backdrop of glinting sunlight. He tried to speak again, but with great effort only managed to say unsteadily, "I do. . . ."

"Good, because I want you to listen to me," Tuesday said, lowering her voice even though the riders had begun to move off along the trail. "I know who you are. You're Fast Larry Shaw. You ride with Marshal Crayton Dawson and his deputy Caldwell, *the Under-taker*."

"Not anymore," Shaw said, his own voice sounding weak and distant to him.

"Whether you do or not makes me no difference," said Tuesday. "I'm in this for what I can get out of it. Do you understand me?" She eyed him with scrutiny, seeing the blankness about him. "If you do, just nod your head."

Shaw nodded his head, but he also answered, coming around now that he had to focus on his job, and on staying alive. "I understand, ma'am," he said.

"Good," said Tuesday, her voice even lower and more guarded. "I'll keep who you are a secret, but only if you promise not to mess up anything I've got going for myself. Deal?"

Shaw didn't answer. For just a second as she'd spoken, he'd had a hard time comprehending anything she'd said. In that same second he had lost all memory of what had happened to him or what he was doing here. Then it all came rushing back to him. "What is it you've got going for yourself?" he asked, hoping she had no way of noticing that his mind had gone temporarily blank.

She stared at him for a moment, then said, "As soon as this is over, Dex and I are clearing out. Far as we'll be concerned, the law can track down this bunch and Madden Corio's gang and do whatever they want with them."

"After what is over?" Shaw asked, working hard at keeping his mind clear and sharp and able to grasp the conversation.

She hesitated. "Well, I'm not sure what we're going to be doing. Corio is playing things awfully tight-lipped. But Dex is meeting with him today and finding out. Whatever it is, it's going to big, as many men as Corio is bringing in on it."

"I hope so," said Shaw, playing his role as outlaw. "I can use the money."

Tuesday cocked her head slightly. "I'll be finding out

about it as soon as he gets back. Maybe you and me can keep one another informed on things." She gave a grin. "I always liked you."

"You did?" Shaw asked, not understanding what she was implying right away.

"Yes, I did," she said; then to help him out, she added, "You did me once, remember?"

Not wanting to offend her by saying he didn't remember, Shaw said, "I hope you'll overlook me, ma'am. This head wound has me—"

"Call me Tuesday," she said. "It's all right that you don't remember it, you was pretty drunk. But you was a gentleman all the same."

"Oh," Shaw said. He stared at her. "Well, I'm glad to hear that."

She shrugged and put the matter aside. "How bad is your head? You look like you're doing well to keep from falling over."

"I'm getting over it quick enough," Shaw said, his hearing once again taking on a distant tone.

"Yeah?" Tuesday looked doubtful. "How well does your gun hand work?"

"Well enough," Shaw said confidently.

"Yeah? Well, I'd like to see just how fast—"

Before Tuesday got the words from her mouth, Shaw's Colt streaked up from its holster, cocked and ready. The tip of the barrel pressed firmly against her large left breast.

"My God!" she said, completely stunned by his action as well as his speed.

"I—I'm sorry," Shaw said, staring at the gun in his

hand, looking as stunned by his action as she was. He lowered the barrel and uncocked the weapon, still staring at it in confusion. "I don't know why I did that."

Tuesday recovered quickly from her surprise. "You did the same thing in Colinas Secas when Dex asked you to shoot Bell Mason."

Shaw stared at her. He didn't want to admit it but he had no memory of the incident, no image or clue as to what she was talking about.

"You were ready to blow daylight through him, if Dex had given you the word," Tuesday said. She gave a dark little giggle. "Dex liked that you was going to. It might be why he hired you." She gave a questioning look. "You do remember it, don't you?"

"Yeah," Shaw lied, "I remember it."

"I hope so," said Tuesday. "If you and me are going to be sharing information, I want to know I can count on you."

"I don't know what information I might come upon that would be helpful to you," Shaw said.

"It's not just information I might need from you, Fast Larry," said Tuesday. As she spoke she put her hand over onto the barrel of his Colt and stroked it back and forth slowly, staring at Shaw. "In country like this who knows when a man with a big gun might come in handy?" Her voice had softened, and warmed. "Can I count on you if the time comes when I need to? Can we be secret friends?" She squeezed the barrel tightly, then relaxed her grip on it.

"I'm sure we can," Shaw said. "But if it's going to be a secret, you and I best get back with the rest of the riders, before they start thinking something they shouldn't." He eased the Colt down from under her hand and slipped it back into his holster.

Tuesday smiled. "I'm glad you and I had this little talk, Fast Larry," she said, backing her horse a step and turning it back toward the rocky trail. "Come on, we'll tag along behind the others for a while. Let them think what they want." She smiled as she gestured him toward the trail. "I've been wishing I had a big gunman I could count on. I never dreamed it would be Fast Larry Shaw."

Madden Corio and Dexter Lowe had spent the day going over parts of the plan that would involve Lowe and his men. In the afternoon, Corio, Bert Jordan and Willard Dance sat atop a ridge and watched Lowe ride down and out across a stretch of flatlands. Making sure he hadn't been followed, either coming or going, Dance said as Lowe's rise of dust settled behind him, "What was stuck in *Dangerous* Dexter's craw, Madden?"

Corio kept watching as Lowe disappeared out of sight over the edge of the flatlands. "He thought him and his men should be doing something more important than driving freight wagons," Madden replied.

"The son of a bitch has sure some nerve on him," Dance said. "What does that little punk want, to run the show, make us his teamsters?"

"Yeah," said Bert Jordan, "have *us* driving the wagons for *him* while he sits perched up watching us, like a hawk or something."

"How'd you get him to change his mind?" Jordan asked Corio.

Corio smiled. "I explained that somebody always has to drive the wagons."

"Explained, ha," said Dance. "I bet you explained it to him with your gun stuck in his ear."

"No," said Corio, "there were no threats made. He saw it my way . . . after he realized this was the only deal around that would make him and his boys the kind of money he's looking for."

"Dexter Lowe has never been more than a hand-to-mouth sneak thief. What's got him so greedy for money all of a sudden?" asked Jordan.

Without taking his eyes off the flatlands, Corio said, "He's gone staggering mad over some young Missouri whore. I expect she's got him turning ambitious. We all know how a whore can be."

"Don't we, though?" said Dance with a chuckle.

"Lowe and his men are meeting Harvey Lemate tomorrow night in Yellow Moon Canyon." To Bert Jordan he said, "Bert, you get over there and take charge, get those stolen wagons over to the draw where I told Lowe to pick them up from us. Then ride hard and get on back here. I'm going to need you at my side."

"You've got it, Madden," Jordan. He and Dance gave each other a look.

"Dance," said Corio, "you ride along with me."

"Sure thing," said Dance, turning and catching up alongside Corio as he rode away.

Jordan sat for only a moment watching with a grim expression as the two rode away. Then he shook his head, turned his horse and rode to where the rest of the men sat sipping coffee, awaiting orders.

Lemate stood up and slung coffee grinds from his cup and asked Jordan, "Where's Madden going?"

"Why don't you catch up and ask him?" Jordan returned.

"Just wondering, is all." Lemate shrugged. "What about these freight wagons?"

"We're taking the wagons over to Yellow Moon tonight, Harvey, getting everything ready to go," Jordan said, "so get everybody off their asses and on their feet."

"All right!" said Lemate, getting excited, dusting the seat of his trousers. "That sounds good to me. We've been sitting still too long, far as I'm concerned."

Chapter 10

Darkness had set in by the time Corio and Willard Dance reached the shack outside the abandoned settlement of Astro Rock. A few chickens roosting along a hitch rail rose in protest, batting their wings and scurrying out of sight as the two men stepped down from their saddles, spun their reins and walked onto a rickety porch through a striped glow of candlelight spilling through a plank door.

At the sound of the disturbed chickens, a startled voice called out, "Who goes there?" before either man could knock.

"It's me, and him," said Madden. He gave a wry grin in the dim glow light.

"Ma-Madden?" said the voice.

"Yeah, it's me, Oakes, open up," Madden commanded.

Inside, a shotgun uncocked. A latch bolt grated across metal and the door squeaked open on dry hinges. "I weren't expecting you, Madden," said an old white-bearded railroader in a pair of faded red long johns. "Have you already done it? I ain't heard it if you have."

"No, we haven't done it, not yet," said Madden. "I'm just going around tying up loose ends first."

"Oh? What loose ends is that?" The old railroader looked concerned.

"Relax, Oakes." Corio gave an easy grin. "I promise I'm not here to kill you." He looked all around the dusty, cluttered shack. "We're going to make ourselves scarce once this thing happens. I wanted to get you taken care of before we cut out."

"You're paying me off, ahead of the game?" He looked surprised. "That's mighty dang thoughtful of you," the old man said. He looked relieved as he shut the door and motioned them inside toward a bare wooden table with only one chair under it. "I always said you're a man of his word." He rubbed his weathered hands together in anticipation. "Can I get you something to drink? One of you can sit, I reckon." He gestured a hand toward the only chair. "You could arm-wrestle for it." He gave a broad half-toothless grin.

"A drink, yes," said Corio. "But we'll stand." He looked at Dance and nodded toward a whiskey jug sitting on a wooden floor cupboard beside a wooden crate of airtights and dried food supplies. Dance stepped over and got the jug while Corio pulled out the chair with the toe of his boot. "You have a seat, Oakes," he said.

"Well, all right, then, if it ain't too impolite of me," said the old railroader. He sat down and watched

Dance pull a wooden stopper from the jug and hand it to Corio, who smelled it, then raised it to his lips.

"Whew, you make good whiskey," said Corio, wiping his lips and passing the jug back to Dance.

The old man chuckled and watched Corio take a leather bag from inside his duster and pitch it onto the battered tabletop. "There's five hundred dollars gold, Oakes," said Corio. "I'd give you more but folks would think it strange."

"Five hundred suits me just fine," said the old man. He opened a drawstring and shook out a line of coins onto his palm.

"Count it some other time," Corio said in a firm tone of voice.

"Yes, I will," said the old man, hurriedly pouring the coins back inside the bag. "No offense intended," he added.

"None taken," said Corio as Dance took a long swig of whiskey. "Let's talk some."

"Yes, sir, sure enough," said the old railroader. He sat as if at attention, his palms lying on either side of the leather bag. "Anything you want to talk about suits me."

"Good," said Corio. He drew a long knife from his boot well and tested its sharpness with the pad of his gloved thumb along the glistening blade. "Who did you tell about this job?" he said bluntly.

"Whoa!" said the old man, terror coming into his eyes at the sight of the knife. "I never told nobody about it, Madden, I swear I never."

"You don't lie to me, Oakes," Corio warned, stepping in closer with the knife. "Now, who else knows about it?"

"Lord, nobody, Madden!" said Oakes. "Please don't kill me. You said you wasn't here to—"

"I know what I said," Corio replied, cutting him off. He leaned down into Oakes' face and dragged the sharp blade effortlessly across the man's brow. Blood ran down behind the path of the blade. Dance watched, transfixed. "I can show you things worse than death," Corio said almost in a whisper, "and still not kill you even if you beg me to."

"Madden, so help me, I ain't told nobody a thing! I'd be a fool to!" Oakes pleaded, feeling his warm blood flood his eyes, afraid to even lift a hand.

Corio stared at him, evaluating his words. Then he said to Dance without turning to him, "Get me that rope hanging by the mantel, Willard."

"Rope?" Dance was as surprised as Oakes at what was going on. But even as he questioned it, he stepped over, took a rope from alongside a blackened mantel, walked over to Corio with it and held it out.

"Tie him down, good and tight," Corio said, still staring menacingly into Oakes' eyes.

"Tie him down?" Dance asked in disbelief.

"Are you going to repeat every damn thing I tell you to do?" Corio growled. "Am I going to have to tie you down too?"

Without a word Dance quickly circled Oakes with the rope and tied him down tight to the chair. Oakes put up no resistance, other than a sobbing plea for mercy to Madden Corio. "Please, Madden . . . I would never mention any—"

"Ah, come on now, Oakes," Corio said, cutting the trembling man off, "I know how it is with you old rail hounds. You get with some pals, pass the jug a round or two, pretty soon you've got to swap stories, the bigger the better."

"But never nothing like this," Oakes said. "I know what would happen if the law found out! This was my retiring money!"

"Lying to me is going to cost you your nuts first off, old man," Corio said. "Then we'll see what you've got to say from there. The sooner you tell me the truth, the sooner I'll stop carving."

"Good Lord, Madden! I ain't lying! I swear to God I ain't!" the old man screamed, feeling the knife go down to his lap and slice his belt open, then the front of his trousers.

"Here they come, Oakes," said Corio, "on the table, right there for you to see. You best confess up."

"If I had told anybody I would admit it!" the old man sobbed.

"You would?" Corio asked matter-of-factly.

Dance winced and shut his eyes as Corio made a wicked upward slash along the old man's privates. Oakes felt the burn of blade and screamed loud and long, not realizing that Corio had turned the blade over at the last second and used the dull edge.

"Now, listen to you, Oakes," said Corio, "wailing and carrying on that way. I didn't even break the skin." He chuckled and forced the sobbing old man to lower his head and look at his exposed lap. "See? You've got everything you started out with."

The old man trembled and choked and could not collect or right himself.

Corio gave Dance a slight grin, but Dance was too shaken to offer anything more than a grimace and a worried look.

"Damn," said Corio, "I didn't realize my own man here was so squeamish." He straightened up. "Are you going to be ill, Willard?"

"Hell no," Dance managed to say, trying to get himself settled down. "It takes more than a nut cutting to throw me off."

"I sure as hell should hope so," said Corio. He turned to the old man and wagged the knife at him for emphasis. "See, Oakes, here's what worries me. If you known anything to tell me, you would have, wouldn't you?"

"Well, I—"

The trembling old man started to answer, but Dance cut in, saying, "Hell, Madden, anybody would under them circumstances."

Corio gave him a cold stare.

"I mean . . . you know. *Maybe* they would," Dance corrected himself.

"Would you, Willard?" Corio asked flatly.

"No, I wouldn't," Dance said without hesitation.

"Good," said Corio. He patted Oakes on his shoulder and said, "This man is telling the truth. He hasn't told anybody anything. I can say that now without a doubt in my mind."

Oakes looked relieved, but only for a moment.

"So right now is a good time to make sure that he never does," said Corio. To Dance he said, "You'll have to kill him for me, Willard. You heard me give him my word that I wouldn't."

At the hitch rail, Corio checked his pocket watch and looked over as Dance dragged a dried fallen pine into the shack, threw it atop a stack of other fallen limbs and dry bracken and struck a match to it. "Let's give it a minute to make sure it gets going real good," he said as Dance walked back out of the shack. He took two cigars from his duster and handed one to Dance. "You didn't like what I did in there, did you?"

"Let's just say I saw no reason for it," Dance replied. He had kept his right hand close to his holstered Colt even as he'd gathered fuel for setting the fire.

"You felt wrong killing that old man, didn't you, Willard?" Corio asked.

"No, not particularly," said Dance. "But I saw no need in it either." He bowed his head to the lit match in Corio's gloved hands and rolled the tip of the cigar back and forth in the flame, puffing on it.

"It's as important to clean up before a big job like this as it is afterwards," Corio said, "and believe me there's going to be lots of cleaning up after this one's over."

"That ole man would not have said anything," Dance said, blowing a long stream of smoke.

"That's where you're wrong," said Corio. "We both know how these old fools are. As soon as word gets around about a big job like this, he'd be taking credit for the whole damn thing, just to make himself feel important."

Dance let out a breath and considered the logic of what Corio said. "Hell, I guess you're right." He gave Corio a level stare. "Am I going to be one of the things that has to be cleaned up after this is over?" His hand rested close to his gun butt.

"No," said Corio, watching the flames lick upward inside the shack, Oakes' slumped body still tied to the chair. "You won't have to worry about what happens after this job, you have my word."

"That's good to hear, after seeing all this," said Dance.

Corio shook his head slowly. "I am not to blame for this man's death. Neither are you," he said soothingly, letting go a stream of cigar smoke.

"Oh?" said Dance.

"That's right, my friend," said Corio. "If you want to blame somebody for Old Man Oakes' death, I'll tell you who's to blame. It's those damned lawdogs who've been working this border on both sides. Can't you see how they've got everybody edgy and overly cautious?"

"Yes, of course I've seen that," said Dance, relaxing a little, smoking his cigar. "I'd have to be blind not to see it. They've got everybody out here not knowing who to trust and who not to."

"That's what I'm talking about," said Corio. "Those damn lawmen . . ." He took a deep breath and watched the flames in grim reflection. "Blame them. If I hadn't had to be so concerned about them learning what we were up to, we would not have killed old Oakes. Hell, we just wouldn't have. They killed him just as sure as if they'd pulled the trigger." He dusted his gloved hands together while the fire began to rage inside the shack. "Far as I'm concerned our hands are clean."

"Whatever you say, Madden," said Dance. "You're the boss."

"That's right." Corio grinned. "I am the boss." He turned to the horses and said, "Now let's get out of here. There's nothing more we can do for Oakes. He's one less thing to be concerned about."

As they both started to step up into their saddles, Corio stopped abruptly. "Damn it, I left that bag of gold in there." He stepped away from his horse and looked inside the open door of the shack at the flames licking wildly. "Run in and grab it and get right back out here," he said quickly.

"Run in there?" Dance said in disbelief.

"There you go, repeating me again," Corio said crossly. "Hell, never mind, I'll get it myself." He gave Dance an angry look and started to walk into the shack.

"No, I've got it," said Dance, not wanting to ride the rest of the afternoon with Corio in a dark and sullen mood. He handed him the reins to his horse and bounded onto the porch and into the open doorway.

"Careful, now," Corio cautioned him. "If it's too hot, just forget about it."

"I got it," said Dance, ducking his head against the scorching bellowing heat.

"Good man," said Corio. As he saw Dance make a run for the table, he raised his Colt and fired three shots into Dance's back. Dance let out a scream as the bullets hit him. Then he fell forward into the roaring flames and disappeared.

Corio patted the bag of gold coins that rested inside his duster. He grinned, watching as the fire consumed the shack. "Now you've *two* less things to worry about afterwards," he said quietly.

Chapter 11

━━━◆━━━

As darkness fell across the badlands, Lowe's men sat near a fire playing poker with a battered deck of cards that New York Joe Toledo had rummaged from the bottom of his saddlebags. Off to herself, Tuesday Bonhart sat near the fire sipping coffee from a tin cup. She wore a heavy men's coat, but with the dingy white wool lapels hanging halfway open down her chest. Beneath it she wore one of Dexter Lowe's wool shirts, its front hanging open in the same manner.

From the circle of cardplayers, Bell Mason shot a glance at the woman and then shook his head and said to the rest of the players, "It's hard being this close to something that warm and wiggly and not squeeze on it a time or two, just for luck—especially the way my luck's been running."

"Huh," said Toledo, hunched over the cards in his hands, "if you thinks your luck's been bad so far, squeeze that one. You won't believe how much worse your luck will turn."

"I see your point," said Mason, holding the deck in his bob-fingered jersey gloves. He licked a thumb and dealt two cards around. "But still, it's unnatural for a man to be this close to something like her and not want to rub her all over himself."

"It might be unnatural, but so is a bullet in the head," Joe Toledo warned.

"Speaking of a bullet-in-the-head," said Mason, glancing around, "where's the drifter?"

"He's over there, sleeping like a dead man," said Toledo. "I've been keeping an eye on him. A while ago he was kicking like a dog having a running fit," he added.

"I had a dog like that once," said Mason. "Sonsabitch would kick and growl and carry on something awful. You couldn't make him stop. Wake him, he'd look at you, go back to sleep and start kicking all over again." He arranged his cards in his hand and shook his head just thinking about it.

"I says let the man sleep," said Toledo. "The more he sleeps, the less time we got to wonder if he's going to go nuts and start shooting."

"You afraid of that scarecrow, New York Joe?" Earl Hardine asked.

"I'm not if you're not," Toledo retorted, knowing that everybody had walked wide of the man with the thick bandage around his head, and the Colt that seemed to streak upward from its holster too fast to be seen.

"Good answer," Mason chuckled, seeing the bested look on Hardine's face. He adjusted the cards in his hand and concentrated on the game.

"I ain't afraid," Hardine offered weakly.

"I know," Mason said idly. "Cards . . . ?"

Hardine slipped three cards from his hand and dropped them onto a spread blanket. "Two . . . ," he said.

"Look at this," Toledo said, turning their attention toward the woman as she stood with a filled cup steaming in hand and walked away from the fire toward the spot where Shaw lay on the ground.

"Fellows, this is nothing but trouble in the brewing if Dexter Lowe finds out," Mason said in almost a whisper.

"If she does it with this drifter, I say she has to do it with the rest of us, before Lowe returns," said Earl Hardine.

"Damn, Earl," said Toledo, "is my bay mare safe around you?"

Hardine gave a sly grin. "If you ride a mare, you take your chances."

Twenty yards away, at the outer edge of the fire's glow, Shaw lay loosely wrapped in a ragged blanket. His saddle served as a pillow; the battered stovepipe hat lay upside down on the ground, his thrashings having discarded it from covering his face.

The pain inside his head had dissipated, but in its wake he felt a strange pressure that made him awaken with a start, as if remaining asleep would cause something vital to burst inside him. When he felt the presence of the young whore drift in between him and the thin glow of firelight, his eyes snapped open. *Who— who's there . . . ?*

Shaw's words had not been spoken aloud, but seeing his reaction caused Tuesday to stop in her tracks. She heard the click of a hammer cocking beneath the blanket. "It's me, Fast Larry," she said quickly but in a lowered voice. "I thought you'd want some coffee."

"Coffee . . . ?" Shaw's eyes searched all around, across the men at the campfire, then back to the young woman standing over him. He considered her words for a second, then replied, "Tuesday, I'm sleeping." But his hand relaxed around the butt of the Colt beneath the ragged blanket. His thumb lowered the hammer.

"I know," she said, "but you didn't eat much. I saw you didn't take any coffee. I just thought . . . well, you know." She held the steaming cup out to him.

Shaw eased out of the blanket and sat up carefully, so as to keep his head from starting to hurt again. Touching a palm to his bandaged head, he looked over at the campfire and saw the men all turn their faces away in unison and concentrate on their cards. "Is Lowe back?" Shaw asked, having a feeling he already knew the answer.

"No, but he should be back any minute," Tuesday said. She held the cup down to him.

"Obliged," Shaw murmured, taking the cup, seeing that nothing else would do. "Let me ask you something, Tuesday," he said. "Do you think this is a good idea, you being over here, knowing how jealous Lowe is, knowing he's riding in any time?" He set the cup on the ground, reached over, picked up the stovepipe hat and put it on over his bandage.

"Probably not." Tuesday smiled, letting her lapels open a little wider. "You just looked so lonesome, lying over here all by yourself. I thought I'd come see how you're feeling."

"I'm feeling all right, Tuesday," Shaw said as she stooped down in front of him, allowing him to see an ample portion of her breasts behind the sheep wool lapels. He nodded toward the campfire, seeing a guard come walking into the firelight ahead of Dexter Lowe. "I think you need to get away from here."

"Oh, shit!" Tuesday said, standing quickly, snapping the coat shut across her and even holding it closed at the top of the collar. "I just came to bring you some coffee, okay?" she whispered as if setting herself up an alibi, even though it was true as far as Shaw was concerned.

"Yes, now go," Shaw said.

At the fire, Dexter Lowe stepped down and handed his horse's reins to the rifleman who'd walked in with him. Upon looking over and seeing Tuesday standing over Shaw, he said to the cardplayers, "What the hell is this? What's she doing over there?" His voice took on an accusing tone toward all of them.

The men shot one another a look. Trying to change the subject and get down to business, Toledo asked, "What'd you find out? What's our part in things?"

"I already told Hatcher everything," Lowe said in a testy voice, keeping his eyes on the young whore. "I'll tell the rest of yas in a minute."

"Yeah, he told me all right," said Able Hatcher, the

rifleman holding the reins to Lowe's horse. Toledo and
the others noted a look of disappointment on Hatcher's
beard-stubbled face.

"Oh, you're unhappy with what we're going to be
doing?" Lowe growled at Hatcher, his hand gripped
around his gun butt.

Hatcher, finding himself on dangerous ground, raised
his hands chest high in a show of peace. "Whoa, I'm
happy just being alive."

"Good," said Lowe. He faced the rest of the group
and asked again, "Now, what the hell is Tuesday doing
over there with that drifter?"

"She just walked over there, Dex," said Sonny Lloyd
Sheer, hoping to keep down any trouble this close to
pulling off a big job. "Hasn't been more than two minutes, right, hombres?"

"Yeah, that's right," said Mason.

"No time at all," said Joe Toledo. There had been
a time when he'd thought it might be fun watching
Dexter Lowe and the drifter lock horns over the whore.
But that time had passed. Now it was time to get down
to business.

Dan Sax and others nodded in agreement.

But Lowe would have none of it. He stomped back
and forth, seething as Tuesday walked over to him. When
she drew closer he shouted at her, "Can't I be gone a
day without you throwing your heels in the air for any
gun-slinging drifter in sight?"

Tuesday stopped a few away and threw a hand onto
her hip. She huffed and batted her eyes as if in disbelief, then shouted back to him, "Oh, I get it. You

think I can't be friends with a man without *doing it* with him?"

"From all I've seen and heard, you can't," Lowe snapped at her, "not if he's got as much as two bits in his pocket." He gestured a hand in Shaw's direction. "Or in this man's case, not if he's packing a big gun, something you think can do *you* some good!"

"You bastard!" Tuesday screamed shrilly.

Shaw sat listening from his blanket. He shook his head and sipped his coffee. *Jesus, what an outfit. . . .*

As Tuesday came closer to the campfire, Mason tried to direct Lowe toward business by saying, "Think maybe we ought to talk some about—"

"Stay out of this, Mason!" Lowe shouted. "I've had a bellyful of you as it is." He turned back to Tuesday just in time to catch her hand before it slapped him in the face.

"Hit me? You worthless little whore!" Lowe shouted. He backhanded her to the ground and kicked at her viciously as she scooted backward away from him, screaming. "I'll carve your heart out!" A knife appeared in his left hand as he snatched at her with his right.

Tuesday scooted backward faster, her heels digging into the ground; she screamed louder, shoving herself with the palms on her hands. "Help, he's going to kill me!"

Shaw had seen things start to get worse. He'd already stood up and started walking toward the campfire, putting on his battered stovepipe hat and carrying his gun belt looped over his shoulder. When he saw the knife come into play, he quickened his pace.

Seeing Shaw coming, the men rose slowly and stood facing him, unsure of what might happen next, out of the drifter or Lowe, either one.

"That's enough, Lowe," Shaw said in a strong voice, even though the pain filled his head at the sound of his own voice.

But Lowe had lost all reasoning. He spun from Tuesday on the ground to Shaw standing before him. "You're telling me *that's enough*, Shaw?" he raged, his hand poised near the pistol on his hip. "You ragged has-been sonsabitch!"

"Yeah, I'm telling you," Shaw said, seeing that Lowe wasn't going to be satisfied until there was blood on the ground. "Drop the knife and back away."

"Oh yeah?" said Lowe, his eyes wide, glistening with fury in the flicker of firelight. "I'll drop it." He spun back toward the downed woman. "I'll drop it in her damned black heart—"

Before Shaw even went for the Colt in the holster hanging from his shoulder, the loud pop of a derringer resounded in Tuesday's upstretched hand. Lowe stopped abruptly; his head jerked back to one side; a ribbon of blood uncurled in a spray from the back of his head. He crumbled to the ground at her heels; the knife flew from his limp hand.

The men stood stunned, their mouths agape, staring, at Lowe lying in an odd-looking position. He'd landed slightly on his knees, his right cheek pressed to the ground, his arms splayed out on either side, like a man who had tried unsuccessfully to fly.

"Holy God! She's killed Dex," said Bell Mason, who seemed to be the first to grasp the situation.

"She put it on him," Joe Toledo said flatly.

"Before he could kill her," Shaw put in quietly. Not knowing what the men might do, he eased his Colt from the holster and kept it hanging loosely at his side, letting them know where he stood should they make a move toward the woman. "Everybody saw it. . . ."

"Yeah, but damn it . . . ," said Toledo. Hands spread, he stared back and forth as if lost for words and looking for help.

Sonny Lloyd Sheer and Dan Sax stood staring coldly at Shaw. Shaw expected trouble from Sheer, knowing that Lowe had left him in charge. But so far so good, he thought.

"She had no choice," said Shaw, stepping sidelong over to Tuesday without taking his eyes off the men. He reached a hand down, took hers and lifted her to her feet. Tuesday appeared to be as stunned as the men.

"I didn't mean to kill him, Fast Larry," she said in a voice filled with shock and disbelief. "I didn't know what else—"

"What'd she call you?" Sheer asked.

" 'Fast Larry,' she said," Toledo cut in before Shaw could answer.

"Fast Larry Shaw," said Sheer, a thin puzzled smile coming to his lips.

"Dex called him *Shaw*," said Jimmy Bardell, standing quietly to the side.

Hardine cut in and said in a voice lowered to a whisper, "I'll be damned. What's going on here? Last I heard, you were working for the law."

"Do I look like I'm working for the law now?" Shaw asked, taking a threatening step forward. "I was a hired gunman long before I ever carried a badge." He needed to take control, get back to his job and find out about Madden Corio's upcoming job. "Do you think Dexter Lowe would have partnered with me if he thought I still worked for the law?"

"He's got a point," said Toledo, staring intently at Shaw.

"Dex knew he'd been working for the law," Tuesday put in quickly. "He didn't care. He told me him and Shaw were going to run the gang as partners. He just wanted to keep it a secret for a while. Of course he had no idea Shaw had been head-shot, or that he'd have a run-in with Thornton, Stobble and Mason here." She nodded toward Bell Mason.

Shaw cut her a glance. He'd never heard a woman lie any better, or faster, in his life.

"Fact is," Tuesday continued, "if Shaw hadn't been on Lowe's side, he'd have killed all three. As it is, this idiot killed the other two." Again she gestured toward Bell Mason.

"Dex never told me nothing about you, Shaw," Sheer said, sounding suspicious of the whole story.

"But he told me about you, Sonny," said Shaw. "I'm keeping you second in charge now that Lowe's dead, unless you want out."

Sheer didn't want out. He needed time to decide

what he believed and didn't believe. But meanwhile, he wanted to keep his hand in the game. He cut a glance to Dan Sax, then said to Shaw, "I'll stick, for now. I've been waiting too long for this big job. I'm not cutting out now."

The rest of the men stood staring, adding uncertainty to their shock. Finally Hatcher scratched his head up under his hat brim. "Damn, lawman . . . outlaw. I don't know what to make of all this."

"Make what you want of it," Shaw said, making a bold attempt at taking over. "But right now, you best get to telling us what it was Lowe told you before he got the chance to tell me."

The men stood in silence a moment longer and Shaw saw he was in good position. Pain pounded in his head, but he had no time to think of it. Now was the time to put matters to test and see where he stood. He reached out with the toe of his scuffed boot and shoved Lowe's body over onto its side. To Sheer he said, "Sonny, get somebody to drag Dexter out of here, get him underground. Rock him over so the 'yotes can't get to him."

Sonny stared at Shaw for a moment; then he looked at Earl Hardine and Joe Toledo. "You two heard him. Get Dex drug out of here and get him buried. The quicker he's underground, the quicker we can get down to business."

Chapter 12

———

As soon as Hardine and Toledo had removed Lowe's body from the campsite, Sheer, Sax, Shaw and the others huddled in a half circle around the flames. Tuesday joined them as Hatcher relayed the information Lowe had shared with him on the way into camp. Off to the side of camp, they heard the sound of shovels clinking in the rocky ground.

"You might not like hearing this any more than I did, Shaw," Hatcher said. He paused and looked warily from one man to the next. "Dex told me we were going to be wagon drivers."

It took a moment for the news to sink. Then Mason spat with contempt and said, "Wagon drivers? What the hell kind of job is that?"

"I know how you feel," Hatcher said. "I told him, if I wanted to be a teamster, I'd have gone to work for Wells Fargo or something." He looked to Shaw for support. "Ain't that how you feel, Fast Larry? Do you want to be a wagon driver?"

"That depends on what the wagons are hauling," said Shaw, considering the matter. "Did he tell you what the big job is?"

"Yes, he did," said Hatcher. He looked all around in the darkness as if to make sure no one could hear him outside of their own circle of thieves. "It's guns and ammunition," he added in a quieter tone of voice. "It's a big army shipment. They're hitting it at Hueco Pass, the other side of Yellow Moon Canyon. That's where we're to meet them with the wagons, at Yellow Moon."

"It's about damn time," said Sax. He gave a sly grin. "I said when they built that high trestle it was only a matter of time before somebody put it to good use." He rubbed his hands back and forth together in eager anticipation. "Who'd have ever thought I would turn out being a part of it?"

"Even as a wagon driver?" Hatcher said, still not happy with the role they would play in the job.

"Hell, I've done lots worse than drive the haul-away wagon," said Sax. "The gangs I've ridden with, everybody had to do their part, whatever it is."

"And he's ridden with some of the best," Hatcher threw in. "We all have. Just so you know."

Shaw only stared in silence.

Sax gave a curt nod of appreciation and continued. "So long as I get my share, I don't care what I have to do to get it." He too turned his gaze to Shaw for support.

"Sax is right," Shaw said, having been considering the matter ever since Hatcher brought it up. "It doesn't matter what job we're going to be doing, so long as the money is right." Pain pounded inside his head, but he disregarded it.

"What are you getting at?" Tuesday couldn't keep from asking.

Some of the men gave her a dubious look, but Shaw answered her in the same way he would have answered any of them. "We might start out driving the haul-away wagons," he said, "but who knows? Maybe we pull ourselves up a notch and get a pay raise to boot." Again he looked from face to face as Hardine and Joe Toledo returned out of the darkness, rolling their shirtsleeves down.

"I like working for a man who's always out to better our position," Sonny Lloyd Sheer said sidelong to Dan Sax, making sure Shaw heard him.

"Then you'll like working with me," Shaw said modestly, but with confidence. His head still pounded relentlessly.

Tuesday listened intently; so did the others. Shaw looked at Hatcher. "Where do we find the wagons?"

"We're supposed to meet tomorrow night in a draw not too far from here," said Hatcher. "The wagons will be there waiting for us."

"When do we show up at Yellow Moon?" Shaw asked.

"The next night," said Hatcher. "Dex said around midnight."

"All right, we'll go get the haul-away wagons," Shaw said, still working it all over in his throbbing head. He paused long enough to make sure the men wondered whether or not he'd finished. Then he raised his lowered head and said, "We're just drivers going in, but that's all going to change once we get our hands on those wagons."

Shaw gave Sonny Lloyd a look that told him it was time for him to take over.

Sonny picked right up on it and said with authority, "All right, hombres. That's all the talk we're going to do for tonight. Tomorrow starts early. Everybody get a good night's sleep, dream about how rich you're going to be. It might be a long while before the next time we stop to rest." He ended his words with a gaze toward Shaw. "We've got ourselves a new leader. Let's show him we're all worth our salt on this job."

In the night, the pain in his head eased up, enough for him to do some clear thinking about where this strange turn of events had put things. Recounting, he knew that Dawson and Caldwell were somewhere on his back trail, but how far back? If he'd thought riding back and warning them about the big job might thwart it, that would have been his first move. But there was no time for that. This was the hand he had to play.

Now that his luck had landed him not only into Lowe's gang, but in charge of it, he had to take advantage of his situation. *So far, so good . . .* , he reminded himself, relaxing, his eyes closed, his stovepipe hat tilted down, covering his eyes. He had to keep a good solid grip around the situation and keep everything in check until the two lawmen caught up to him. Could he do that? Yes, he believed he could.

"Fast Larry, are you asleep?" Tuesday asked in a whisper, interrupting his thoughts.

Shaw sighed under the cover of his battered hat, hearing her walk quietly up to him from the direction of the campfire. "Are you going to keep waking me up all night?"

She stooped down beside him. "There are men who would spend their whole roll to have me waking them up in the night," she whispered in a suggestive voice. "I just wanted to tell you how good you did, getting everybody to follow you—and to thank you for saving my life."

"Saving your life?" Shaw tipped his stovepipe up above his eyes. "Tuesday, you're the one who put a bullet through Dangerous Dexter's eye."

"I didn't mean you saved me from Dex," said Tuesday. "I meant you saved me from the rest of the gang. I hate to think what Sonny Lloyd and Dan Sax would have done to me if you hadn't been there. I'm most grateful to you."

"You're welcome, Tuesday," Shaw replied, pulling the hat brim back down. "We've all got a long day tomorrow. You best get yourself some sleep."

"You're not sleeping," Tuesday said.

"That's true," said Shaw, "and there's a reason for that."

She giggled under her breath. "I'm sorry I woke you again. I just wanted to know how you're feeling, see if you'd like me to show you just how *grateful* I am."

Shaw heard the rustle of her coat; he raised his hat brim again and batted his eyes. Looking at her in the pale moonlight, he saw her open the coat, revealing her nakedness beneath it. "Whoa . . . ," he said under his breath.

"Well? What's your pleasure, Fast Larry?" Tuesday asked. "You're not going to leave me out here exposed to this chilled night air, are you?" Even as she asked, she lifted the edge of Shaw's blanket and stretched out alongside him.

"No, Tuesday," Shaw said, coming alive at the sight of her as he'd looked her up and down. "It would take more than a head wound to make me crazy enough to do a thing like that." He held the blanket up for her until she had settled in against him, slipping out of the coat. Then he pulled the blanket down over them both and held her to him.

"There," she whispered, pressing herself against him with an urgency, "isn't that better than sleeping over here alone?"

Shaw didn't answer, feeling the heat of her through his clothes as she unbuttoned his shirt, his belt, his trousers . . .

From across the campfire Dan Sax and Sonny Lloyd Sheer sat huddled near the glowing flames, the rest of the men having taking to their bedrolls scattered about the campsite. "I have to say, I'm surprised you stood still for this man taking over the gang," said Sax.

"Don't go getting the wrong idea. It wasn't the right time for me to step in and fill Dexter Lowe's boots," said Sonny. He discreetly slipped a pint bottle of rye whiskey to Sax even through there was no one around to see him do it.

"Fill them?" said Sax. "Hell, Dex wasn't even out of his boots yet."

The two gave a slight grin. "He was going to die before long anyway," said Sheer. "I was getting ready to see to that. All the whore did was speed things up a little."

Sax took a swallow of whiskey and licked his lips. "Damn shame this gunman was here, though. Hadn't been for him, we could have shot the whore and you could have taken everything over clean and simple. These boys would have been begging you to do it."

"I ain't complaining," said Sheer, taking the bottle back from him as he stared out across the fire at the darker form of Shaw and Tuesday on the ground outside the circle of waning firelight. "This is no time to fool with things. This big job is all set to happen. Let Fast Larry Shaw lead the show for now. Once it's over we'll take it all and jerk the ground out from under him."

"Yeah, if this really is Fast Larry Shaw," said Sax, introducing a thread of doubt.

"Even if it is," said Sheer, "I can't understand why Lowe never mentioned taking on a partner to me."

"Neither can I," said Sax, "unless he was out to undermine you, which you said a time or two that you thought he might be."

"I had a bad feeling not to trust the sonsabitch, that's for sure," said Sheer. He spat and corked the bottle and put it away. "Now I guess I'm understanding why."

"So, you believe he did bring Shaw in as a partner?" Sax probed.

"I don't know what I believe right now," said Sheer. "But we'll go along with things 'til it suits us both to do otherwise." He continued to stare out across the fire toward the couple wrapped in each other's arms beneath Shaw's blanket. "I do know one thing. He's bedded down with that fleshy warm whore. We're sitting here having to wonder what he's up to next."

"Yeah, it's hard to take," Sax said quietly, also staring out across the glowing fire. . . .

Moments later, beneath the blanket, Shaw turned over onto his side and gazed up at the stars strewn across the purple night sky. Tuesday sighed, shoved her hair from her face and adjusted her head onto his chest. "Now, wasn't that worth waking up for?" she whispered.

"Are you going to start talking now?" Shaw asked quietly.

"No," she said. But then she corrected herself and said, "Well, a little maybe. You have to admit this is an unusual situation we're in together, us two running the Dexter Lowe Gang."

Shaw cut his eyes down to her. "How do you figure *us two* are running the gang?"

"I'm forever grateful to you sticking up for me. But I already had a stake in all this with Dex before you even got here, Fast Larry," Tuesday said.

"Right," said Shaw, "but putting a bullet in his eye had a way of dampening the spirit of any relationship you two might have had."

"But don't forget I'm the one who made it sound real, the part about you and Dex being partners. I put you right on top of his gang, ahead of men like Sonny

Lloyd Sheer, who's been with Dex for more than two years now."

He couldn't tell her that there was no future for her here. As soon as Dawson and Caldwell caught up with them, the Lowe Gang was gone for good, the Corio Gang too with any luck. "All right, I'll give you that," Shaw said. "You put me on top. But I don't want to stay on top. I'm only running this big job on out so I can get paid. I only stood up when I did so they wouldn't shoot you dead before Dexter Lowe was even in the ground."

"Okay, what's your point?" she asked, raising herself enough to turn and lean on his chest, looking him in the face.

"The point is that I'm the only one running the show here, not *us*," said Shaw, his tone serious. "When this job is over I want you to get away from here, as far away as possible."

"I will, I promise," said Tuesday, but her tone told him she wasn't taking him seriously. "Dex was going to take me to Paris. We were going to kick up our heels. Couldn't you and me do the same thing?"

"We could," Shaw said, realizing that warning her too much might cause her to suspicion why he was here. "Let me think about it."

"All right, then," said Tuesday, moving against him again, her hands going down his stomach. "While you think about it, I'll see what I can do to convince you it's a good idea."

PART 3

PART 3

Chapter 13

Badlands Territory

When the single rider appeared and stopped between the high rock walls of the narrow canyon, Bert Jordan turned to Harvey Lemate beside him. "Fan those two away some," he said. "I don't recognize this jake."

Lemate turned in his saddle and waved a hand at two gunmen, Max Skinner and Dade Watkins, who sidestepped their horses away a few feet away from each other and sat watching intently. Each of them held a rifle propped on his thigh, and each held a ready finger on the trigger, thumb across the hammer.

"I don't like this," Lemate said, righting himself forward in his saddle.

"Nor do I," said Jordan, keeping his eyes on the single rider in the battered stovepipe as the man nudged his horse forward at a walk.

The two sat watching in silence until the rider drew

within thirty feet; then Jordan called out, "That's close enough, stranger."

Shaw stopped and sat perfectly still, eying the two riders farther back and the line of five freight wagons sitting beyond them, a man sitting aboard the one in front.

"Who the hell are you?" Jordan called out after checking the empty narrow trail behind Shaw.

"I'm the man sent to pick up the haul-away wagons," Shaw called out in reply.

"You, by yourself? Where's Lowe?" Jordan asked, sounding agitated.

"I brought drivers." Shaw raised a hand and as if by magic conjured up riflemen on either side of the rocky canyon walls.

"This son of a bitch," Jordan whispered sidelong to Lemate. "This ain't the way it was supposed to be." To Shaw he called out in a stronger tone of voice, "I asked you, where's Lowe?"

"Lowe's not coming," Shaw called out. "He made a change of plans. He sent me instead."

"A change of plans," Jordan whispered. "Leave it to a punk like *Dangerous* Dexter Lowe to start making changes right when everything is set to go."

"What are we going to do now?" Lemate asked.

"Damn," said Jordan, "what can we do? We've got to have the wagons on the job. Madden is already on his way to meet that train."

"Say the word," said Lemate. "We'll kill this jake and the ones above us and drive the wagons ourselves. To hell with Lowe."

Jordan considered it for a moment, his eyes moving along the canyon walls, taking in the riflemen above him. After a tense moment he let out a breath. "No. We let them take the wagons. I don't know why Lowe is doing this. But it'll be his ass on the line, not ours."

"Madden will kill him for this once we get this job finished," said Lemate, turning and motioning for the men to relinquish the wagons to Lowe's men.

"I hope to hell he does," said Jordan. He raised his voice and called out to Shaw, "Ride on in. Let me get a look at you."

Shaw gave a hand signal to his riflemen, then nudged his speckled barb forward.

"Keep me covered," Jordan said to Lemate, nudging his horse forward to meet Shaw.

When the two drew within a few feet of each other and stopped, Shaw turned his barb sideways on the trail to indicate he was coming no closer.

Eying Shaw closely, Jordan said, "Who did you say you are?"

"I didn't," Shaw replied. "Lowe sent me to gather the wagons, not to socialize."

"Yeah?" said Jordan, knowing he was on a spot, knowing the wagons had to be on time, ready to go. "You can tell Dangerous Dexter that he's going to answer for this. I don't like last-minute changes." Jordan looked him up and down and added, "Madden will like it even less."

"I'm following orders," Shaw offered. On either side of the canyon the riflemen came down and started walking to meet the line of wagons that Skinner and

Watkins had begun helping to bring forward. "Once this is over, I don't care what Dexter and Madden Corio have to say to each other about it, do you?"

Jordan noted how confidently the stranger's hand lay on his thigh, near the butt of the holstered Colt. "No," he said, "not if all goes well. I'm in it for the money, same as you."

"Then we're in agreement," said Shaw.

The two sat in silence as the men with Shaw climbed aboard the wagons. "Here's another change in plans," Jordan said to Shaw as Lemate rode up closer. He turned to Lemate and said, "Tell Skinner and Watkins they're riding alongside these wagons, to make sure Dangerous Dexter knows the trail to Yellow Moon Canyon." He stared back at Shaw. "Any objections with that?"

"None," said Shaw. "If Lowe doesn't like it, he can take it up with Madden Corio himself. Like you said, we're in this for the money." He touched the brim of his stovepipe hat in respect.

From a high ledge at the far end of the canyon, Tuesday lay with a pair of binoculars to her eyes, watching as the wagons moved forward, Joe Toledo, Jimmy Bardell and Bell Mason in the drivers' seats. Mason's wagon drove along with a tag line leading the fourth wagon behind him. Behind the wagons rode the two men Jordan had sent to keep an eye on things.

"They're coming!" Tuesday said over her shoulder to Sheer, Sax and the others who stood out of sight behind the cover of rocks. "Shaw's got the wagons for us without Lowe even being there!"

Dan Sax and Sonny Lloyd Sheer gave each other a guarded look. "Good for Shaw," said Sheer. Turning to where the horses stood on a stretch ten feet below them, he said to the others, "All right, everybody mount up, let's ride down and meet them. We've got an all-night ride if we're going to get those wagons over to Yellow Moon Canyon."

"That's right, let's get to Yellow Moon," said Tuesday, excitedly standing and brushing herself. "That's where we make our fortunes."

On the flatlands, beyond the canyon walls, Dade Watkins and Max Skinner both tensed at the sight of the riders appearing up ahead of them. "What the hell is this?" Skinner asked Shaw, riding near him, his hand poised on the rifle across his lap.

"It's exactly what it looks like," Shaw replied in a calm tone. "It's the rest of the Lowe Gang coming to join us." He gave the man a bemused look. "You didn't think we were riding onto this job unguarded, did you?"

The two looked at each other. "Lowe sending you instead of coming himself has got us strung a little tight, Mister," said Watkins. "It's to be expected when you change the plans like this at the last minute."

"I understand," Shaw said. "But you best get used to Sheer, Sax and me showing up from now on. Dexter is going to be lying low, staying out of sight."

"Yeah?" Skinner asked, looking suspicious. "For how long?"

"From now on, would be safe to say," Shaw replied.

"What makes him think he can drop out of sight and still do business with men like us?" said Watkins. "The Corio Gang ain't a bunch of small-time sneak thieves he can treat any way that pleases him."

"Neither are we, not anymore," said Sonny Lloyd Sheer, riding up in time to hear what Dade Watkins said to Shaw. He swung his horse to stop, facing Watkins and Skinner. He stared coldly into Watkins' eyes.

Skinner cut in, saying, "You can't blame Dade for being riled over this, Sonny. I'm riled too. What the hell is going on anyway? Lowe decides to send this man instead of showing up himself?"

"You better *unrile*, fellows," Sheer warned. He gave a nod toward Shaw. "This man speaks for Dex and all the rest of us."

Shaw relaxed a little, knowing that these men's seeing Sonny Lloyd with him gave credibility to the matter. Sheer was known as Lowe's right-hand man.

"It's good to see you here, Sonny," Skinner said, settling a little.

"But what was we supposed to think?" said Watkins, settling, but more slowly than Skinner.

"I don't give a damn what you think, Dade," said Sheer. "Neither does Dangerous Dexter." He gave them a short unrelenting grin, something in it letting them know it was all right. "But whatever you think, you best do it while we ride. I better not miss my payday because you two don't like the way we run our part of the show."

"All right, forget it, Sonny," said Skinner, jerking the reins on his horse, turning it toward the passing wagons. Beside him, Watkins did the same.

As the two rode away alongside the empty stolen wagons, Sheer looked at Shaw and said, "We've all put ourselves on the line to make this job work for us. You better be as straight-up as you say you are."

Shaw didn't answer, nor did he touch his hat brim or give any other form of acknowledgment. Instead he sat staring as Sheer and Sax also turned their horses and rode away. Sheer looked back over his shoulder at Shaw, then said to Sax, "The son of a bitch only speaks when it damn well suits him."

As soon as the riders were a few yards away, Tuesday rode and stopped her horse beside Shaw and said, "That went pretty well, don't you think?"

Shaw didn't answer.

Tuesday tried again. "I said, don't you think that all went well?"

This time when Shaw didn't answer, she reached over, took his forearm and shook it, saying, "Hey, Fast Larry. Are you all right? Do you hear me?"

Shaw jerked his eyes toward her in surprise, like a man who had just snapped out of a trance. "Huh, what?" he said, his eyes looking lost and confused.

Tuesday gazed at him for a moment. "I said, that went well, didn't it?"

"Yeah, it went well," Shaw said in a strange tone of

voice. He sounded like a man who'd just returned from a trip afar.

Wondering still if he'd heard a word she'd said, Tuesday called out in a louder voice, "Fast Larry? Larry Shaw? Are you all right?"

Again Shaw failed to answer. Tuesday could only watch him with concern as he nudged his speckled barb forward and rode off alongside the wagons.

Outside the town of Colinas Secas, Jane stood in her stirrups and looked back at a thin rise of dust that had been closing on their back trail all morning. "Whoever it is, they're still there," she said to Dawson and Caldwell, who rode their horses at a walk beside her.

"Shaw, do you suppose?" Caldwell asked.

"I don't see how," said Jane, gesturing toward the hoofprints on the ground beneath them, "since it's Shaw's trail we've been following for two days." She glared at Caldwell and added, "Unless you're implying that I don't know bobwhite shit about tracking."

"I'm not saying it," Caldwell said, a bit tight-lipped on the matter. "But you have led us in a string of circles from the minute we left Wooten."

"Excuse the hell out of me, Undertaker," Jane said acidly. "If you'll recall, we're tracking a man who is head-shot and doesn't know his ass from a shotgun butt. Every circle we've made, he made before us." She looked back and forth from Caldwell to Dawson, then said, "Or maybe you'd both feel better if you didn't have a drunken saddle bum like me tracking this—"

"That's enough, Jane," Dawson said sharply, cutting

her off. He gestured toward a low stand of rocks less than thirty yards to the right of the trail. "Get over there and cover up. We're going to see who this is."

Turning to Caldwell, Jane said with sarcasm, "Would you like to lead us over there, or am I still the woman for the job?"

"After you, Janie," Caldwell said, not letting her abrasiveness anger him. He knew that part of her surly attitude was the whiskey still working its way out of her system.

The three left an easy-to-follow set of tracks from the trail to the stand of rocks. Once inside the rocks, a few feet above the flatlands, Jane crawled forward on her stomach, stretched out a battered telescope and held it to her eye. The two lawmen stood back and watched in silence until finally she said without turning to them, "Damn it, it's that young Creole gal from the hotel bathhouse."

"The one called Raidy?" Caldwell asked.

"Yep, Raidy Bowe," said Jane, scooting back and standing, holding the telescope out for Caldwell to take from her. Then she stepped forward and leaned against a tall rock, her arms crossed, staring back along the dusty trail.

"What does this girl want?" Caldwell asked no one in particular. Then he asked Dawson, "You and she didn't have any time to—"

Standing beside him, Dawson gave him a light gig in his ribs, enough to get his attention. Dawson gestured toward Jane. Caldwell got it and shut up.

After moment of silence, Jane said, "All right, gentlemen, it's me she's following. But damn it to hell, I had nothing to do with her . . . nothing to be ashamed of, that is." She sighed and shook her head. "I've never known why, but for some reason I draw that kind of person right out of the woods."

Dawson and Caldwell looked at each other. "When she gets here, get rid of her," Dawson said. He and Caldwell turned and walked to their horses.

Fifteen minutes later, Jane walked over and took the reins to her horse. "You say get rid of her, I'll get rid of her," she said. Turning, she led her horse away, out onto the flatlands with a look of determination on her face.

A few minutes later the lawmen heard raised voices, followed by a shrill scream and the resounding crack of a pistol shot. "Oh no!" Caldwell said in stunned disbelief. "Jane's shot her!"

They ran out onto the flatlands and saw the two women standing twelve feet apart. On the sandy ground their footprints had met, then backed away. Jane stood with her big revolver drawn, held drooping toward Raidy Bowe, smoke curling from its barrel. In the sand a foot in front of the young woman, Jane's bullet had upturned a dark hole in the ground. Raidy stood staring down at the bullet hole with her hands covering her mouth in terror.

"Jane, take it easy," Dawson said, approaching her with caution, knowing that her latest whiskey binge had left her shaken and unstable.

"She won't go," Jane said stiffly without turning to

face Dawson as he approached her. "I can't make her."

"Can't you see, it is because I love you, Janie!" Raidy called out tearfully.

"I've done everything short of sticking a bullet in her ass," Jane continued, ignoring Raidy's words. She started to level the sagging pistol toward the young woman again, but Dawson made it over in time to grab the gun from her hand. She gave it up without resistance, Dawson noted, watching her drop her empty hand to her side.

Caldwell ran to the young woman and looked her up and down for any signs of blood. "Ma'am, are you all right?" he asked.

"*Oui*, I am all right," said Raidy. "She did not intend to harm me, only to scare me."

Jane shook her lowered head and said to Dawson, "I don't know why it is, my whole life, I've attracted women like her. I try to tell them I ain't like them, but it makes no never mind. You saw me try to get rid of her, didn't you, Cray?" she asked. "You saw, didn't you?"

Dawson thought she was trying too hard to convince him, but he put the matter aside and took Jane by her fringed doeskin shirtsleeve. "Yes, I saw it, Janie," he said. "Now come on, let's get out of this sun and cool off. We've still got to find Shaw. That's the main thing."

"Yeah, find Shaw . . . that's the main thing," Jane agreed in a trancelike state as he led her off toward the shelter of standing rock.

As Dawson helped Jane along, leading her horse out of the sun, Caldwell came up beside him, the young woman in tow. "The gunshot scared this one's horse away," he said.

Dawson shook his head in disgust. "That figures," he said. "They'll have to ride double."

"I can't do that," Jane said, "not with things being as they are."

"Nobody is judging you, Janie," said Dawson. He gave Caldwell a look and walked on.

Chapter 14

In Colinas Secas, the old livery hostler met the lawmen and the two women riding double as they rode off the badlands toward the barn. "Welcome to Dry Hills, Marshal . . . ," he said, seeing the two badges glint in the sunlight. "Deputy . . . ," he added, touching the brim of his sun-faded derby hat toward Caldwell. "I'm Caywood Radler, at your service."

"Obliged, Mr. Radler," said Dawson, touching his hat brim in return. "I'm Marshal Dawson. This is Deputy Caldwell. Have you any horses for sale?" He gestured a hand toward Jane, who sat atop her horse with Raidy pressed against her back. Raidy slept with one arm around Jane's waist, the other arm up across the fringed bosom of her doeskin shirt.

Radler gave the two women a curious look.

Jane growled at him, "What the hell are you staring at, old man? We need a horse!"

"What's wrong with the horse following you?" Radler said, pointing a gnarled finger at the far edge of town where the spooked horse Raidy had been riding walked forward slowly, shyly, its reins dragging the ground.

"I'll be a son of a bitch," Jane said, her face reddening. To Dawson and Caldwell she said, "I didn't know that horse was following us, I swear I didn't."

"Neither did we, Jane," said Dawson, stepping down from his saddle, Caldwell doing the same.

Radler cackled aloud. "Good thing it weren't some ambusher tracking you."

"Yeah," said Dawson, "a good thing it wasn't." He and Caldwell looked at Jane as she woke Raidy and helped her down from behind her. Caldwell stepped over and helped the waking woman.

"Say, you lawmen should have been here the other night," said Radler. "We had more fireworks than a Chinese funeral. One drifter beat the living hell out of three men with a long-handled shovel, caused one of them to kill the other two. I never seen nothing like it."

Dawson and Caldwell looked at each other. "A man with his head bandaged?" Dawson asked.

"Yep, he's a daisy, that one," said Radler. "Turns out the barkeeper recognized him as Fast Larry Shaw. Said he'd seen him before over in Somos Santos." He beamed at having such knowledge. "Anyhow, Fast Larry Shaw told me you two would be coming along directly. Said to tell you he's gone off with the Lowe Gang." He grinned. "What's left of them anyway. After the drifter was through with that shovel, I expect Dangerous Dexter found himself short of guns."

"That's good to know, Mr. Radler," said Dawson. "Again we're obliged to you."

"Hey, you two can just call me Caywood," said the proud old hostler. "I hope whatever it is you are searching for Fast Larry for ain't too bad. I mean, you ain't out to hang him or nothing like that, are you?"

"No," said Dawson, "it's nothing like that."

He and Caldwell both handed Radler the reins to their horses. When the old man had taken them, he stepped over to Jane and took hers. "Did Fast Larry happen to mention anything about me, Jane Crowley?" she asked almost hesitantly, for fear of what his answer would be.

"I know who you are," said Radler. "I recognized you by your skins as soon as you rode in, Miss Crowley."

"Well, did he?" Jane asked as Radler turned to walk away.

Radler looked back over his shoulder at Jane. Then he looked Raidy up and down knowingly and said, "No, ma'am, Miss Crowley, not a word."

When they had watered, grained and rested the horses, Caldwell led the animals out into the evening sunlight, where Jane and Dawson stood talking in the dark shade of a thick ancient saguaro cactus. He heard Jane saying to Dawson, "Crayton, I can't help what impression this girl has gotten of me. I didn't do anything to lead her on. Leastwise I did nothing intentionally. I didn't set out to break her heart. You know me, I ain't that kind of person."

Listening, Caldwell caught a certain underlying pride in her voice, as if she liked having a man's kind of conversation, with a man, about a woman.

"Get rid of her, Jane," was all Dawson offered in reply. "We've got no time for this."

Caldwell walked up and stood with them. "The horses are all ready to go," he said. "Where's the woman?"

"I'm right here, Undertaker, are you blind?" Jane said, immediately taking on a testy attitude toward the deputy.

"You know who I mean, Janie," said Caldwell, not allowing her to turn anything he said into some childish sobering drunkard's argument.

"Yes, I guess I do, Undertaker," Jane said, taking a different approach toward him. "We were just talking. I was telling Dawson that I don't want to hurt that poor girl any more than I have to, you know, to get rid of her?"

"Yes, I understand," said Caldwell. He gave Dawson a look.

"What was that?" Jane said, catching the gesture. "What are you two thinking? If either one of yas has something to say, spit it out. If you think I've done something to be ashamed of with the young woman, don't be bashful, tell me about it." She glared at Caldwell.

"Nothing, Janie," he said. "She's your friend, not mine."

"Friend?" Jane flared, red-faced and wild-eyed. "She's not my damned friend, Undertaker!"

"She's certainly not your enemy either," Caldwell offered. "I use the term 'friend' because I have no idea what she is to you."

"She's just a girl I happen to know," said Jane, "same as you two know women all over these badlands. Is there anything wrong with that?"

The two lawmen shook their heads.

"Good," Jane said, "because if it's any of your business, or if you haven't noticed as yet, I am in love with Lawrence Shaw."

The two lawmen saw Raidy Bowe walk up behind Jane as she spoke, but there was no time to warn her until it was too late. "Jane," Dawson said quietly, giving a nod past her to where the young woman stood with a hurt, stunned look on her face.

"Oh, hell," Jane said under her breath. She turned to say something to Raidy, but the woman had turned, her eyes welling with tears, and ran away around the corner of the livery barn. "I better go talk to her," Jane said.

As soon as she was out of sight, Caldwell asked Dawson, "Does it appear she's enjoying this in some strange way?"

"Yes, but I don't even want to let myself think about it," Dawson replied. "Jane's an odd one—she always has been."

"No wonder Shaw's so hard to find," Caldwell murmured in dark contemplation.

Jane caught up to Raidy behind the livery barn, having to grab her by her arm to stop her. "Wait, Raidy, I didn't mean anything by what I said. I had to say all that, for the lawmen to hear."

Raidy said in a hurt voice, "You are ashamed to say how you feel for me?"

"If I felt for you the way you want me to, yes, I expect I would be," said Jane. "But I don't feel that way about you."

"Then how do you feel?" Raidy asked.

Jane wrinkled her brow. "It's hard to explain, Raidy."

"I see," Raidy replied. "But it's safe to say that you do not love me, as I do you."

"In that respect, yes, it's safe to say so," said Jane. "But I like the hell out of you . . . you know, in a friendly, sisterly sort of way." She grinned.

"Turn me loose, *sister*," Raidy said in a clipped tone. "I am riding back to Wooten."

Jane let go of her forearm. "I think that's a good idea, Raidy." She brushed a strand of hair from the younger woman's forehead. "When these things I'm doing are settled down some, maybe I can—"

"Do not tell me things that you do not mean again, *sister*, Jane," Raidy said. "I made the mistake of believing you before and it caused me to do stupid, terrible things."

"I never told you *anything* before I left Wooten," Jane said. "I didn't lead you on. I was sober enough by then to remember. I didn't do anything to cause you to follow me here."

"No, I do not mean right before you left Wooten," Raidy said. "I mean before that, when you were drinking so much you could not find your hotel. I took you in. You stayed with me."

"I did?" Jane took on a strange, confused look. "I stayed with you . . . in your room? For how long?"

"It does not matter now," Raidy said, "but you told me things, how you felt about me, when the two of us were in bed together, making love—"

"No—stop it, Raidy," Jane said, aghast. "Nothing like that happened. I wasn't that drunk . . . was I?" she asked with a margin of doubt.

"*Oui*, you were drunk," said Raidy.

"Why didn't you mention this to me when I was sobering up, before I left town with Dawson and Caldwell?"

"I—I wanted you to remember on your own," said Raidy. "I wanted you to be sure of yourself. I wanted you to love me, the way you loved the gunman, Fast Larry Shaw."

"Jesus . . ." Jane hung her head for a moment. When she raised it she said, "Listen, Raidy, nobody can ever know what you've told me here. Do you understand? I was blind drunk and I did lots of things I shouldn't have, including trying to kill the man I love."

Raidy studied Jane's serious expression. "I will never tell anyone. It will be our secret." She lowered her voice to a whisper and said, "And now I will tell you something that you must never tell anyone. It was *I*, not you, who shot Lawrence Shaw."

"On my God, no," Jane said with a gasp of fear in her voice.

"It is true," said Raidy. "I saw how unhappy you were with him. You always came to me, crying about how bad he made you feel."

"Raidy, that was my drunken whiskey talk, getting this thing off my chest. That was just me wanting something from Shaw that he couldn't give."

"I thought with Fast Larry dead, you would be happy with me," Raidy said. "I knew I could make you happy. I still can."

"Oh, Raidy," Jane said, pulling the young woman to her in an embrace, "this is the worst I've ever screwed anything up in my life. I don't know how I'll ever straighten this out with Shaw."

"But it was not you who shoot him, it was me," said Raidy against Jane's doeskin shirt bosom.

"It might have been you who pulled the trigger," Jane said, still having no certainty on the matter. "But if it was, it was only because my drunken carping and crying led you to do it."

Raidy closed her eyes against the warm fringed doeskin. "*Oui*, perhaps it was," she whispered.

On the dirt street out in front of the livery barn, Dawson said to Caldwell, "We've got to get moving while there's enough daylight to pick up Shaw's trail."

"I'll get her," said Caldwell.

He walked around the livery barn and stopped suddenly at the rear corner when he saw the two women standing in each other's embrace. "Whoa," he murmured to himself. "I didn't want to see this. . . ." He backed away out of sight before Jane or Raidy knew he was there.

Out front, Dawson watched the deputy return from around the corner of the barn with a strange look on his face. "What's wrong?" Dawson asked.

"Nothing," said Caldwell. "She's coming." He stood in silence and offered no more on the matter.

A moment later, Jane and Raidy appeared from around the corner and walked toward the horses. Jane stepped to her horse's side, but Raidy walked to the other side of the hitch rail and stood quietly, watching Jane unhitch her horse and mount it.

Dawson and Caldwell stepped over to their horses and mounted without asking any questions. Finally before the three backed their horses onto the dirt street, Jane said quietly, "She's not coming with us."

Dawson and Caldwell only nodded. They touched their hat brims toward Raidy and turned their horses. As they moved away at a walk, Jane looked down at Raidy and said quietly, "Don't worry. Things will work out. I'll see you soon." Then she turned her horse and caught up alongside the two lawmen.

None of the three said anything until they had ridden nearly a full mile from the town and veered onto a trail leading west, across the badlands toward the border trails and rock passes. Finally Jane said, "She's going back to Wooten. I expect she'll be wanting her job back at the hotel baths."

Not knowing what to say, the two lawmen rode on without comment.

The rest of the evening they rode in an awkward silence, having no trouble finding Shaw's trail—the same meandering set of hooves they'd been following. But once they had made camp and boiled a pot of coffee from the crushed beans Caldwell carried in his saddle-bags, Jane leaned back on her bedroll, stared into the steaming brew and said, "Pards, now that I'm sobering up I've given it some thought. I didn't shoot Shaw."

"Then why'd you say you did?" Caldwell asked.

Before Jane could reply, Dawson cut in saying, "She was hungover and shaky that I pushed her into think-ing she did it."

"I wasn't going to blame you, Crayton Dawson," Jane said firmly.

"You don't have to," said Dawson, letting her off the hook. "I saw I was pushing too hard and I backed off, but not soon enough." He paused, then said, "So, are you saying you didn't shoot Shaw?"

Jane considered it, then said, "I'm saying I might not have, now that I'm sober enough to start making sense of myself."

Caldwell gave her a look. "You might want to de-cide for sure one way or the other. We'll be meeting up with Shaw before long, I expect. For all we know Shaw might be hot on Madden Corio's trail this minute. This is not the time for uncertainty."

"I know . . . ," Jane said, and she fell silent and stared back down into the dark swirl of steaming coffee.

Chapter 15

———

Madden Corio and Bert Jordan stood on the boarding platform at the last water stop along the western edge of the badland territory. Corio wore the finely pressed and dusted uniform of a U.S. Army colonel, with it a wide-brimmed cavalry frontier hat. Jordan wore a trim-fitting major's uniform and a campaign field cap. He and Lemate had ridden all night in order to be back in time to meet Corio and get into the uniforms.

Jordan had told Corio about the change in plans, and about Lowe sending his new partner to gather the wagons. He'd told Corio about leaving Skinner and Watkins to keep watch on things. "Good idea," Corio had told him as he appeared to consider the matter. But he'd offered no further comment. Jordan was certain that Dangerous Dexter Lowe and his whole gang would be killed before the job was finished. Seeing Lowe, his men and his new partner dead suited Jordan well enough.

Behind the platform sitting atop their horses in a column of twos sat Robert Hooks, Irish Tommie Wade and six other members of the Corio Gang who'd met Corio along the trail. The six had brought along the army uniforms that had been burgled over a year earlier from a frontier outpost. At the head of the column, Robert Hooks sat squarely in his saddle, eyes straight ahead as the engine of the train rolled past, coming to a slow stop, a long blast of steam rising from its iron brakes.

"Look sharp, lads," Hooks said over his shoulder. "Our game has commenced."

Speaking without visibly moving his lips, Irish Tommie said jokingly, "Aye, Sergeant, and will it be an extra ration of hardtack for us each at the end of this long day?"

"And then some, I wager," said Harvey Lemate to Arnold Stemms, one of the six who'd brought the uniforms.

"There better be," said another of the six, a young Missourian named Matthew Ford, cousin to the Ford brothers, Robert and Charles, and a longtime friend of Robert Hooks.

The other four men withheld their smiles and stared at the slowing train as faces of soldiers looked out at them questionably through the open passing windows. Ordinarily there would have been greetings exchanged back and forth from the troop car to the column, but the presence of a colonel brought with it a more serious, attentive atmosphere.

From one of the front-most windows, a young captain from Baltimore named William Ploster had looked up from a checkerboard in time to see the stoic passing faces of the colonel and major staring straight at him. "Damn it to hell, Webster!" Ploster shouted at his sergeant. "Why didn't you warn me?"

"I didn't see them myself, sir, until it was too late," the sergeant said in his own defense. "What the hell is a colonel doing out this far?"

"I'll be sure and ask him for you, Sergeant," the young captain said sarcastically over his shoulder as the sergeant guided the sleeves of his tunic onto his arms from behind and hiked it onto his shoulders. "Now hand me my sword, Sergeant," the captain barked, frantically buttoning the tunic up the front. "Jesus, there's enough brass out there to start a band!"

"Let's not worry, sir," said the sergeant. "I recognize neither of these men. If they were higher-echelon officers on any renown, I would know them both by name."

"That offers me small comfort, Sergeant," said the captain. "I make it a point that no rank higher than my own should ever see me uncovered, with my guard down." He jerked his battered hat from the hands of a private who held it out to him as the train lurched to a final halt.

"Yes, sir," said Sergeant Webster.

"Let us go see what this is all about, shall we, Sergeant?" said Ploster, regaining his military bearing.

"Yes, sir," the sergeant repeated, gesturing for two privates to follow him. The privates snatched their rifles from against the wall and held them at port arms.

Pulling the hat down levelly onto his forehead, Captain Ploster walked briskly toward the car door, the sergeant right behind him, the two privates following the sergeant in perfect step.

Corio stood with his chest out, his hands behind his back, as the captain stopped four feet from him and snapped his hand to his forehead in a salute. "Sir, Captain William Ploster, Fifth Calvary, Frontier Service Detail, at your service, sir."

But the make-believe colonel's return salute was not immediately forthcoming. Instead he kept his hands behind his back, leaving the captain with his hand raised while he looked the young officer up and down slowly. "Let me ask you something, Captain. Do you know where you are?"

"Where I am, sir?" Ploster asked.

The colonel stared fiercely at him.

"We are in Badlands Territory, sir," Ploster said quickly. "Our exact coordinates might be best described as two miles below the rail trestle at Hueco Pass, headed in a northeasterly—"

"Yes, Badlands Territory," said Corio, cutting the captain off midsentence. Now he brought his hands from behind his back, raised his right hand as if grudgingly and returned the attentive captain's salute. "No one should have to tell you how dangerous this place is. Shouldn't the fact that we have posted guards aboard each flatcar be enough to inform you?"

"Yes, sir. It is, sir," said Ploster, not knowing what else to say.

"This is no place to be either undressed or playing

poker, Captain," said Corio with disgust. "What if you had suddenly found border trash, American land pirates or Mexican banditos awaiting you here instead of the United States Army?"

Captain Ploster searched his brain rapidly for an answer, yet found himself only able to offer, "It was checkers, sir."

"It was what, Major Clinton?" Corio asked, turning to Jordan as if for a translation.

"*Checkers*, Colonel Winthorpe," Jordan replied with a harsh stare centered on Captain Ploster. "The captain was out of uniform, playing checkers with his men, sir."

"Checkers, indeed," said the fake colonel. To Ploster he said, "Captain, have your sergeant relieve all your guards. We have brought a detachment of special sharpshooters who will accompany the cargo on to Arizona Territory."

Relieve the guards . . . ? Sharpshooters . . . ? Captain Ploster had chosen these guards himself; each of them was a crack shot. Moving only his eyes, he looked the colonel up and down, taking note of the gold colonel insignia on each of his broad shoulders. "Sir, begging the colonel's pardon. But if I might ask—"

"You *might not* ask, soldier," Corios growled in a scorching tone, appearing to advance on the young captain like an angry dog. "I did not ride eighty miles across the barren wasteland to answer the questions of some subordinate checker player. I too follow orders. My orders come from General Tolliver himself. Perhaps you might care to ask him why we're doing this, then be so kind as to enlighten me when you find out! Meanwhile, have your guards *stand down!*"

"Sergeant Webster," Ploster said quickly.

"Yes, sir," said the sergeant, not having to have the order repeated to him. Turning on his heel, he and the two privates moved away toward the flatcars at a trot.

Behind the platform, as if on cue, Hooks, Irish Tommie and the rest of the make-believe soldiers stepped down from their saddles and stood at parade rest, awaiting their next move. Staring toward the engine, Corio folded his hands behind his back once again and said to Jordan in a more pleasant tone, "Major Clinton, believe it or not, I have never ridden in one of these iron horses. This trip I believe I shall."

"Yes, Colonel," said the phony major. "Shall the captain and I accompany you, then?"

Corio turned and looked Captain Ploster up and down again as if gauging his worth. Then he looked to Jordan and said, "You join me, Major, but only for a time. I want Captain *Checkers* here with his men, awake and in uniform, without his checkerboard. I feel it must take your presence to assure me of that." With no more on the matter, he turned with his hands still behind his back and walked away toward the engine.

As soon as the phony colonel was out of hearing range, Jordan stuck his hand out to Captain Ploster and introduced himself with a more agreeable smile. "Major Markus Clinton, Captain. I hope you'll overlook the colonel's abrasiveness. This unusual task was thrown upon him by the general quite punitively, I'm afraid."

"Oh?" said the captain, shaking hands. He actually felt a bit relieved hearing that the colonel would not be riding in the troop car with him. Even more relieved that he now saw a much friendlier side to the major.

"Yes," the phony major went on, "apparently Colonel Winthorpe questioned the readiness of the troops guarding the shipments of armaments along the badland rails, not realizing that the general himself had a personal hand in things, along with the rail owners."

"Ouch," said Captain Ploster, letting himself breathe a little easier.

"'Ouch,' indeed," the fake major said with a slight chuckle. "So the general sent him out here to see for himself. It's just the sort of innocent blunder that can freeze even a colonel in today's army, I'm afraid." He raised a cautioning finger and advised, "So take heed, Captain. We are under watchful eyes."

"Yes, sir, Major Clinton," said Ploster. "I'm grateful you're telling me. I intend to avoid any such *innocent blunder* myself." Gesturing a hand sidelong toward the troop cars, the young captain escorted the phony major toward the idling train.

From inside one of the open windows, a young trooper watched Hooks, Lemate and the rest of the phony soldiers step down from their saddles as one and unsnap their Winchester repeater rifles from their saddle hooks in the same manner. To his comrade beside him the young man said quietly, "These must be some of them special troops I've heard about. Now, there's some fellows who *know* how to soldier."

Any suspicions Captain Ploster might have had would

have gone away as he and the major walked aboard the train and looked out the window to see the phony soldiers lower the loading ramp on the stock car. As Ploster and the major took a seat, the captain watched the soldiers lead their horses inside the stock car and close the doors. Sergeant Webster and the two privates stood in the aisle waiting to be dismissed.

Sitting down beside Captain Ploster, the fake major took two cigars from inside his tunic, handed him one and sat expectantly until Sergeant Webster produced a long sulfur match and lit each man's cigar in turn, Major Clinton's first.

"There's no reason why we can't get civilly acquainted before I go join the colonel, is there, Captain?" he asked with a smile, letting go of a long stream of smoke.

"None at all, Major," said Ploster, feeling better now that the colonel was up front in the engine, and his reason for being here was better understood.

"So, Captain?" the fake major asked with the same friendly smile. "West Point, I presume . . . ?"

"On the contrary, Major Clinton," said Ploster, "I'm strictly field command—Comanche wars."

"*Comanche* wars," said the phony major with an impressed look. "I commend you, sir."

Ploster gave a humble nod. "And yourself, West Point?" He also let go of a long stream of smoke, and relieved the sergeant and the two privates with the toss of a hand. They stepped away and took seats across the aisle from the two officers.

"Ah yes, West Point. I graduated in the same class

as Philpot, Custer and Dowd . . . ," the major said a bit wistfully. It was the only true thing he had said so far, he reminded himself, recalling the years before he'd ridden off to fight for Lee's Southern forces.

In the engine, Corio stood back with a hand raised and wrapped around an iron bar for support, steadying himself as the train began its slow departure. Leaning and looking out the door back along the train, Corio saw Hooks reach out and wave his hat up and down slowly, signaling that everything had gone well in relieving the guards, who were now resting in the troop cars farther behind him.

Corio watched as Jordan stepped down from the troop car, trotted forward past the flatcars and hopped up onto the iron ladder at the engine's door. Taking Corio's hand for support, Jordan hopped aboard and said with a smile clamped around half a cigar, "That certainly went well, Colonel Winthorpe."

"Just as I anticipated it would, Major," said Corio, still going along with their ruse. "I hope you and the captain had a nice chat over your cigars?"

"*De*-lightful," said Jordan with exaggeration. "It was like taking a short trip home."

"And how did you leave the captain?" Corio asked.

"Resting as comfortably as a child," said Jordan, his voice below the roar, pulse and pound of the big steam engine.

Glancing back over his shoulder, the engineer, an older man named Foster Brady, looked the two up and down, and said, "Begging both your pardons, but I never had a high-brass colonel and a major in this sweatbox before."

"It's unlikely you ever will again," said Jordan.

"That's right," said Corio, unbuttoning the collar of his tunic as he spoke. "We're not what you'd call your typical high brass." He took off the cavalry hat and hung it on an iron peg.

"Oh . . . ? You two are just some good ole down-to-earth boys at heart, eh?" the old engineer asked with a crooked grin.

"That's us to a fault," said Jordan, slipping his Army Colt up from beneath its holster flap and holding it down at his side, his thumb over the hammer. "My colonel here has a keen interest in trains."

"Does he sure enough?" the old engineer asked, glancing back at Corio.

"I fear he'll be bending your ear on the matter most any time now," said Jordan.

"Well, bend away," said the engineer. "I know more about trains than I'll ever know about women." He cackled at his own little joke.

"To begin with . . . ," said Corio, looking around and judging the speed of the train. "How far back would you have to begin braking in order to stop this train at, say, halfway across the trestle at Hueco Pass?" he asked.

As he asked, Corio also slipped his Colt from beneath the holster flap and held it down at his side, ready to bring into play when needed.

"At the speed we'll be going when we get near there, I'd have to start braking down ten or twelve minutes before we go out onto the trestle."

"Which is it, ten or twelve?" Corios asked in more a demanding tone than a simple question.

Without looking around, the engineer recalculated his speed and judged his answer closer. "All right, ten minutes, then, if you want to get to the fine line." He shook his head slightly, then said, "But that's not something anybody would ever want to do, stop out there on the middle of a trestle that way."

"Why's that?" Corio asked.

"Well, there's no reason too. It's high up, and dangerous. There's barely room for a man to walk. If you was walking, a hard wind would blow you away." After a silent pause he asked, "Why'd you ask such a thing as that anyway, Colonel?"

"Because that's where you're going to make this train stop," said Corio. He smiled and raised the Colt and cocked it. "The back half of it anyway."

The engineer looked around and saw two cocked Colts pointed at him. "Ah, hell, I'm robbed, ain't I?"

"That's the story," said Corio, a pocket watch in his left hand. "If you don't do what I tell you, you're not only robbed, you're dead."

"I don't want to die, but I can't promise to stop this thing exactly where you want it," said the engineer.

"Then you better start calculating," said Corio. "I want you to tell me where we have to pull the pin, to cut the troop cars off and leave them out on the trestle."

"Damn," said the old man, hesitating, "I can't be a party to something like that."

"Then we shoot you and do it ourselves." Corio shrugged. "I've got a man waiting for my signal. If we do it, there's no telling how it turns out. You do it, you can leave them boys with no more than a high walk back to the other side. What's it going to be?"

"Hell, I don't want to see nobody hurt," said the engineer. "I'll tell you when to cut them loose."

Chapter 16

An hour had passed since the train had taken on its water and gotten back under way. Captain Ploster had leaned back in his seat and allowed himself to doze, leaving the sergeant to warn him should the major or the colonel walk back to the troop car, which was something he doubted now that the train was rolling along at a good fast click.

He couldn't picture either of the higher-ranking officers wanting to walk along the open edge of the flatcars in order to reach one of the two troop cars, especially now that they would be heading over the long trestle at Hueco Pass. *Hallelujah for that. . . .*

Yet, no sooner had he fallen into a light but fitful sleep than he heard the lowered voice of Sergeant Webster say close to his ear, "Captain Ploster, wake up, sir. The train is slowing down over the pass. There's something wrong up there."

As the captain awakened and stood up, a young soldier called out from an open window where he had leaned far out and looked ahead at the flatcars of arms and munitions pulling away from them across the deep gaping chasm below them. "Sergeant Webster, we've been cut loose from the train!" he shouted, drawing others to the open windows to see for themselves.

"Oh no," said Ploster, already getting the picture before even looking out the window.

"Out of my way, lads, step lively!" shouted the sergeant, shoving and elbowing his way through the excited soldiers until he could lean out the window and look ahead across Hueco Pass. Gripping the open window frame with rage, Webster said, "The lousy sonsabitches are waving at me!"

On the last of the flatcars, Irish Tommie stood dancing a lively jig. He and the others waved their cavalry hats at the slowing troop cars left drawing to a slow halt almost halfway across Hueco Pass. Almost as one the men sailed their cavalry hats out across the canyon.

The soldiers could only stare, watching the hats circle and careen downward out of sight.

In the engine, the engineer heard the revelry of the outlaws on the flatcars. "Not a danged shot fired!" he exclaimed. He breathed a sigh of relief, then grinned and added, "That was as slick as socks on a rooster, if I do say so myself."

Corio and Jordan lowered their Colts and let the hammers down, but kept the guns in hand. From atop the train a fireman named Lowell Kirby had walked down across the carload of firewood into the engine when he noted the cars behind them beginning to lose speed and separate from the train. Now he stood with his hands chest high and a worried look on his face. "Can I put my hands down now?" he asked. "I'll need to stoke us up here in a few minutes." He nodded toward the iron door on the boiler.

"Yeah, drop them," said Corio. "Do what you need to do to speed us up and keep us moving, and we'll let you out of this alive."

"Thanks, Mister," said the fireman, lowering his arms and taking a deep breath. "Just tell me where we're headed, so I'll know how far to stretch my wood supply."

"Yellow Moon Canyon," said Corio. "Get us there before midnight."

"That'll be the new rail spur headed toward the border, you're wanting?" the fireman asked.

"That's the place," Corio said with a faint smile of satisfaction. "Now take us to it."

The fireman shook his head in consternation. "That's a dangerous place out there around Yellow Moon," he said in a fearful voice. "There's outlaws from both sides of the border, would cut a man's throat for his—" He stopped short, considering his present company.

"You're not going to be a talker, are you?" Jordan asked in a harsh tone, his lowered Colt easing back up to level. "Because we both *hate* talkers."

The fireman cleared his throat and ventured, "All's I meant was—"

"Shut up, Lowell," the engineer said over his shoulder, keeping his eyes on the rails ahead. "Can't you hear him? They hate talkers."

Back on the abandoned troop cars that had now

come to a complete stop almost halfway across the deep canyon, the second fireman, a younger man named Huey Sadler, walked carefully along the narrow walkway beside the train. He stopped as the captain and the sergeant stepped out and looked down at the dizzying space stretching downward beneath them. "They've taken one stock car of horses with them. There's not enough room to lower a ramp and get our horses off the other, Sergeant!" said Ploster, assessing the situation.

"Right, sir, I'd say that's the gist of it," said Sergeant Webster. Looking at the second fireman, he asked, "Any notion what a man's to do in this kind of situation?"

"I've never even seen a situation like this," said Sadler. He stood scratching his head up under his cap brim. In the open windows the soldiers stood looking all around, and down at the yawning canyon below. "I say we've got to walk off of here," Sadler concluded. He looked at Ploster and said, "Leastwise that's what I'm going to do. I advise all of yas to do the same."

Looking embarrassed, feeling humiliated and helpless, Captain Ploster asked humbly, "When will another train be through here?"

"Tomorrow at noon, or thereabouts," said Sadler. "I'm going to walk back and warn them as far back as I can."

Across Hueco Pass, Irish Tommie continued his jig on the rear of the flatcar. As he dipped and twirled he raised a flask to his lips and drank deeply, in spite of the fact that Madden Corio had given strict orders against it. "Look at me, I'm fat as a Christmas goose but lighter than a pillow feather!"

"You best settle yourself down, fool," Harvey Lemate called out to him.

But Irish Tommie would have none of it. Instead of heeding Lemate's advice, he reeled with laughter and jumped higher and higher as he shrieked toward the wide blue evening sky. With his eyes closed he finally jumped so high that when he came down, the flatcar had sped out from under him.

"Good Lord!" Boxer Shagin, one of Corio's men who'd brought the uniforms, called out to his brother, Lindsey Shagin. "The idiot's jumped off the train!"

Irish Tommie's shriek had intensified, then stopped short as he hit the cross ties feet first, bounced high, flipped in a full circle and bounced twice more until he landed headfirst and came to a limp and broken halt between the two gleaming rails. "He's bashed his bloody brains out!" shouted Richard Little, one of the men standing and gawking in awe as the train sped onward.

Brule Kaggan, another of the six who'd brought the uniforms, stood beside Little and Matt Ford. "Somebody tell Corio. We've got to go back for him."

"In a pig's eye," said Ford. "Corio wouldn't stop this train for his own mother." He added with a wicked grin, "Hell, neither would I. Ma and I never got along that well."

The train rolled on into the long shadows of evening, the surrounding terrain growing more rugged and mountainous until darkness sank down and enveloped the land. "Won't be long, we'll be coming to the starting edge of Yellow Moon Canyon, Mister," the engineer called out in the dim glow of lantern light, above the deep, steady hypnotic throb of the steam engine.

Madden Corio pretended not to have been dozing and just awakened. Instead he forced his voice to sound strong and alert. "Good work, men," he said to the two railroaders. "Don't be surprised if there's a bag of gold coins waiting for both of you once we get to where we're going. How would that suit you?"

The engineer and fireman looked at each other in the dim flickering light. "That would suit me fine," said the engineer. "But I'm afraid it wouldn't set well with my employer."

"Me neither," said the fireman.

"You'd tell him about it?" Corio mused, giving Jordan a look of disbelief.

"He'd ask," said the engineer, "and I would not brand myself a liar over a bag of gold coins."

"Neither would I," the fireman said as the train made its way along the beginning of a deep canyon.

"I say man's honor is all he's got," said the engineer. "I stand good to my word whatever it takes."

"My hat goes off to you," said Corio. "I feel much the same way myself. When I give my word I refuse to crawfish on it." He and Jordan gave each other a knowing look, then chuckled between themselves.

Lawrence Shaw, Sonny Lloyd Sheer, Dan Sax and Able Hatcher sat atop their horses at the top of a steep trail leading down into Yellow Moon Canyon. They watched the round globe of the train light meander up as if from out of the earth and straighten itself into a long harsh beam of light across the rocky ground.

"Here it comes now," Shaw said sidelong to the men beside him. "Bring Corio's gunmen up behind us," he said to Hatcher. "Get ready to cut them loose when I give you a signal."

As Hatcher turned and rode away at a gallop, Shaw reached out and turned up a dimly lit lantern into a high glow. He raised the bright lantern over his head and waved it back and forth slowly toward the approaching train.

"Can't they see us?" Sheer asked after an anxious moment.

"Oh yes, they see us," Shaw said with confidence, still waving the lantern. No sooner had he spoken than they watched the bright headlight shudder atop the engine as the train began its long, screeching, grinding, steam-blowing halt.

"They damn sure do," said Sax, restlessly gripping the stock of the rifle lying across his lap.

"All right," said Shaw, "be ready to back up anything I tell them."

A moment passed as the train sat pulling and pounding and blowing off steam into the desert air. Then the heavy thud of a boarding ramp dropping resounded in the darkness, and horses' hooves shuffled and clanked down onto the rocky ground. As Shaw and the others watched, figures began to move toward them in the shadowy moonlight. Shaw held the lantern low and gave a short signal wave to Hatcher and the others waiting just off the trail behind them.

In the darkness, Madden Corio saw the short wave of the lantern and said to Jordan and Lemate, who rode close beside him, "They've gotten themselves ready for us. Keep me covered."

As the three rode closer and Corio saw the lantern go out altogether, he said to the shadowy images sitting their horses before him, "You better hope our wagons are ready and waiting. I'll hear no ifs, ands or buts about it."

"The wagons are ready, Corio," Shaw said, on the hunch that it was Corio talking to him.

Corio stopped his horse, the other two following suit beside him. They were barely able to make out the three figures in the pale moonlight. "Bring up the wagons, let's get them loaded," he commanded.

"Real soon, Corio," Shaw said calmly. "First let's talk about it."

"What is there to talk about?" Corio asked, his hand on the rifle across his lap as he nudged his horse forward at a slower, more cautious pace. "Your partner and I agreed to the payback before you become a part of this deal."

"That was then, Corio," said Shaw, "this is now. Things have changed."

"Oh, have they?" Corio asked, moving forward and stopping fifteen feet away, his two men flanking close on either side. "In what way has anything changed?"

"Lowe is dead," Shaw said.

"What happened to him?" Corio asked, but his eyes kept moving back and forth, trying to see in the darkness down along the canyon trail.

"His gal killed him," Shaw said. "They had a lovers' spat, you could say."

In the darkness, Corio fell silent for a moment. Then upon making out the faces of Sheer and Dan Sax in the grainy moonlight, he said to Sheer, "Is that true, Sonny Lloyd? Dexter Lowe's whore killed him?"

"She killed him deader than hell," Sheer replied.

"And it's true this man was his partner?" Corio asked, sounding wary of the whole idea. "And you believe all this, you being Lowe's right-hand man?"

"Yes, I believe it," said Sheer. "I heard the words come straight from Dangerous Dexter Lowe's own mouth," he lied. "There's not a doubt in my mind."

Corio stepped his horse in closer for a better look at Sheer's and Sax's faces. "What about you, Dan?"

"No doubt in my mind either," Sax said.

"With Lowe dead, where does that put you two?" Corio asked, testing the two gunmen's loyalties.

"You see where we're sitting, Madden," said Sheer, nodding toward Shaw. "We're with him, all the way."

Corio considered what *all the way* meant. "We don't have all night to sit jawing about this," he said. He turned to Shaw. "If these two say you're all right, then you're good in my book. Now get my wagons up here, let's get loaded and gone. We'll finish talking about the money once we're under way. We're going to have soldiers down our shirts soon as they figure out what's hit them."

"We talk about the money now, else there won't be any wagons brought up," Shaw said.

"I left Watkins and Skinner with them," Jordan said

to Corio. "I call out to them, they'll start killing these saddle tramps quicker than—" His words stopped as he saw the two walk up from the trail, out of the greater darkness, their hands tied behind their backs.

"Saddle tramps, are we, Jordan?" Sonny Lloyd Sheer asked in a sharp-edged voice.

"Shut up, Jordan," said Corio, seeing that this was getting him nowhere. He calmed down and watched Skinner and Watkins walk up closer and stop. Watkins' forehead bore a swollen imprint of a rifle barrel. Skinner's nose and upper lip were swollen and bloody. "It looks like you're trying to deal yourself in deeper into my business, Mister," said Corio, ready to go along with anything so long as he got his wagons and got them loaded.

"Now you're starting to get the message," Shaw said. "My men get even splits the same as you pay you're regulars."

"Okay, that's them," said Corio. "Let's hear about you."

"This time out I get the same as your man here gets," Shaw said, nodding toward Jordan. "Next job, whatever my men get will come off of my end."

"Off of *your* end?" Corio said, with a slight bemused grin.

"That's right, my end," Shaw said. "Next job we pull I ride as a full partner."

"You've got sand. I'll say that for you, stranger," Corio said, still knowing that it didn't matter what he said, so long as he got moving across the border. "Hell, all right, it's time I take on some new guns, expand on my horizons, so to speak."

Behind Shaw, Sonny Lloyd Sheer and Dan Sax looked at each other in amazement.

"You men heard my partner," Shaw said. "Get those wagons up here. Let's make some money."

Chapter 17

In a grainy glow of moonlight and torches, Corio's men and Lowe's men made quick work of unloading the flatcars onto the big wagons. Upon first arrival, Shaw climbed up and cut the tie-down ropes from a canvas tarpaulin. When he flipped the corner from atop the cargo crates, he stopped for a moment and looked down at the crate markings.

"Gatling guns . . . ," he said in a whisper, wondering how far behind him Dawson and Caldwell might be. So long as these guns stayed in the crate, his lawmen partners were safe enough, but he did not want to draw them into a fight with an enemy armed with Gatling guns.

"That's only part of it," said Corio, stepping up beside him. "On one of these cars we've got a crate of newly designed French hand grenades. All you do is run a striker across the top of it and give it a toss." Seeing the question in Shaw's eyes, he added, "Some high brass always manages to slip in something like this. It keeps them knowing the latest in armament."

Shaw was impressed but he tried to play it down. "Who is this going to?" he asked in an offhand manner, hoping Corio would give something up.

But Corio didn't fall for it. "That's going to remain my little secret, *partner*," he said with deliberation. "I'm not sharing any more than I have to with you just yet."

Shaw just stared at him.

"What do you expect?" Jordan asked, stepping up beside Corio as the men began laying walk boards from the flatcars to the wagons. "We don't even know your name." Behind Jordan came Sonny Lloyd and Dan Sax. "But I say it's time we find out, here and now."

More of Corio's men gathered on the ground beside the low open flatcar. Now that the wagons were in place, Shaw figured it was time for somebody to test him a little more, see how far he might be pushed. He took a moment and looked all around at Corio's men, matching faces to names by memory, by wanted posters. When he turned back to Jordan, before he said anything, Tuesday Bonhart climbed the iron ladder up onto the flatcar.

"His name is Shaw—Lawrence Shaw," she said with no hesitancy. "Some of you might know him as Fast Larry or the Fastest Gun Alive."

"What the—?" Jordan cut himself short; his hand went for his holstered gun.

Tuesday's words caught Shaw by surprise, yet as he saw hands snap to pistol butts and rifle stocks, his own

Colt streaked up fast enough to cause every other hand to freeze in place. Even Jordan hadn't manage to clear the top of his holster before Shaw's big Colt bore down on him and moved back and forth slowly between him and Corio like some steel-eyed serpent choosing where to strike first.

"See why they call him that?" Tuesday said fearlessly, her hand going to her cocked hip. "I just love watching him at work."

"Everybody hold tight," said Corio. Watching Shaw's gun barrel move slowly back and forth, he raised a calm hand toward his men as if it would keep the blood from spilling. "Are you Fast Larry Shaw?" he asked Shaw somberly.

"I'm Lawrence Shaw," Shaw said, feeling the pounding begin to ratchet up inside his head, induced by the suddenness of his move. "I don't go by Fast Larry anymore."

"You're a lawdog," Jordan said, a bit brazenly considering his gun had not even cleared his holster.

"Watch your language," Shaw said. "I wore a badge for a while. I still carry it. But I'm a gunman, always was, always will be." Even as he said the words, it dawned on him that he was not lying. The pain in his head had grown intense; he hoped it didn't show on his face. Yet with his pain came the truth. The two seemed intertwined. There was a sudden rush of clarity in calling himself a gunman, as if it had been something he'd denied for too long.

Corio saw the look on Shaw's face and eased in to take things over before Jordan worked this into a killing. "You rode with that U.S. marshal and his deputy," he said, but not in a harsh, confrontational manner. "You killed friends of ours along the border."

"This is gun country, Corio," Shaw said, feeling more like himself than he had for a long time. "I live here. Killing is what I do."

"But you are the law," said Jordan, venturing his words in, his finger stabbing toward Shaw like some short saber. "You put on a badge and killed our own kind down here."

"I kill for money," said Shaw, "same as every other man here. I put on a badge for the law, or a uniform for the army, or a monkey suit for some high-rolling money baron." His gaze bored into Jordan.

"But still . . ." Jordan let his words trail, but his accusing finger drooped a little.

"Let me say it again, this time slower for you." Shaw cocked the Colt's hammer as he held the big gun leveled at Jordan's chest. "This is gun country. I live here. Killing is what I do. Any questions?" His eyes looked dark and dead with resolve as they moved slowly from face to face.

A tense silence set in. Sonny Lloyd Sheer, Dan Sax and the others watched in awe. Tuesday stood rapt in fascination. Corio took a tight breath and said, "And it's a damn good job you've done of it, from all I've ever heard." He paused with a slight smile, still holding the upper hand, he thought, so long as only he knew where the armament was going. "Now can we get these damned wagons loaded?"

"Yeah, let's get to it," Jordan said, glad to put aside

differences now that Corio had given his approval to do so.

Corio gave his men a look. The men eased back into motion, their hands coming away from their guns and going to the business of reaching for crates and rolling tarpaulins. In a moment everyone had gotten busy again, too busy to note that Shaw still stood with the same look frozen onto his face. But Tuesday saw that Shaw was in trouble. He seemed to be stuck in place.

"Hey, you're coming with me, Fast Larry," she said, moving in quickly and hooking her arm through his, drawing his forearm away from the big Colt. "We're going to do some celebrating in private." She turned and gave a wink to Corio to keep him from seeing Shaw's condition. "I get hot all over when I see him sling his big gun around," she added, and she tried to turn and walk to the iron ladder.

But Corio blocked her way. "Hold on," he said, without noticing Shaw's lost and frozen eyes. "I take it you're the young whore who killed Dexter Lowe?"

"Yes, what of it?" Tuesday asked in a bold voice, ready at any second to grab the derringer from inside her dress if she needed it.

"Dexter and I did lots of business together," said Corio. "He was a good man. I don't like the idea of you killing him."

"Get used to it," Tuesday said. She stepped forward, using Shaw's presence to get Corio to move aside. "How do you think I feel killing him? The son of a bitch said he'd take me to Paris."

Corio took her by her forearm to keep her from walking away. "Why'd you kill him?" he asked bluntly. "I've got a right to know."

"I killed him because . . ." Tuesday took her time, staring down at his hand on her arm before raising her eyes to his. "He put his hands on me," she said with a knowing look. "You might want to keep that in mind, Madden Corio."

As Shaw and Tuesday stepped onto the iron ladder, neither Corio nor Jordan saw the change that had come over the wounded gunman. "I suppose we should've figured on some whore killing Lowe someday," Jordan said between the two of them. Then in a lowered tone he said, "What about Shaw?"

"What about him?" said Corio, watching Shaw and Tuesday step away into the moonlit darkness. "We've got a deal going with Bocanero. Until we've gotten our money, we leave Shaw and Lowe's men alone, let them do the job they're paid to do."

"Which is to be decoy targets for the Mexican army while we get away with our firearms," Jordan said with a sly grin.

"That's right," said Corio. "You heard Shaw." He quoted, " 'This is gun country.' He lives here."

"He can die here too," said Jordan.

"Only when the time is right for it," said Corio. "Any time him or these men get on your nerves, remind yourself of that, and keep your head clear. We can kill Shaw any time we're ready, like snuffing out a match. But for now, let him burn."

Outside the circle of torch and lantern light, Tuesday sat Shaw down on the rocky ground and helped him lean back against an ancient ironwood tree. "Damn it, Shaw, don't break down on me now," she said in a harsh whisper. She took off his tall stovepipe hat and examined his bandaged head as best she could in the pale moonlight, as if looking at it would reveal anything about his mental condition. "What comes over you, makes you act that way?"

Shaw only stared blankly, knowing he'd drifted away, and knowing he'd been powerless to stop himself. He tried to speak, to answer the woman's voice he'd heard, but he couldn't get the words to form and move through his lips. He sat slumped for a moment, yet he saw himself lying on a bed. He saw a woman move toward him as if through a dark veil. He saw her hand reach out and slip his Colt from his holster; he heard the gun cock. Then he heard an explosion too loud and powerful to be real.

Coming to with a start, Shaw clamped his hand tight around Tuesday's throat. But then a fog seemed to lift; he caught himself and stopped.

"Jesus, Fast Larry!" said Tuesday, jerking her head back from him as he turned her loose. Her hand had almost gone to the derringer in her dress. But she stopped and looked into Shaw's eyes. "Hey, are you with me?"

"Yes—I'm all right." Shaw sat gasping breath after breath, like a man who had forgotten to breathe and now had to catch up.

"Do you remember what happened back there?" Tuesday asked.

"I remember," Shaw said, though he was stretching the truth. "You mean Corio, the train, all that?"

"Yes . . . all *that*," Tuesday said dubiously, watching his eyes, gauging his senses. "You remember shooting Bert Jordan?"

Shaw had to consider it for just a second before he realized what she was doing. "Stop it. I told you I'm all right."

"Okay." Tuesday smiled and took a breath and laid his hat on the ground beside him. "I worry about you, is all. You sit here. I'm going to get a blanket and have you lie down and rest."

She started to turn away but Shaw said, "What about loading the wagons? Corio will think something's wrong if I'm lying out here when I should be there with the wagons."

"No, he's going to think we're out here *doing* each other," she said, "sort of celebrating the job. I left that impression. Don't you remember me saying I wanted you to do something for me in private?" She watched his eyes in the darkness.

"Yes, now I remember," Shaw said, leaving her unable to tell whether or not he was lying.

"Sit still," she said, "I'll be right back."

"I saw a woman just now," Shaw said, recounting what had just gone on in his confused mind. "She took my gun out and shot me."

Tuesday stared at him for a moment, then said, "Well, it wasn't me, if that's what you're thinking."

"No," Shaw said, "I know it wasn't you. . . ." He slumped back against the ironwood tree, closed his eyes against the pain in his head, feeling it subside a little. He had an idea who the woman was, but he didn't want to allow himself to consider it. He tried forcing himself to think more clearly, but he did so in vain. It would take time, he told himself. Meanwhile, Dawson and Caldwell would be depending on him. He couldn't let them down. . . .

From a ridge higher up, Crayton Dawson gazed down through a pair of binoculars at the stranded train sitting out on the trestle above Yellow Moon Canyon. In the early morning light, he saw two soldiers carrying grain bags into the stock car to horses trapped inside. Gazing back along the rails, he saw soldiers sitting strewn out along the rails. They stared off along the tracks as if expecting help most any time.

Among the soldiers sitting on the rocky ground, a young officer stood erect and vigilant, his hands clasped behind his back—in charge, in spite of their helpless predicament. "Corio's gang got the train," Dawson said to Caldwell and Jane, who stood back holding the reins to their horses.

"What do you mean, they *got* the train?" Jane asked, irritated. "You mean they robbed it, they stole it, they *ate* it, or what?"

"Take your pick," Dawson said in retaliation to her sarcasm. He stood and dusted his knees and chest. He walked back to Jane and handed her the battered binoculars. But as he spoke he turned to Caldwell. "They've stolen it."

"A nice fat arms shipment," Caldwell muttered, gazing out with his naked eyes, seeing very little through the remnants of gray morning.

"That's my guess," said Dawson. "I figure the officer in charge sent some troops back to warn any oncoming train and get some help out here. These others stayed here to take care of the horses and keep an eye on things."

Looking down through the binoculars at the half of a train sitting out on the trestle, Jane said, "Pretty damn clever of Corio. Now he's unloaded his booty and is hightailing it to Old Mex."

"Yep," said Dawson, "and we're right behind him."

"What about these boys?" Jane asked, gesturing toward the soldiers below.

"They'll be all right without us," said Dawson. "By the time we ride down and see if we can help them, then ride back up here to circle Hueco Pass, Corio and his gang will be long gone."

"Do you suppose Shaw is on Corio's trail," Caldwell asked, "or riding with him and Lowe's gang?"

"Good question," said Dawson. "I wish I knew the answer for you."

The three mounted up and rode off around the high rim of Hueco Pass. An hour later, they descended a trail and followed the rails until they saw Irish Tommie lying where the train had left him in the night. "Damn! It looks like this fool is alive," Jane said, hearing the large man let out a groan.

"Good, let's see if we can keep him that way," said Dawson, the three of them reining their horses down together. Taking his canteen from his saddle horn, he stepped down and hurried over to the downed man, seeing blood smeared and puddled all around him.

Dawson stooped down and rolled the heavy man over onto his back. Opening his eyes, Irish Tommie said weakly, "I shouldn't been . . . jumping."

"Easy, big fellow," said Dawson. He raised the big man's head onto his lap and held the canteen to his parched lips. "We'll get you fixed up here. Have some water." He poured a thin trickle onto his fingertips and touched them to Tommie's lips. Then he carefully poured a bit into his mouth. From the looks of the man's bashed and bloody head and his broken, twisted body, Dawson saw little hope for him.

Swallowing and letting out a gasp, Tommie noted the badge on Dawson's chest. "You are . . . the lawmen who's dogging . . . everybody. . . ."

"That's me," Dawson said. "Where's Corio headed with this train?"

"Don't you want to know . . . where I'm headed?" Tommie said with a grim bloody chuckle.

"You're headed for hell, Irish Tommie," Jane cut in, recognizing the big rotund outlaw. "So tell him what he wants to know. Maybe the devil will show a little mercy, not stick you in the ass with his pitchfork—"

"That's enough, Jane," Dawson said, cutting her off.

"Yell-Yellow Moon . . . ," Tommie said, grasping Dawson by his shirtfront, unable to finish his words.

"Yellow Moon Canyon?" Dawson asked. "They're taking the train to Yellow Moon Canyon? They'll unload it there?"

Irish Tommie gave a bloody grin and tried to nod his head. "Got to . . . go now," he gasped.

"And good riddance to you, Tommie!" Jane shouted

down at him, as if wanting hers to be the last words he would ever hear.

"That's uncalled for, Jane," said Caldwell as Dawson eased Tommie's head from his lap and let it down on the rocky ground between the two steel rails.

"You can say that, because you don't know this sonsabitch the way I do, Undertaker," Jane grumbled.

"Let's drag him off the tracks and get going," said Dawson, ignoring Jane and Caldwell's bickering. "We'll be tracking Corio into Mexico by the time we catch up to him."

Chapter 18

———

By the time the wagons were loaded, sunlight had begun to glow in a silver wreath along the eastern edge of the earth. Corio watched as Shaw and Tuesday walked back to the flatcars. To Jordan he said quietly, "Here comes our new partner now."

"Yeah," said Jordan, "he's no doubt bred, fed and ready to ride."

"Good for him, then," said Corio. "Maybe the whore will keep him on top of his game, the way she seemed to do with Dangerous Dexter."

"Yeah, maybe," Jordan said grudgingly. "As whores go, I've seen worse looking. She's young, strapping and robust. I like that."

"As do I myself," said Corio, watching the sway of Tuesday's hips as she walked nearer. "Maybe we'll save her for ourselves when we've finished this job. Have a *celebration* of our own."

"I'm going to hold you to that," Jordan said.

When Shaw got closer, Corio said down to him from

atop the flatcar, "As soon as we get across the border, we're going straight across the desert to the hill country. Once the wagons make it there without the *federales* spotting them, it'll be easier traveling until we have to come back down."

Shaw looked up at him. "Where are we headed once we come back down?"

"It's not time for you to know that," Corio said.

"It *is time* for me know which way for these wagons to run if my drivers get hit by an ambush crossing the hill trails."

"No matter where the wagons are," said Corio, "my men and I will be a level above them. They will be in our gun sights at all times. If they get ambushed, we'll cover them and pull them through it. You have my word on it. Don't forget what this cargo is worth to me . . . to all of us." He stepped onto the iron rung of the flatcar ladder and climbed down the four rungs to the ground.

"Or, don't you trust Madden's word, partner?" Jordan asked, staring down at Shaw.

"I have no reason not to trust his word," said Shaw. "I'll be riding up there myself, making sure my drivers are covered."

"Your men are covered, Shaw," said Corio, gesturing a hand toward the line of five loaded wagons. "See for yourself."

Sheer and Sax had climbed up into the first wagon, one driving and one riding shotgun. In the second wagon sat Jimmy Bardell and Earl Hardine. Behind them in the third wagon sat New York Joe Toledo and Able

Hatcher. In the driver seat of the fourth wagon, Bell Mason sat alone, a shotgun propped against his leg. The fifth wagon carried two of Corio's men, the Shagin brothers, Lindsey and Boxer.

"Show us something, Boxer," Jordan called out. Before the words were out of his mouth, Boxer Shagin scrambled over the seat into the wagon bed and threw a green tarpaulin off a mounted Gatling gun and crouched behind it, ready to fire.

"Feel better, *partner*?" Jordan asked, stepping down from the flatcar himself and dismissing Boxer Shagin with a short wave of a hand.

Shaw didn't reply. Instead he looked at the faces of the men on the wagons, making sure they were satisfied with the setup. Seeing them give him a short nod, he looked toward Tuesday Bonhart, who came running from where she'd watched over him on the blanket until his pain had subsided and his dull stupor had worn off.

"Wait for me!" she called out, adjusting her clothes as if she'd just thrown them back on. Giggling, she gave Shaw a suggestive look and wiggled up hurriedly into the wagon seat beside Bell Mason. "My goodness, Fast Larry, give a gal time to catch her breath!" She picked up the short-barreled shotgun from against Mason's leg and ran her hand back and forth along its barrel with a glowing secretive smile.

Shaw looked at Corio and said, "All right, ready when you are." He walked to where Bardell had formed all of the wagon drivers' horses into a string in a column of twos. He took up the lead rope, gathered the reins to his speckled barb and climbed up into the saddle. The pain in his head was gone. His mind felt clear and focused. He gigged the barb forward and rode along beside the wagon where Tuesday sat with the shotgun lying across her lap.

While Corio and his men mounted and headed up into the hillsides surrounding them, Shaw looked down at Tuesday and said, "Obliged, I needed that."

Knowing Bell Mason could hear them, Tuesday giggled and replied, "No more than I did, Fast Larry." She rose from the wooden seat, reached over to him and said with a laugh, "Lift me onto your lap. I want to see if I left anything behind."

Mason gave an excited sidelong glance as Shaw drew her from the wagon onto his lap. She threw her arms around his neck and nuzzled her face close to his ear. "The arms are going to Sepio Bocanero."

"Bocanero, the rebel leader?" Shaw pulled her away from his neck and looked into her eyes, amazed. "How did you find that out?"

She giggled coyly. "How do you think?" She pressed her large warm breasts against him and rolled her shoulders slowly back and forth.

Shaw stared at her. "But you couldn't have. There hasn't been time."

"It doesn't take a gal long, not with these randy gunmen," she said. "It's all right isn't it, I mean you don't mind me doing that?" she asked, moving back close to his ear.

"Tuesday, I'm not your boss," Shaw said, riding along with her pressed against him. "I won't tell you what you can or can't do."

"I know, and that's what I like about you," she cooed in his ear. "Dex was a stupid jealous prick. I'm glad he's dead."

"What about Sepio Bocanero?" Shaw asked, changing the subject from the late Dexter Lowe. "Did you happen to hear where we're supposed to meet him?"

"No," she said. "But I figure with the *federales* hunting for him and his men, he won't stick his head up for long. I thought you'd want to know. Did I do good?"

"You did real good, Tuesday," Shaw said, sidling back to the wagon. "Now get back over there."

"How about you? Are you sure you're feeling all right?" she asked as Shaw started to lift her back over to the wagon seat.

"I'm sure I am, thanks to you," Shaw said in almost a whisper. "You keep your eyes open and your head down. Be ready for anything. I expect the worst out of Madden Corio." He left her on the wagon seat and nudged his barb forward behind Corio and Jordan. He followed a good distance behind them.

On his way past the engine, he saw the body of the engineer and the fireman lying sprawled in the dirt beside the tracks. The engine sat with its headlight black, silent in the gray morning light, except for the metallic click and thump of the cooling iron boiler.

By midmorning the wagons had ridden down into a stretch of lower-lying hills and crossed the border. Once across the border, Shaw stayed up inside the cover of scrub juniper and cholla cactus, keeping a watch on the five slow-moving wagons below as they ambled along on narrow switchback trails.

At noon the wagons had made good time and stopped to rest and water the horses at a thin runoff stream. Shaw looked all around and watched Corio's men scout upward and ride away into the rocky hillsides. Looking down at the wagons, he gave Tuesday and the wagon drivers a signaling wave. When both Sonny Sheer's and Tuesday Bonhart's return wave told him everything was all right, he turned his barb and rode away, taking the opportunity to scout farther along the high trail and the sand flats that lay ahead.

From across the ridge, Bert Jordan and Madden Curio watched Shaw ride forward. "There goes our *partner*," said Jordan. "What do you say?"

Corio said nothing. But he gave a short nod of his head.

"Adios," said Jordan with a wicked grin. "It's about time." He jerked his horse around and batted his boots to its sides.

Corio waited a full ten minutes longer before he took out a palm-sized piece of a broken shaving mirror and expertly cocked it at an angle against the noonday sun. A moment passed as the flash of white light glistened out three hundred yards across the jagged ridges. Then, with no show of surprise, Corio watched as three of Sepio Bocanero's rebels eased forward from the cover of juniper and dry bracken and looked down on the wagons below.

Corio waited until he was certain Bocanero's rebels had seen him. He gestured a hand toward the wagons below, letting them know to tell their leader that the arms were here, that he was ready for Bocanero to take possession of the shipment. He said as if the Mexicans could hear him from two hundred yards across the canyon, "Tell him his guns have arrived, gentlemen, as promised."

Corio lowered the angle of the mirror away from the rebels as they turned and vanished back into the rocky hillside. He cocked the mirror in a different angle and sent the white light flashing down onto the trail below where Boxer and Lindsey Shagin sat in the wooden seat sharing a canteen of tepid water. "Time to get it done, men," he said quietly to himself.

Lying stretched out in the dirt and leaning back against the wheel of his wagon, Dan Sax saw the beam of mirrored sunlight streak across the toe of his scuffed boot and said to Sonny Lloyd Sheer lying bedside him, "What the hell was that?"

"I don't know, but I saw it too," said Sheer, scrambling to his feet as he capped the canteen he'd been drinking from.

At the next wagon, Jimmy Bardell and Earl Hardine saw Sheer and Sax stand up quickly, and they did the same. Behind them Toledo and Hatcher followed suit, Toledo with his shotgun in his hands. "What's going on?" Tuesday asked Bell Mason as she hurried to her feet, grabbing the shotgun on her way.

"Injuns!" said Mason, his eyes bulging with fear. He

reached over into the wagon and snatched a rifle he'd kept lying beneath the wooden seat.

"Indians? You're crazy, Bell!" said Tuesday. "That's not Indians!" Yet even as she spoke she crouched near the wagon wheel and looked all around on the ridges lining both hillsides above them.

A tense dead silence gripped the narrow valley for a moment as each of the wagon divers looked back and forth along the rock walls and ridges surrounding them. But the silence was suddenly broken by the rustle of the tarpaulin being slung off the Gatling gun. The next sound they heard was the clank of an ammunition stack slamming into place atop the gun as it swung around toward them.

"A trap!" shouted Bell Mason. But before the words left his mouth, a rifle shot from the hillside above them nailed him in the chest and sent him flying backward, a ribbon of blood curling in his wake.

"Oh, hell! Look out!" shouted Sonny Lloyd Sheer.

As if the rifle shot that killed Mason had been a signal, the Gatling gun began its wild, deadly chatter. Huddled beside the fourth wagon, splattered with Bell Mason's blood, Tuesday screamed, "*Shaw!*" But her words were engulfed by the exploding gunfire. As bullets whistled past her, she dove under the wagon and hugged the ground.

A half mile ahead on a higher trail, Shaw did not hear Tuesday's scream, but he did hear the endless firing of the Gatling gun and the cacophony of rifle fire from the rocky canyon walls. Turning the speckled barb quickly, he raced back along the trail toward the sound of raging battle. But before he'd gone a quarter of a mile, he caught a glimpse of one of the rebels in a dirty white peasant shirt looped with a bandoleer of bullets.

The man rose quickly from the rocks alongside the trail. He heaved a lit grenade toward Shaw, then flung himself out of sight before the iron sphere hit the middle of the trail and rolled and bounced closer. With no time to turn the barb and ride out of the grenade's blast, Shaw did the only thing he could; he jerked the reins hard to the side, veered the barb sharply and sent both horse and himself plunging headlong off the edge of the trail.

Even before the steep hillside rushed up and met them, Shaw felt the bone-crushing blast of the grenade lift dirt and rock from the middle of the trail and launch it like buckshot in every direction. He felt it pepper him and the barb in that split second before the two of them dropped out of sight.

The sound of the grenade blast was quickly taken over by the barb's long whinny as horse and rider separated in midair. The two of them rolled and bounced, thrashed, slammed and slid, finally coming to a stop in a spray of dust, broken juniper branches and loose rock, on a ledge over a hundred feet below.

Shaw landed on his chest and felt the air explode out of his lungs. Twenty feet away the barb's long terrified whinny turned to a low guttural chuffing and spluttering as the battered animal tried to catch its breath and struggle up onto its hooves.

On the edge of the trail, two of Sepio Bocanero's rebels, both wearing dirty white shirts and bandoleers of ammunition, stood looking down the hillside through a dusty haze. "I think he must be dead, this gringo," one said to the other. He took off his straw sombrero and fanned it in front of him, stirring a cloud of thick dust.

"I will make sure," said the man beside him. He took another grenade from inside his loose dirty shirt and hefted it in his hand, grinning. "God bless the wonderful French, eh, Migio?" he said to his cousin in his native tongue.

"What are you doing, Paco?" the first one called out loudly. He saw the man strike the fuse on the grenade and light it. It was too late to stop his comrade from heaving the sizzling grenade, but his shouting had distracted the man enough that his throw went awry. The grenade fell short and far to the right of the ledge where Shaw and the barb had landed.

"Yii-hiii," shouted the one who'd thrown the powerful hand bomb. Down the rocky hillside a spindly fifteen-foot pine took the brunt of the blast at its trunk base. It lifted straight up over a foot, toppled down and slid a feet few before it lodged against another tree.

"We can't be wasting these, Paco!" said Migio. "We have been ordered to use only what we must."

"And that is what we did." Paco shrugged. "We had to make sure he was dead, *sí*?"

"*Sí*, and he *is* dead—that much is certain," said Paco, turning and putting his sombrero back on. "Come—we must help with the wagons." The two walked away toward the place on the hillside where their horses stood hitched to a creosote bush.

PART 4

Chapter 19

Madden Corio, Bert Jordan and three Mexicans sat atop a cliff overlooking the canyon floor. On the trail below lay the bodies of men and horses strewn about as though dropped from some high summit. The five wagons moved forward now, their dead and wounded horses replaced by mules the rebel forces had brought along, knowing that the fresh animals would be needed.

Four of the wagons were now driven by rebels. The fifth wagon still held the mounted Gatling gun, Lindsey and Boxer Shagin still in control of it.

"Well, General Bocanero," said Corio to the tallest of the three Mexicans sitting atop horses beside him, "that's how to take an arms shipment, the quick and easy way."

Sepio Bocanero gave a hand gesture, and one of the other two Mexicans stepped his horse forward and hefted a heavy saddlebag off his shoulder and into Jordan's waiting hands. When Jordan had spread the saddlebags over his cantle and flipped open each flap and looked at the gold coins, he gave Corio a nod of approval.

The third Mexican nudged his horse forward and hefted a saddlebag to Jordan, who smiled and checked it in the same manner as the first.

Looking at Corio, Sepio Bocanero said in good border English, "I must admit, you have surprised me, Corio. I hope we will do much business together in the future."

"I see nothing stopping us," said Corio. "We are both serious men with the same purpose in mind."

"Purpose . . . ?" Bocanero gave a slight grin and said in a mock rehearsed voice, "My *purpose* is to rule my beautiful *Mejico* with a fair hand, so all of her people will know justice and freedom."

Corio returned the grin. "Yeah, that's exactly what I meant," he replied knowingly. He gestured a nod toward Jordan, who had lifted a handful of gold coins from the second saddlebag and let them spill from his fingertips.

Both the Mexicans and the outlaws gave a laugh. Then Bocanero turned serious and asked Corio bluntly, "When will we get the other big gun, and the French hand bombs?"

"Tonight," said Corio, staring levelly at the Mexican rebel leader. "I'm leaving the brothers here to guard our back trail. Anybody comes trailing us before sundown is going to have to get through Lindsey and Boxer Shagin. Sometime after dark, they're going to just up and slip away, leave the wagon, the Gatling and the grenades for your men to take over. Sound fair enough?"

"Fair enough." Bocanero nodded. "I will personally ride back with a detachment myself after dark." He looked closely at Corio. "Soon we will know one another better and such caution can be put aside, eh?"

"I'm certain of it, General," said Corio, knowing full well that he would never trust this man, not after a hundred years of dealing with him.

Bocanero nodded over toward Tuesday Bonhart, who lay half conscious, her hands tied in front of her, blood running from a welt on her forehead. "What about this one?" he asked. "My men would like nothing better than a fine young woman at the end of this hard day's work."

"She's not part of the deal, General," said Corio. He grinned. "She's already been spoken for." He jerked a thumb toward Jordan. "My *segundo* here has a sweet tooth for her. Besides, she's not looking any too spry. I'm not sure the girl will make it through a night of hard celebration."

Bocanero eyed the woman closely. Tuesday's blouse had been ripped half off her, revealing most of her large firm breasts. "It is a pity," said Bocanero. "Perhaps next time you will bring along a young *puta* for my men as well."

"I'll ask if she's got a sister." Corio touched his hat brim and backed his horse. "Watch out for those damn border lawmen, *mi amigo*," he warned. "They're getting more brazen all the time."

"Always, we watch for them," said Bocanero. "But we watch, hoping we will meet up with them, so we can make them bleed." He and his men turned their horses and rode away on a narrow trail, keeping a watchful eye on the wagons rolling along below.

As soon as they were gone, Corio let out a breath, stepped down from his saddle and walked over to Tuesday lying on the rocky ground. "Wake up, little darling," he said in a cutting tone. He reached down, grabbed her roughly by the short rope tied between her wrists and pulled her to her feet. She stood, wobbly and weak. "It looks like you've got a hard ride coming tonight."

"In more ways than one," said Jordan, who sat staring at the exposed white flesh with a dark gleam in his eyes.

Corio lifted the helpless woman like a sack of grain and tossed her up behind his saddle. "You are one lucky whore," he said to her, not knowing whether or not she could even hear him speaking. "Everybody died down there but you."

With Tuesday sitting limply in the saddle, Corio laid the reins up onto the saddle horn with his hand and started to step up into the saddle. But suddenly as if driven by a bolt of lightning, Tuesday let out a blood-curdling scream and kicked Corio sharply in his chin.

"Jesus!" shouted Jordan, his lap bogged down by the dual sets of heavily laden saddlebags. It took him two tries to grab the gun on his hip and raise it from the holster without losing his hold on the gold. By the time he'd brought the gun up, Tuesday was hightailing it out along a thin game path into the rocky hillside.

"She's stolen my horse. Kill her!" shouted Corio, coming up onto his knees, blood running from the deep cut on his chin. He raised his Colt and fired. Tuesday stiffened in the saddle just as she rounded a turn out of sight.

"Damn," said Jordan, "she's getting away."

"I got her," said Corio. "I saw it hit her." Rubbing his bloody chin, he barked at Jordan angrily, "Why didn't you shoot her while you had the chance?"

"I tried to, Madden!" said Jordan. "Look at me, I'm covered with saddlebags! By the time I got my gun up to fire, she was gone." He wagged the Colt in his hand. "I couldn't just turn loose of all this gold, now, could I?"

Corio settled down and let out a tight breath. "No, I suppose you couldn't." He looked along the trail, then said, "Throw the saddlebags down here and go get her."

"Huh?" Jordan looked down at him as if wondering whether or not he meant it.

"Damn it, go on," said Corio, "before those Mexican's grab her up." He stepped backward behind Jordan, giving him a clear trail. "A little bullet hole won't slow down our party much, 'less she dies underneath us."

Jordan grinned. "I hear you." He hurriedly hefted the saddlebags off his saddle and let them drop to the dirt with a heavy thud. He started to nail his boots to his horse's sides, but before he could, a bullet from Corio's Colt sliced through him from behind and exploded out of his chest in a gout of blood. Jordan looked down at his shattered chest in wide-eyed disbelief, then melted down his horse's side like a man made of soft candlewax.

"I saw what you did, you sonsabitch," Corio said down to Jordan, who lay gasping on the ground. He cocked the Colt again and pointed it down at Jordan's head. "Choose a piece of hot-tail over me? Now look at you."

"Madden, please . . . we're friends," Jordan rasped, staring up into the Colt's open bore, a sliver of gray smoke still curling from it.

"Adios, then, *friend* . . . ," said Corio. The Colt bucked in his hand; a blast of fire exploded from the barrel. Bert Jordan sank to the dirt, silent as stone.

Higher up along the narrow meandering trail, Tuesday shook her head as if to clear it and tried to ignore the pain and the nausea that tried to overtake her. She had felt the bullet slam into her back moments ago, but she hadn't slowed down. She had stiffened for a second from the impact of the slug, but then she'd lain forward and ridden on, reckless and fast, along the twisting rock trail.

Her life was ending too soon, she thought, feeling the stream of blood run down the center of her back. For a moment it had looked as if she would make it to Paris with gold to spare. Now, within an amazingly short time, it had all ended. She would die soon, and the most she had managed to do in life was to become a two-dollar line whore in a frontier saloon.

Who said she was dying . . . ?

She shook off the numbness and forced herself up-right in the saddle and fought against the sensation of falling down some deep dark hole. She had no idea where she was heading or what she would do next. But she wasn't giving up, not yet. There was something holding her here, she was convinced of it.

As the horse rounded a turn in the trail, instead of straightening out, the animal veered far right to avoid the upturned earth and rock left by the grenade explosion. To keep from falling from the saddle, Tuesday jerked back on the reins and shouted, "Whoa, horse!" until the animal slid to a stop and reared slightly.

As the horse settled with a jolt that Tuesday felt deep in her wounded back, she heard Shaw's voice call out from down the steep hillside, "Tuesday? Is that you up there?"

"Fast Larry?" she said, recognizing his voice even with an echo surrounding it. "Where are you?"

Shaw had pulled himself upward along the downed pine tree that the second grenade had lifted from its roots. As he'd climbed he'd pulled the barb along by its reins until he and the animal had reached a sharp drop thirty feet below the trail's edge. "Down here, Tuesday, me and my barb. Can you give us a hand?"

Tuesday shook off the dizziness caused by a loss of blood. "Yes, what do you need?"

"I need a rope . . . some way to help me and the barb up over these rocks."

Tuesday looked at the coiled rope hanging from Corio's saddle. "I've got one," she called out. Then she had to stop for a moment until a wave of dizziness

went away. "What—what do you want me to do?" She
slid down from the saddle, coil of rope in hand, and
staggered to the edge of the trail.

Shaw peered up at her, the barb standing beside him
on steep treacherous ground. "Tie the end of it to your
saddle horn and pitch the rest of it down to me," he
said. He saw her sway and almost fall. "Are you all
right? I heard shooting back there."

"I'm . . . all right—just a little back wound," Tuesday
forced herself to say. She turned and tied the end of the
rope around the saddle horn.

A little back wound . . . ? Shaw listened and waited,
hoping she was able to do what he needed her to do. If
not he would have to shoot the barb rather than leave it
down here to die; he would have to take his chances on
climbing the rest of the way up without losing his grip
and tumbling back down the hillside.

When Tuesday came back, further weakened by loss
of blood, she staggered again before she pitched the
rope out and watched it fall almost into Shaw's gloved
hand.

"Good throw, Tuesday," Shaw said. He hurriedly
looped the end of the rope around the barb's neck and
tied it, knowing the wounded woman might lose con-
sciousness any moment. "All right, get in the saddle
and ride your horse away real slow and steady. Help
me to get this scared horse moving up with me."

Tuesday didn't answer; she needed to save her
strength. She struggled up into the saddle and nudged
the horse forward, but not as slow and steady as Shaw
would have liked. Instead, she let the horse beneath her

move away at its normal walk, tugging hard against the weight on the other end of the taught rope.

"Good Lord, Tuesday, wait," said Shaw, both him and the barb having to scramble up over the edge of the deep drop-off back onto the steep hillside. But Tuesday had slumped forward onto the horse's neck. The horse trudged on relentlessly.

"Come on, boy, or else she's going to hang you!" Shaw shouted at the barb, slapping its rump hard with the barrel of his Colt until it finally dug its way up over the edge of the trail and shook itself as it continued walking along behind the other horse.

Shaw hurried ahead of the barb, grabbed the horse's reins from Tuesday's hand and stopped the animal in its tracks. Pulling Tuesday down from the saddle, he carried her over to a flat spot alongside the trail. In the commotion she awakened some and looked dreamily at him.

"You made it, Fast Larry . . . ," she managed to say weakly.

"Only because of you, Tuesday," Shaw said. He pulled off the torn remnants of her blood-soaked blouse and tore two long strips from it. He wadded the rest of the cloth and held it ready as he examined the bullet hole near the center of her back. Blood ran freely out and over his hand as he pressed his fingers down on the flesh surrounding the wound to see if the pressure slowed the bleeding. It did, but only a little. Yet feeling the hard knot of the bullet lying wedged in between her ribs made him breathe easier. The bullet itself wasn't life-threatening.

"How . . . is your horse?" Tuesday said sleepily.

"He's good," said Shaw, pushing the wadded-up cloth down onto the wound and holding it in place. "Keep talking to me, Tuesday," he said, patting her firmly on her cold cheek. "I want you to stay awake."

"I—I don't think I can . . . ," she said in her weakening voice.

"Come on, you've got to," said Shaw. "Stay alive," he demanded. "Be the toughest little whore you know how to be."

Tuesday turned her head and smiled up at him weakly. "You say the . . . nicest things, Fast Larry . . . ," she whispered.

"I know," said Shaw, "it's my nature." He quickly looped the torn strips of cloth around her and tied them tight into place across the wadded-up blouse. "Don't die on me, Tuesday. I've got all this gold I managed to steal from Corio . . . you've got to stay alive and help me spend it," he said, lying to her to keep her attention.

Her eyes opened as she considered his words. Even in her weakened state, she managed to say, "Fast Larry . . . I love you . . . so much."

Chapter 20

––––––

The sun had sunk below the western hill line as Shaw led the speckled barb and Corio's big bay horse down silently from among the rocks. Tuesday lay slumped on the big bay. Her back wound had all but stopped bleeding. But the bullet was still inside her and needed to be cut out soon, before infection set in.

Shaw looked at her, trying to keep his concern from showing. She wore his swallow-tailed coat and nothing under it except for the bloody bandage and the strips of cloth holding it in place. "Do you think . . . we could both go?" she asked quietly. "To Paris, that is?"

"Sure," whispered Shaw. "Why not?"

"That sounds fine . . . ," she cooed.

The young woman had remained in a weak half-conscious state all the way down the hill trail, yet she had managed to keep herself in the saddle. When Shaw stopped at a small clearing, he lowered her to the ground. "I need you to keep quiet now, Tuesday," he whispered.

She didn't seem to hear him. "Are you . . . carrying the gold with you?" she asked, looking around bleary-eyed in the dimming evening light.

"Don't talk crazy," Shaw whispered. "In fact, don't talk at all. I wouldn't be carrying that much gold around right now."

"Why are . . . we whispering?" Tuesday asked, even as she continued to do so herself.

"Because Lindsey and Boxer Shagin are sitting at the Gatling gun less than fifty feet from us. That's why I want you to keep quiet."

Tuesday gasped, and gazed out through the spindly branches of a creosote bush at the single wagon still sitting in the middle of the trail. She looked back and forth in horror at the bodies of the Lowe Gang lying where they had fallen.

"Give me a gun, Fast Larry," she said, her thirst for vengeance seeming to strengthen her. "I'll kill them both."

"No," said Shaw, reaching up and lowering her down from the saddle. "I want you to wait here, watch the horses and keep quiet."

"You're going to kill them?" she asked, holding on to his forearms to steady herself while she sat back against a large rock. "I . . . I want to help."

"Shhh, be quiet," said Shaw. He took a canteen down from his saddle horn, uncapped it and handed it to her. "If this doesn't go well for me, slip away from here and don't look back."

"But what about the gold?" Tuesday asked with a dull shine in her eyes.

Shaw didn't answer.

"If something happens to you—" Tuesday began to say more on the matter, but Shaw raised a finger to his lips, coaxing her to keep quiet. Then he backed away and slipped into the cover of rocks and disappeared like a snake.

In the wagon, seated behind the mounted Gatling gun, Boxer Shagin kept a steady gaze fixed through the falling darkness onto the trail ahead, in the direction the rebels had taken the wagons farther out along the high winding trail. "I heard something out there," he said to his brother in a lowered voice. "I heard it a while ago, and again just now."

Lindsey Shagin sat staring in the same direction. "If it's Mexicans, I doubt we'll hear anything at all," he said. "They're just like Apache. You don't hear nothing until it's too late."

Boxer gave him a grim look. "Then why the hell did Madden leave us here, to get us killed?"

"Straighten up, brother Boxer," Lindsey said, correcting him. "It's getting that time of evening when you always get spooked about what you've done during the day."

"I ain't spooked, and I ain't done nothing," Boxer said in his own defense.

"Yeah?" Lindsey grinned and gestured toward the bodies still lying strewn in the trail. "Try telling these poor dead bastards that." Blood on the bodies of man and horse had blackened and dried in the heat of the day. "They'd say you've done plenty."

"Don't start trying to make me feel bad, Lindsey," said Boxer. "You killed them too. I killed them because it's my job. It wasn't because I didn't like them or was mad at them. Anyway, look how dark it is. Ain't we waited long enough? Can't we get out of here now? We've got gold to spend." He patted a pair of saddlebags lying at his side, their share of gold from the gun deal that Corio had given them before he'd left.

Lindsey gave a dark chuckle at the nervousness in his brother's voice. He shook his head. "You're a real daisy, you are, brother Boxer." He stood up from beside Boxer in the wagon bed and stretched and started to step over to the open tailgate. "Yep, a real daisy, short the petals of course. . . ."

"Hey, where are you going?" Boxer asked, sounding anxious. He reached up and snatched his brother by his arm.

"To relieve myself before we ride. Damn, are you really that scared of the dead?" He pulled his arm from his brother's grip.

"You can go right there," Boxer said, nodding down at the rear wagon wheel.

Lindsey gave him a look. "Yeah, but you know me, I always prefer pissing against a tree when there's one handy. Of course I could wait until it gets even darker, these bodies get up and start walking around and—"

"Shut up and go on," said Boxer, cutting him off, waving him away. "I don't like talking that kind of nonsense. Hurry up and let's get going."

Lindsey jumped down to the ground and walked away from the wagon, laughing under his breath. A few yards farther away, Shaw moved in close, walking along with him in a crouch in the cover of low rocks and brush. When the big outlaw stopped at an ancient cedar, unbuttoned his fly and began to relieve himself, Shaw rushed forward, his knife out of his boot well and gripped tightly in his hand.

Lindsey heard the last few running footsteps coming toward him from behind. At the last second he swung around, but only in time to feel a hand clamp over his mouth and a blade slide expertly into his heart. His eyes bulged above Shaw's hand; he sank back against the big cedar and slid down its trunk.

When Shaw saw the outlaw's bulging eyes turn dull and lifeless, he eased his hand from over his mouth. Silently he placed a boot on Lindsey's chest, pulled the knife free and wiped the blade back and forth on the dead man's slumped shoulder.

On the wagon bed, Boxer looked around over his shoulder, seeing the figure walking toward him in the grainy evening darkness. Standing and dusting his trousers, he said, "Hurry up. I'm ready to get the hell to a cantina somewhere and spend some—oh, my God!" His words tuned into a loud yell as he began to see that this wasn't his brother, Lindsey, at all. This was one of the bodies from the trail risen from the dead and coming at him.

The front of Shaw's shirt was black with dried blood from attending to Tuesday's back wound. A long smear of the dark dried blood ran from his ear to the corner of his mouth. "Stay away from me!" Boxer screamed, his deep voice turning shrill in his terror.

Shaw came forward at a run the last few yards and bounded up onto the wagon bed and onto the outlaw like a mountain cat. The big outlaw had become so paralyzed with fear that he hadn't made a move toward the Gatling gun, or even for the Colt holstered on his hip. He caught Shaw in his big arms and fell backward onto the wagon. Shaw snapped his big head back, exposing his throat, and brought the knife into play with one vicious backstroke.

From where she waited in the cover of rock, Tuesday had heard Boxer Shagin cry out. Then she sat in tense silence for what seemed to be a long time until she heard footsteps walking toward her across the rocky ground. In spite of her weakened condition, she managed to hold her derringer out at arm's length, cocked and pointed, until she heard Shaw say, "Tuesday, it's me. Come on, I'm getting you out of here."

"Getting me . . . out of here?" said Tuesday. "What about you?"

"I'm staying until Bocanero's men come back for the big gun," said Shaw.

"You're going to give it to them?" she asked, looking at the saddlebags slung over his shoulder.

"Yes," Shaw said, "just as much of it as they can stand." He stepped over to the horses and pitched the Shagin brothers' saddlebags up behind the bay. He opened a bag, ran his hand in and brought up a palmful of Mexican gold coins. Tuesday's eyes widened.

"Is that . . . ?" She let her words trail.

"It's the gold I told you about," Shaw said, realizing

that in spite of his lying about the gold, he'd come out of it smelling like a rose. Letting the coins dribble from his fingertips back into the saddlebag, he asked, "How are you feeling?"

"Not nearly as bad now as earlier," she said. "I'll be okay once I get . . . this bullet out." She nodded stiffly toward the saddlebags. "That helps a lot."

"I hoped it would," said Shaw. For all the blood she'd lost and for the bullet lodged in the back of her rib cage, Tuesday looked only a little worse for the wear.

"There's nothing like the glitter of gold . . . to put a whore at the top of her game, Fast Larry," she said with a weak, tired smile. She held her arms out to him.

Shaw picked her up and helped her up into the saddle atop the bay. "Think of me while you're in Paris," he said.

"Wait," said Tuesday, "aren't you coming with me, aren't you going to . . . catch up to me when you're finished here?"

Shaw gave her a serious look. "I might never get finished here, Tuesday. You need to get somewhere and get that bullet cut out."

"But I thought you and I—"

Shaw cut her off with a raised hand as his attention drew toward the trail where he'd heard the slightest sound of hooves on stone. "There's no time to talk about it," he said in a whisper. "Get out of here, they're coming." He slapped the bay on its rump and sent it hurrying away in the opposite direction of the approaching hooves.

As Tuesday Bonhart rode away quietly, Shaw jumped

up into the wagon bed and stepped over Boxer's body. Looking down at only a half dozen stacks of ammunition lying beside the Gatling gun, he murmured, "Madden Corio, you cheap bastard." But then he saw a half dozen grenades and nodded in satisfaction. *That helps. . . .*

He took off the tall stovepipe hat and filled it with the grenades. Then, heavily loaded hat in hand, he stooped down, cradled the Gatling gun in his arms and stood up with it, tripod and all, as the sound of the distant hooves drew closer.

On the trail, Sepio Bocanero halted his six-man detachment long enough to light torches before riding into the empty clearing where he knew the wagon with his last Gatling gun and his hand grenades awaited him. "Raul, light a torch for me also," he said to the tall Mexican riding at his side—one of his top officers, who had been with him at the exchange of gold for guns earlier.

"But, Sepio," said Raul, "is it wise for you to ride in there like some ordinary soldier?"

"It is wise if I say it is wise," Bocanero snapped. "Now light me a torch and bring it to me. If I am to remain a leader, my men must see me *lead*, not wait in the shadows. Besides, there is nothing for Madden Corio to gain by pulling a trick at this stage of the game."

"As you wish," said Raul. He turned and took two lit torches from the men as they busily passed them around and lit them one from the other until the trail was aglow in flickering light. The men watched respectfully as Bocanero took a torch from Raul and nudged his horse ahead of the others.

"Follow me," Bocanero commanded.

The men waited for only a second until Raul quickly nudged his horse up beside Bocanero and waved them forward. With nothing to fear, the seven men rode into the wide spot in the trail and looked all around, paying close attention to the dead still lying scattered on the ground. As Bocanero spurred his horse over to the wagon and looked over into the bed, Raul said to two men, "Paco, Migio, your horses will pull the wagon. You two will take turns driving—"

Raul stopped short as Bocanero turned his horse quickly at the sight of Boxer Shagin lying in the empty wagon bed, his throat cut deep and wide. "No, Raul! Put out the torches! It is a trap. Put out the torches!"

You caught on quick, Bocanero. . . .

In the darkness on the hillside above them, Shaw lobbed a grenade far to the right of the clearing. Before it even exploded he lobbed another far to the left, pressing the men between the two. The other two grenades he tossed into the middle of the clearing among the panic at the center of the trail. Then he settled in behind the Gatling gun and braced himself for its impact.

He held one hand firmly on the big gun's handle and his other hand on the firing crank. He clicked the safety lever off with his thumb and started cranking, bringing the lead-belching monster to life.

On the trail, stunned by the blasts of grenades, the men tried to retaliate and defend themselves, but their rally had come too late. The gun raked across them in the glow of torchlight, making a terrible sound of lead thumping, ripping and slashing through human meat and bone. In the torchlight Shaw watched the blood fly. He saw dirt kick up high from the trail and splinters and chunks of wood explode from the wagon.

Some of the men ran, almost making it out of the flickering light. But *almost* wasn't good enough. Shaw swung the gun along with them. He followed them, cranking steadily on the firing handle until the big gun hammered the helpless men in place and left them lying dead on the ground, scattered among the corpses left from earlier in the day.

In a moment it was over. Shaw could not recall any of the men getting a shot off before the Gatling gun ate them alive. Looking down at the five remaining stacks of ammunition, the half a stack remaining atop the gun and at the two grenades lying at his feet, he said to himself, "I guess this was enough after all. . . ."

Chapter 21

———

Shaw walked down into the flickering light of the fallen torches still lying about on the ground. He picked one up and walked among the dead, his Colt hanging loosely in his right hand. At the rear of the wagon he saw Sepio Bocanero lying hatless and bloody on the ground. The dying rebel leader had managed to prop himself up on one arm, and draw a long Remington revolver from his holster. He struggled to raise the pistol, but his failing strength would not allow it.

"Uh-uh," Shaw said, clamping a boot down onto Bocanero's wrist. "Turn it loose."

The wounded Mexican opened his fingers from the pistol and looked up at Shaw with a string of bloody saliva swinging from his lips. "Do you . . . know who I am?"

"I've got a pretty good hunch," Shaw said.

"Then you must know, I can make you rich . . . ," Bocanero said, his voice broken and shaky.

"Don't you get it, Sepio? It's all over." Shaw raised his boot from Bocanero's wrist and kicked the Remington away from his hand.

"It is not over," Bocanero demanded. "I am the leader of my people. I am like a king . . . like God to them!"

"No," said Shaw, "you're no king, or God." His gun hand rose slightly. "You're just one more gun-buying bandit who died bloody in the dirt."

The big Colt bucked once in Shaw's hand, then dropped back to his side, smoking and silent. Looking around, he walked to the outer edge of torchlight and gathered two of the soldiers' horses to pull the wagon. When he'd hitched the animals and led his barb out from the rocks and hitched it to the rear of the wagon, he stepped up into the bed and rolled Boxer Shagin's body out onto the dirt beside Bocanero.

Moments later, Shaw had carried the Gatling gun and the grenades back down from among the rocks and loaded them onto the wagon. Hitched to a wagon for the first time, the two saddle horses writhed, kicked, neighed and grumbled. But finally, realizing what was being asked of them, the animals settled into their task and moved out along the trail.

Before Shaw and his wagonload of guns, grenades and ammunition had gone a thousand yards, he caught a glimpse of a single rider on a horse standing in the middle of the dark trail, silhouetted by the moon. Silently he stopped the wagon as he drew his Colt and held it ready at his side.

"Fast Larry?" Tuesday Bonhart called out in a wary tone from the darkness. "Is that you?"

Shaw let out a breath. "Yes, it's me, Tuesday. What are you doing here?"

"Oh, Fast Larry!" Hooves clicked lively toward him from the darkness as she rode into sight. "I knew it was you! I knew you'd be all right!"

"How did you know?" Shaw asked.

She reached down to him for support from her saddle to the wagon. As Shaw helped her over from the saddle to the wooden seat, the swallow-tailed coat opened down the front, revealing her naked breasts above the cloth strips holding the bandage to her wounded back.

"Oh, don't forget my bags," she said, wagging a dainty but bloodstained finger toward the saddlebags behind the bay's saddle.

"But how did you know it was me?" Shaw asked again. He reached over, loosened the saddlebags and hefted them over to the wagon floor between his boots.

"I don't know." She shrugged. "I heard all the firing, and then I heard the single pistol shot . . . and something just told me that you were okay! I knew it was you!"

"What if it hadn't been me?" Shaw looked at her pointedly, a little peeved because she hadn't done as he'd told her to.

"But it *is* you!" Tuesday, said, looping her arms in his and snuggling up against him in spite of the pain that was beginning to grow stronger in her back now that the numbing impact of the shot had begun to wear off. "Don't be cross with me, Fast Larry," she said, feigning a pout. "Don't forget I'm an injured gal." After a pause, she said, "Anyway, I didn't want anybody cutting into my back but you."

Shaw let out another breath. "All right, I'm not cross. There's an extra shirt back there in my saddlebags." He nodded toward the barb hitched to the rear of the wagon. "I'll get it for you."

"Not right now," said Tuesday. "Let's get away from here. I like being close to you this way without my blouse on."

Shaw shook his head.

"Am I being too lewd, for a whore with a bullet in her back?" She smiled in spite of her pain and the weakness she still felt from the loss of blood.

"You're doing fine," Shaw reassured her, glad that she was in such good spirits and rebounding so well from the gunshot.

"Is it going to hurt?" she asked, her tone suddenly turning a bit concerned.

"It will," Shaw said. "It would be better if we had some whiskey to dull it a little. There's a village a day's ride—"

"No," Tuesday said, cutting him off. "This is my *first* gunshot wound. I want you to be the *first* to cut my bullet out. It will be sort of like starting all over for me, don't you think?"

Shaw winced a bit, having a hard time understanding her thinking. "Yes, if that's what suits you," he finally said. He let the two wagon horses ride on at their own slow walking pace.

Within minutes, the slow rocking of the wagon and the weariness from the loss of blood had caused Tuesday to fall asleep against Shaw's shoulder in the hard wagon seat. Without waking her, Shaw waited until he'd reached a wide pull-off along the trail and reined the horses over into it. Stopping the wagon as gently as he could, he eased Tuesday over onto the seat and set the long hand brake.

He stepped down from the wagon and, within only a few feet from the trail, managed to rake together enough twigs, short downed pine limbs and dry bracken to build a small fire. Into the edge of the licking flames he stuck the blade of his boot knife. Atop the fire he boiled water from his canteen in a tin coffee cup while he spread his ragged bedroll blanket on the ground.

He walked to the wagon, pulled the slumbering woman into his arms, carried her to the blanket in the firelight and laid her down gently, hoping not to wake her just yet. Then he removed the tin cup from the fire, picked up his knife and stuck the blade down into the bubbling water.

The knife blade sizzled in a rise of steam.

Picking up a short piece of hardened cedar, he walked over, knife and cup of boiled water in hand, and kneeled down beside Tuesday Bonhart. She awakened slightly as he rolled her carefully over onto her stomach and peeled the swallow-tailed coat from her back. "Are— are we ready to do it . . . ?" she asked sleepily, her head turned to the side looking up at him.

"We're ready to do it," Shaw said in an apologetic tone. He reached down and slipped the piece of cedar crosswise between her lips. "Bite down on this when you need to."

But Tuesday rejected the piece of wood and spat to rid her mouth of any trace of it. "No," she said adamantly, "I'm through having things stuck into my mouth that I don't want there."

"I understand," said Shaw, "but this part is the worst." As he spoke he loosened the two strips of cloth and removed the dark sticky bandage. He stuck the edge of the bandage into the water and shook it to cool it, then wiped the wound in order to better see the bullet hole.

"It'll be all right," said Tuesday. "I'm the toughest little whore you've likely ever seen in your life."

Shaw nodded and patted her bare shoulder. "Here goes," he murmured.

In the darkness on the winding upward trail, a long, loud, bloodcurdling scream echoed down from the higher ridges, causing Jane Crowley's spooked horse to rear beneath her.

"Mother of God!" she shouted as the frightened animal twisted in midair and tried to turn in the opposite direction in order to bolt away as soon as its hooves touched ground. "Somebody's being skinned alive!"

But Caldwell reached over and grabbed her horse by its bridle as it came down, assisting her in getting control of the animal even as his and Dawson's horses also tensed and recoiled at the shrill terrible sound. "Easy, boys," said Caldwell in a strong yet soothing voice, settling both his and Jane's horses.

"I don't need help with my damned cayuse, Undertaker! Thank you very damned much!" Jane said angrily, jerking her horse away from him. Without missing a note she asked the two lawmen, "What the hell was that anyway?"

"It sounded like a woman screaming," Dawson said as he and Caldwell stared up along the dark ridges in the light of a pale half-moon.

"I'm sticking with somebody 'skinned alive,'" Jane said, staring up with them, "until something convinces me otherwise."

"How far away do you say it was, trail scout?" Dawson asked Jane without taking his eyes down from the high dark ridges towering above them.

Liking the respect that his question showed, Jane considered it. "An hour, maybe less." She pondered the matter a second longer. "It come from the same direction as the gunfire we heard earlier, only much closer, I make it."

Caldwell gave a short wry grin. "We've had gunfire, we've got screaming. I'd say Shaw is somewhere close at hand."

"Yep, let's go," said Caldwell, turning his horse back to the trail ahead. "He might need our help."

"Hmmph," Jane said under her breath as she nudged her horse along behind them, "he ain't so far. . . ."

The three rode on.

Atop the winding trail, in the glow of firelight, Shaw felt the white gooseflesh on Tuesday's back shiver beneath his bloody left hand. In his bloody fingertips

he held the misshapen bullet he'd picked out from between her ribs. In the last attempt at removing the bullet, he'd held the wound open with the blade of the
knife and reached into her back with his fingers and
gripped it between his short nails.

"Now, now, breathe deep, relax," he coaxed her soothingly. "It's all over. I got the bullet out. It was wedged
deep—that's why I had to keep digging, loosening it."

"Oh my God," she sobbed, "I never had anything
hurt so bad in my life. If I ever see Madden Corio, I'm
going to kill him an inch at a time."

"You did good, Tuesday," Shaw said. He patted her
naked shoulder and brushed aside her dark hair from
her face as she turned and looked at him tearfully.

"I wasn't nearly as tough as I thought, was I, Fast
Larry?" she said.

"Nobody is," Shaw said quietly as he began dabbing
the corner of the bandage at the wound, hoping the
heavy bleeding would not start anew. "Most times a
person passes out from the pain. You didn't."

"So I am a tough a little whore like I said?" she
asked, her voice less trembling now that the ordeal was
over.

"If that's what you want to call yourself, yes, you
are," said Shaw. Now that the bullet was out, he squeezed
the wound shut and tied one of the strips of cloth
around her back to hold it shut. Then he put the bloody
bandage back in place over the wound and tied it
down with the other cloth strip.

"Well, it's what I used to be," Tuesday said, her voice

sounding even more relieved. She turned herself stiffly onto her side and looked up at him, her face resting on an arm folded under her cheek. "I don't have to be a whore any longer. I've got money to burn."

Shaw brushed her dark hair from her cheek again. He spread the swallow-tailed coat over her. "Yes, you do," he said gently. "Now get yourself healed up and ready to start spending it."

"What about you, Fast Larry?" she asked. "How's your wound healing?"

"I'm healing right along," Shaw said. He touched the dirty bandage at his forehead. "Another day or two, this is coming off. I'm coming back to my senses, clear as ever."

"Good," Tuesday said, her eyes closing for a moment, then coming slightly open again as she caught herself drifting off. "I want you to come with me to Paris. . . ."

"We'll see," Shaw said. She moved just enough to cause her large firm breasts to peep from behind the coat. Shaw reached out and tried to adjust the coat, but it didn't help for long. He breasts soon exposed themselves as if willfully.

"No, I mean it," she said, realizing that he was only placating her. "I want you to come to Paris with me."

"What would I do in Paris?" Shaw said, placing a hand on her shoulder as she drifted off to sleep.

"We'd do all sorts of things," she said, her eyes closed, her voice turning relaxed and dreamy. "We'd visit the Roman Coliseum . . ."

"The Roman Coliseum, in *Paris* . . . ?" Shaw cocked his head dubiously. "Tuesday, you might want to think about that some. . . ."

"And we can see the Great Wall . . . ," Tuesday said, drifting further.

"The Great Wall. . . ." Shaw smiled to himself and tried once again to cover her bare breasts. Again his effort failed. "I'm no historian," he offered to the sleeping young woman, "but I don't believe the Great Wall is in Paris."

"Yes, it is . . . it's been there a hundred years," she offered.

"But, Tuesday—" Shaw's words stopped short.

"Well now," Jane Crowley's voice boomed from the outer edge of firelight, "I hope to hell we're not interrupting something here."

Shaw looked at Jane, and the two lawmen flanking her. Rather than have them think they'd caught him off guard, he said, "You're not interrupting. I heard you coming a while ago, but I was busy with my fingers in this young woman's back."

Jane stared, enraged, seeing Tuesday's bare breasts beneath Shaw's coat. "I'm damn certain you had *something* of yours in *something* of hers."

"We've no time for this," Dawson said, stepping his horse in ahead of Jane in an attempt to keep down any further heated words from her. "Shaw, are you all right? We've been tracking you for a long time."

"Much of it in circles," Caldwell added, also stepping his horse forward, the two now sitting ahead of Jane Crowley.

The lawmen looked down at the woman, then at the blood on Shaw's fingers, then at the dark dried blood all over his chest. Dawson said, "All the shooting earlier, I take it that was you, and the Gatling gun lying there in the wagon?"

"That's right," said Shaw. "I wandered around in the desert after getting shot in the head. But I knew we were searching for Madden Corio and his gang. I stumbled onto Dexter Lowe and hooked up with Corio in the midst of a big gun-running deal with Sepio Bocanero."

"Madden Corio's gang *and* Sepio Bocanero and his rebel army . . . ?" said Dawson. "That's some big game. The Mexican government is going to want to know where to find Bocanero."

Shaw shrugged. "That's easy enough. Last I saw him he's lying dead up the trail." He nodded over his shoulder.

"You killed him?" Caldwell asked, surprised.

"Him and a few of his men," said Shaw. "They came back to get the Gatling gun and some grenades they'd already paid Corio for."

"But Bocanero wasn't even our concern," said Dawson. "That should've taken the whole Mexican army, somebody that big. What made you do something like that?"

Shaw considered it. "I've been a little off my game with this head wound. Maybe I wasn't thinking real straight." He paused in reflection, then continued. "Anyway, the Mexican army wasn't there—I was. Bocanero is dead." He stood up. Picking up the cup of water with him, he poured the warm water over his bloody hands, washing them.

"Who is this?" Dawson asked, nodding toward the sleeping woman.

"This is Dexter Lowe's gal, Miss Tuesday Bonhart. She has saved my life more than once through all this. She's been my ace in the hole."

Jane sneered under her breath.

"Dangerous Dexter Lowe's gal?" Caldwell asked in disbelief.

"She was until she killed him," Shaw said, slinging water from his hands. "Look, I know we've got lots of catching up to do. But we can catch Corio and most of his men if we get moving."

"What about her?" Caldwell asked, nodding down at Tuesday Bonhart. "Is she going to be able to ride?"

"She hasn't missed a step yet," Shaw said. "She can keep up with anybody here."

Jane stepped her horse forward with a sour expression. "If she can't she'll be left behind."

"Easy, Jane," said Dawson. "Nobody who rides with us ever gets left behind."

"I did," Jane replied to Dawson, giving Shaw a harsh stare.

"No, you didn't," said Shaw. "I remember we split up the same night I got this." He tapped his bandaged head.

"That's something the two of you will have to thrash out between you," said Dawson. "But this is not the time or place. We need to get on Corio's trail."

Shaw stood in silence, knowing Dawson was right.

He watched as Jane grumbled under her breath, backed her horse and turned it away into the darkness. "I'll put us on the damn trail. Don't worry about that. Jane Crowley always does her part."

When she was gone, Dawson and Shaw looked at each other and shook their heads. Then Dawson asked, just to get an idea where he stood on the matter, "Who shot you, Shaw?"

"I have no idea," Shaw said, "only suspicions. What about you? Have you heard anything?"

"No," said Dawson, not wanting to fuel any trouble, "no idea at all."

"Any suspicions?" Shaw asked.

"Suspicions can get people killed if they're not well founded," said Dawson, backing his horse to turn it. "So I try to avoid having any."

Chapter 22

———

At a fork in the dark, winding trail down from the hill line, Madden Corio stopped his horse and turned it to face the rest of the men gathering to halt. "Did we make a good pot for ourselves, men?" he asked cheerfully.

As the men nodded and hooted, he added, "You damn well bet we did!" He turned his horse back and forth restlessly as he spoke, and patted his saddlebags. "And there's going to be plenty more coming! Damn soon!"

The men cheered in the darkness. Arnold Stemms reached over playfully and jerked young Matthew Ford's hat down on his forehead. "Hear that, Matt? Did Jesse and Frank ever treat a man any better than this?"

"Hell no," said Ford, grinning, straightening his flop hat.

"Now it's time we split up and leave anybody tracking us to chase their own tails," said Corio. He looked around at their faces. "Matt Ford, Stemms, Little Dick and Dade Watkins—"

"It's *Richard Little*," said an irritated voice, "not Little Dick."

"All right, whatever." Corio chuckled, too excited and keyed up to even mind Little cutting him off, something that might ordinarily get a man killed. "I want the four of yas to ride north to Cedrianno." He nodded toward one fork in the trail. "When you get there, get yourselves and your horses fed, watered and rested. But don't dally around longer than you need to. I want all four of yas to cut out of there in different directions."

The four grinned, each with his share of the gold in his saddlebags. "But you don't mind if we load up some whiskey or mescal for the trail, do you?" Arnold Stemms asked. "It's torture for a man to have gold and a powerful thirst, and not do something about it."

The men gave a chuckle.

"All right, get something to go with you," said Corio. "But get it and get out of there. We've got some big jobs coming up and I can't afford to lose any more men, especially after what happened to poor Bert Jordan."

"Don't forget Irish Tommie, that poor high-leaping sumbitch," said Robert Hooks in a somber tone.

"Yeah, him too," said Corio, offhandedly, already having dismissed the big heavy Irishman's death from his memory. He looked at Hooks and three other men, Brule Kaggan, Harvey Lemate and Max Skinner. "You four are riding with me on into Nozzito. Skinner, now that Bert is gone, you're my new right-hand—my *segundo*. Any objections?" He gave Skinner a flat, level stare.

"None," Skinner said quickly. "You call the shots, I'll make 'em, dead center," he said with determination. He looked from face to face. "I expect everybody here heard what Madden said, loud and clear. So, when I give an order it's the same as it was with Bert Jordan. I expect it to be followed."

"All right, enough said," said Corio. "Let's ride." He turned his horse back to the trail and booted it forward.

Matt Ford, Arnold Stemms, Richard Little and Dade Watkins sat their horses and watched the others ride away behind Corio. "I don't think it's by mistake that he does that," Little said quietly.

"What's that, Richard?" Stemms asked.

"All the time calling me Little Dick," the seething gunman said. "I think he knows it gets to me." He spat in the darkness and ran a hand across his lips.

"You've got no complaints," said Watkins, who'd been smoldering in silence. "Look at me, I've been with Corio since the war. What's he do? He chooses Skinner ahead of me. How would that make you feel?"

"Aw, hell, forget it, the both of yas," said Stemms, turning his horse to the north fork of the trail. "We got gold, and it's less than a three-mile ride into Cedrianno. Let's go live it up some."

Turning his horse alongside Stemms' big bay, Matthew Ford asked, "Are there going to be whores in Cedrianno, you reckon?"

"Oh my goodness, *yes*, lad!" said Stemms. "There are whores there, I reckon."

"Then what are we waiting for?" said Ford. He booted his horse up into a run. Behind him the other three followed suit, laughing and catcalling into the night until the silhouette outline of the town drew closer and closer.

In moments the four horses rumbled onto the dirt street at a full run in the middle of the night. The only light still burning along the row of adobe and weathered clapboard buildings was a lantern sitting atop the bar at Rosas Salvajes Cantina.

Upon seeing and hearing the riders coming, the only working girl still on her feet hurriedly dampened the lantern to blackness as the four rolled out of their saddles at the hitch rail out front. But before the lantern went completely black, or before she had time to go drop an iron bolt in place, the big doors burst open and Arnold Stemms pounced into the middle of the floor like a large bear. "No, you don't, little darling!" he cried out with a crazy laugh. "This night ain't even begun yet! Is the Wild Roses Cantina open to me and my *long-rider* friends or what?"

"Oh, Senor," the young prostitute said, recovering quickly now that she knew she had to. She put on her best and friendliest face in spite of the fact that she'd been ready to retire upstairs and go to bed, alone, for the night. "Of course we are open to your long-rider friends. And for a big handsome bull like you," she added, "we are always open."

From a room atop the stairs another young woman,

this one an American from the plains of Kansas, had been listening. "Damn it, Calisa, speak for yourself," she said to herself, dreading the thought of getting up and attending to a cantina full of drunken border outlaws.

Beside her another girl moaned under her breath and said, "We better go on down, Maggie. If Calisa has to take on the whole bunch, we'll be hearing her cussing over it for a month. As soon as Willie hears them, he'll send us down anyway."

"I know it, Flo," said Maggie, fluffing up her hair and pinching her cheeks red. "I hope you've some of that white powder left. I'm going to need something good and strong to get me going again."

"I've got some in my room," said Flo. "I'll go get it. You go on down, I'll wake up Elnora and Lying Betty and bring them with me. We might as well squeeze what we can out of these idiots."

"Elnora is bedded down with Willie tonight," said Maggie.

"She won't mind. Neither will Willie," said Flo, hiking up her nightdress and hurrying away down the dark hall.

Downstairs at the bar, the four men had already helped themselves to bottles of mescal and tequila. Watkins had grabbed Calisa and wrestled her out of her dress and undergarments and left the items lying strewn out toward a big wooden table in a darker corner. Stemms had opened a bottle of tequila and took a long swig.

He leered toward the stairs and called out in a harsh

singsong voice, "Come down, come down, or Daddy Arnold will come up and drag you down."

He started toward the stairs, but stopped in the middle of the floor when she saw Maggie, a tall redhead, walking down seductively, wearing nothing but a towel around her shoulders.

"Evening, boys," she said, pulling the towel back and forth as if shining her shoulders with it. "I hope you don't mind me dressing *informally.* This time of night I don' like nothing on me but big warm hands."

"By God!" shouted Stemms. Unable to control himself, he snatched his pistol from his holster and fired two rounds straight up into the ceiling.

"Easy, big fellow," said Maggie. "Don't shoot up the ceiling. We've got girls sleeping up there. You wouldn't want to hurt them, would you?"

Stemms shrugged; he didn't care. "Then get the hell over here and cool me down before I bust into flames!" he demanded.

"I don't mind if I do, you big stable stud!" Maggie hurried into his big arms, pitched the towel around his neck and pulled his face to her naked freckled breasts. She wiggled herself back and forth vigorously. "These won't cool you, but they'll for sure keep you *occupied.*"

At the bar, watching Stemms and the naked redhead, Matthew Ford called out, "*Whooo-ee,*" and threw back a long swig of mescal. "All we need now is some music, and we've got ourselves a fiesta!"

As Ford drank, Richard Little said beside him, "Maybe we ought to tend to our horses, then come back here. It looks like this has the makings of an all-night thing."

"To hell with the horses," said Ford. "We've got gold, whores and liquor. If this ain't heaven it has to be right next door." He laughed and wagged a bottle of tequila in the air.

"Holy cats and rabbits!" said Little, seeing a line of three scantily clad women file down the stairs.

Behind the women, a Texan named Willie "the Weed" Weedham shuffled down in his Mexican sandals, hooking his gallowses up over his shoulders. "Did I hear somebody say music? I'll have some coming right up. Flo, you tend the bar 'til I get back." He turned at the bottom of the stairs and headed out the open front door.

"Damn," said Little to Ford, "was that Willie the Weed?"

"I believe it was," said Ford, eying the women.

"I thought they hanged him in Fort Griffin," said Little.

"If they didn't, they should have." Ford laughed without taking his eyes off the half-naked whores.

With the light of a torch held close to the rocky ground, Jane Crowley picked up fresh hoofprints of the eight horses coming from the direction of the place on the trail where Corio and Bocanero had transacted their stolen gun deal. Shaw sat in the wagon seat, Tuesday slumbering against his shoulder. He had taken a wrinkled shirt from the bottom of his saddlebags and put it on her. It helped ease Jane's bitterness toward him some, but not completely.

"How can you be sure these belong to Corio and his men?" Caldwell made the mistake of asking.

"Because I'm not a damned fool like some here might think I am, Undertaker," Jane snapped. "Who the hell else would be riding this trail, eight men strong, except Corio's gang?"

"Just asking," said Caldwell.

"Just don't," Jane snapped.

"How long ago?" Dawson interceded, to keep down the tension.

Jane settled and studied the ground again. She pressed her fingertips into a shoe imprint. "The ground's so dry it's hard to tell," she said. "But I make it six hours, give or take."

"What's ahead?" Dawson asked.

"There's Cedrianno in one direction," Jane said. "There's Nozzito in the other." She gazed off into the darkness ahead. "Both places have everything Corio and his men will be looking for. They want grain and water for their horses. They'll want food, liquor and whores for themselves."

"There'll be a fork in the trail somewhere, then," said Caldwell.

"Yep, Undertaker," Jane said, a bit of sarcasm toward Caldwell left over in her voice, "there will be a slit in the trail a few miles ahead."

Shaw shook his head at her sour mood.

Caldwell and Dawson ignored it. "That's where Madden Corio will split his gang up and try to throw us off *his* trail," said Dawson. He looked at Shaw. "We'll split up too. Caldwell and I will . . ." His words trailed as he gazed back at a flicker of dim light tagging along behind them.

"Who the hell is this?" Jane asked.

"I don't know," said Dawson, "but whoever it is must be begging to get themselves killed." He sat staring for a moment longer as if to make certain he wasn't imagining things. "Shaw, get the wagon out of here." To Caldwell and Jane he said, "All right, let's get into cover. This could be a trick."

"Yeah . . . ," Jane said speculatively, staring toward the bobbing light, "nobody is this stupid."

Shaw drove the wagon forward as quietly as possible. When he'd reached a point thirty yards along the trail, he set the brake handle, carefully eased Tuesday Bonhart over onto the wooden seat and stepped quietly over in the wagon bed behind the Gatling gun. "What's wrong . . . ?" Tuesday asked, waking to Shaw's movement and adjustment of the big gun.

"We've got somebody on our trail," he said.

In the darkness behind Shaw, Tuesday and the gun wagon, Caldwell and Jane had slipped down from their horses on one side of the trail. A few yards ahead of them, Dawson did the same on the other side. The three watched as the lantern light drew nearer. Finally, when the swaying light revealed its carrier, Jane let out a breath of relief and disgust, and said, "I'll be a son of a bitch. It's Raidy Bowe. She's following me."

Hearing the raised voice from the side of the dark trail in front of her, Raidy gasped and said, "Jane . . . is that you?"

"Damn it," Jane said to herself. Then to Raidy Bowe she said, "Hell yes, Raidy, it's me. You better thank your lucky stars it is me. Now trim down that damn lantern unless you're throwing a part for every gun-toting son of a bitch this side of hell."

At thirty yards away, Shaw heard every word being said. So did Tuesday. "That's Raidy Bowe?" said Tuesday.

"That's what I heard them say," Shaw replied.

"Why is she following us?" Tuesday asked.

"Beats me," said Shaw. "Do you know Raidy?"

"Yes," said Tuesday, "she and I worked the line together when we both started whoring. She quit the line before I did." Having been asleep when Jane and the lawmen had joined them, Tuesday asked almost in a whisper, "Is that's Jane Crowley I hear back there?"

"Yes," said Shaw, "the mouth with all the black-guarding flying out of it."

"Is everything she says a profanity?" Tuesday asked with a short giggle, still hearing the loud cursing voice as Jane and the two lawmen led the horses back out onto the trail.

"Yes, pretty much," Shaw said. He stood and stepped over beside Tuesday as she made room for him in the driver's seat. "Look, I might need to tell you this. Jane and I were sort of together for a while."

"Sort of . . . ?" Tuesday asked. "You don't sound like it meant much."

"It didn't," said Shaw, "not to me, or to her either." As he talked he turned the wagon around on the narrow trail and began driving it back toward the others. "We went on a drunken spree, is all it really amounted to. But when it came time to get away from each other, she took offense. She's still a little prickly over it. I thought you ought to know."

Tuesday said, "But I thought Jane was, you know . . ." She let her words hang for Shaw's interpretation.

"I heard that too," Shaw said, "but she told me it's not so. I didn't push the subject any further."

"Well," said Tuesday, "Raidy Bowe is."

Shaw looked at her. "How do you know?"

"Oh, I know," said Tuesday. "Believe me, *I know*," she added in a way that made Shaw not want to pursue that subject any further either.

He shook his head and drove the wagon forward. "I'm never getting drunk again," he murmured.

When they stopped in the midst of the dimly lit lantern, Jane looked at Tuesday and said, "Well, well, look who's awake. I hope we didn't interrupt your beauty sleep."

Tuesday ignored her, and looked at Raidy, who recognized her right away. "Tuesday Bonhart, is that you?" Raidy asked.

"Hello, Raidy," said Tuesday.

"You two know each another?" Jane asked warily.

"Yes, we do," Tuesday said. "What are you doing out here, Raidy?"

"I—I'm following my friend, Jane," Raidy said.

"Yes, we're friends," Jane said defensively to everybody. "What the hell of it?"

No one responded. Both Raidy and Jane eyed Shaw as if to see what his reaction might be. But he only stared blankly. "And you, Tuesday," Raidy asked, "what

are you doing out here?" She took note of how close
Tuesday sat to Shaw.

"It's a long story," Tuesday said.

Off to the side, Caldwell whispered to Dawson, "Shaw
draws them from every direction, doesn't he?"

"Yes, he seems to," Dawson said. To Shaw and the
three women he said, "Whatever you four have to talk
about, you best do it on the trail. We've got to get going."

Jane stared harshly at Shaw, then at Tuesday Bonhart, and then she said, "I don't have another damn
thing to say about it." She took Raidy's horse by its
bridle and pulled it over beside hers. "You stay close to
me, Raidy," she said protectively.

"I will, Janie." Raidy beamed.

Jane scowled at Shaw, even though he hadn't said a
word or made any critical sign on the matter. "Anybody doesn't like it, they can go to hell," Jane added,
staring toward him.

Dawson also looked at Shaw. "Are we ready to go
on now?" he asked stiffly.

"I'm ready when you are," said Shaw. He turned the
wagon on the trail and pointed it in the direction of
Cedrianno.

Chapter 23

———

Outside the Rosas Salvajes Cantina, in the grainy blue hour before daylight, the four horses stood at the iron hitch rail, still under saddle, unattended and streaked white with their own dried sweat. Inside the two-story adobe cantina and brothel, Matthew Ford stood up from a ragged blanket on the dirty tile floor and fumbled for his trousers lying on the floor beside him. He looked out at the trail-worn horses through the open front door and cursed under his breath.

"Hey, Watkins, get up. I know you're not asleep," he said to the nodding gunman stretched out on the bar, the young whore Calisa pressed against him, one of her short naked legs slung over him. On the bar two feet from them, a pile of brownish white cocaine powder lay spilled from the open drawstring top of a small leather pouch. Calisa snored steadily through a nose coated with the fine powder. "Watkins, damn it! Get up, let's go," said Ford.

He stepped over, shook Watkins roughly by his shoulder, then walked over to where Stemms lay naked on the bare tile floor between two naked women, his eyes wide and shiny, staring up at the ceiling. A streak of cocaine powder lay across Stemms' hairy chest. "Stemms, get up," said Ford. "You're not asleep." He reached his boot out and wagged Stemms' foot back and forth. "It's time we got moving."

Stemms grumbled in protest. But he snapped to his feet, still in the grip of the cocaine. Beside him the two women stared as if they had never seen him before, as he snatched up his clothes and gun belt and began dressing as if the cantina were aflame. A few feet away, two guitar players and a young accordion player lay in a heap on the floor, their instruments still in hand.

"Damn, Matthew," Stemms said, wrestling himself into his clothes. "You was the one so interested in getting here and finding some women and some hooch. Now you're wanting to leave already?"

"I come to with a bad feeling in my guts," said Ford, glancing with a wary eye though the wide-open front door, toward the empty street. "It's time we get our horses watered and fed and get out of here."

"Listen to me, Matthew," said Stemms. "It ain't likely the law has even gotten on our trail yet. If they did, they turned back at the border. We're in Mexico, my young friend. Enjoy yourself."

"I did enjoy myself," said Ford, the cocaine keeping him as jumpy as a squirrel. "Now it's time we did as we're told and get moving."

"I am moving," Stemms said, "so settle down."

Ford turned and walked quickly back across the cantina floor, behind the bar to where Willie Weedham sat slumped in a tall bartender's chair, his hand folded across his thin, flat belly. "Wake up, Weed," Ford said to the sleeping bartender, the only one in the place who had not snorted or drunk the cocaine powder.

Willie the Weed awakened to a pile of gold coins dumped into his lap. His eyes opened wide as he began gathering the coins with a big openmouthed grin of appreciation. "You fellows come back any time. You're always welcome at the Wild Roses!"

At the bar, Watkins had stepped down onto the floor, scraped his clothes together and begun dressing. As he slung his gun belt around his waist, he said to Stemms from across the cantina, "What's got Ford so agitated?"

"He wants to get going," Richard Little cut in. "So do I. We didn't mean to stay this long. It's not wise." He gestured a nod toward the horses out front. "We didn't even take care of our animals."

"Well, hell," said Watkins, hurrying a bit faster, but sounding cross about being told what he had to do, "I expect we'll just go take care of them right now. Let it not be said that I *ever* slowed this bunch down, not for a damn minute."

In moments the four had dressed and gathered their rifles, and lavished more gold on the whores and walked out, their arms loaded with bottles of tequila and mescal. But out front they stopped and stared back and forth at the empty iron hitch rail in the grainy morning light. "Where the hell's our horses?" Watkins asked, his face smeared with lipstick, his beard flaked with dried saliva.

"What the hell is this . . . ?" Matthew Ford said in a wary voice. "I saw them no more than five minutes—"

"Uh-oh, this ain't good," Arnold Stemms said, cutting him off. Less than a hundred feet away sat the gun wagon in the middle of the empty street. The rear of the wagon faced them, its tailgate down, the Gatling gun aimed in their direction. Behind the gun Shaw stood wearing his tall stovepipe hat and swallow-tailed coat. In one hand he held one of the remaining French hand grenades. In his other hand, instead of a grenade striker, he held a glowing cigar.

"Whoa, ole buddy," Ford called out. "Corio told us you were dead. He said some of Sepio Bocanero's men killed you by mistake."

"Imagine our grief," Watkins threw in, still sailing on cocaine. Even as he spoke he looked all around to see if anyone else had them in their gun sights. "Seemed like no sooner than you joined us, you were dead and gone."

"We were broken up," said Little, wearing a tense, tight cocaine grin. He held bottles of tequila cradled in his left arm, but his gun hand was free, poised near the butt of a holstered Remington.

Shaw offered no reply. He only stood, silent and imposing, the open bores of the big Gatling gun barrels staring blankly at them, like some leering attack dog awaiting its command.

"Hell, I hope you ain't gone cross at us over anything," Ford said, noting the Gatling gun. "All we did was what we was paid to do." He stepped forward with a shrug. "You was just one of us, far as we were all concerned."

Shaw still didn't reply.

After a moment, Stemms stepped forward too, and said in a lowered tone, "The hell with this, Matthew, look out." He elbowed Ford aside and said to Shaw, "If you come here looking for your share, you're out of luck. If you come here spoiling for a fight, you'll get one, sure enough."

"Arnold's right," said Ford. "Too bad, if Corio screwed you out of anything. But we ain't giving nothing up without a fight."

Behind him, Ford and the others heard the big cantina doors slam shut. They heard the iron bolt fall into place on the inside.

"Oh, shit," said Watkins, looking all around for cover, knowing what the Gatling gun was capable of doing at this close distance.

Shaw took the cigar from between his teeth and stuck the glowing tip of it to the grenade fuse. While the four outlaws reached for their guns, he made sure the fuse was burning in a good strong sizzle, then lobbed it in a high arc toward them.

Bullets began flying past him as the grenade arced downward. Before it hit the ground, Shaw ducked down onto the wagon bed and covered his head, tall hat and all, with both forearms. He felt the impact of the blast lift the wagon and drop it with a bone-jarring thump. Heat, dirt, iron fragments and chips of broken rock streaked past him. But no sooner had the blast resounded and debris peppered down on his back than he jumped over behind the Gatling gun and brought it into play.

Watkins, Little and Stemms had all three dived to the ground when they saw the grenade sailing down amid them. But Ford had made a run for it and dived behind the cover of a water trough. As the other three gunmen staggered to their feet, coughing and fanning thick dust in order to get a shot at Shaw on the gun wagon, Ford sprang to his feet and ran around a corner to the livery barn.

"Rush this son of a bitch!" shouted Watkins, not thinking clearly, owing to both the impact of the blast and the long night of cocaine use.

"Kill . . . him," Little called out, choking, coughing and squinting through the dust toward the gun wagon.

Watkins started to yell something, but his words went unheard as the Gatling gun began its loud, deadly chatter.

Shaw saw no clear targets, just dim images through the heavy dust as he swung the gun back and forth. As he made the first pass across the swirl of shouting voices and exploding gunshots, he felt the air around him fill with bullets. But on the backswing of the gun, the shouting turned to screams of pain. The gunfire turned silent as death set in and descended onto the dirt street.

Shaw stood up and stared into the settling dust, his hand poised near the Colt on his hip, the Gatling gun staring straight ahead now, a stream of gray smoke curling up from its hot barrels. To his right and left,

Cedrianno lay as quiet and deserted as a ghost town. But the quiet only lasted for a moment. Around a corner he heard the pounding of hooves and an old man crying out in a plea for mercy.

As Shaw jumped down from the wagon bed and started walking through the settling dust, Matthew Ford came charging at him from around the corner atop a leggy roan he'd run in and stolen from the livery barn owner at gunpoint.

"Senor! Please! My horse! Do not kill my horse!" the liveryman cried out to Shaw, running around the corner shortly behind Ford as the young gunman straightened the roan on the street and made a bold charge.

"I'll kill you, you son of a bitch!" Ford screamed in rage as he rode down on Shaw, his pistol blazing. Two bullets streaked past Shaw and thumped into the side of the gun wagon.

"No, Senor, please! My horse!" the old liveryman shouted again at Shaw. But then he dove out of the way as Shaw raised his Colt at arm's length.

"No problem . . . ," Shaw said. His Colt bucked once in his hand. The shot hit Matthew Ford in the center of his forehead and sent him flying backward from his saddle in a spray of blood, brain and bone matter. Shaw watched him hit the ground and noted that the pain he'd felt for so long in his head wound had not bothered him throughout the gun battle. The realization caused him to breathe a sigh of relief.

Shaw lowered the Colt and watched the roan let down from a hard run into a trot, then circle and slow to a walk. Finally the horse came to stop when the old liveryman ran up to it tearfully, grabbed it reins and threw his arms around its neck. "Oh, Senor! *Gracious, gracious, gracious,*" he repeated over and over to Shaw. The horse only chuffed and scraped a hoof and shook out its mane.

Shaw looked at the Colt in his hand and touched his fingertips to the dirty head bandage beneath the brim of the tall stovepipe hat. His mind was clear, his hand steady; his head not hurting. *Good . . . ,* he thought to himself. *Must be getting better. . . .*

Another elderly Mexican came venturing out ahead of a gathering of townsfolk. He swept a hand around at the dead on the street, and at the five-foot-wide crater the hand grenade had left in the dirt. "Senor, look at our beautiful Cedrianno. How will it ever look the same again?"

Before the man could go any further, Shaw gestured a nod toward the dead in the street. "Go through their pockets. There's enough gold to pay for the damages."

"Ah, that is good, Senor," said the old man with a smile. "And their horses too, of course? To help pay for any damage we do not yet see?"

Shaw looked over, a block away, where he had hitched their horses next to his own speckled barb that he'd led to town behind the gun wagon. "Their horses are yours too," said Shaw, "except for the barb on the end. That one belongs to me."

At first light Dawson and Shaw pulled their horses up at a turn in the trail looking down across a wide valley. A few feet in front of them, Jane sat atop her horse,

Raidy Bowe seated on her horse beside her. Behind the four of them, Tuesday rode along, keeping her horse at a slower gait. Jane looked back, saw Tuesday and said to Dawson and Caldwell, "It looks like Shaw's whore is having a hard time keeping up after all."

The two lawmen ignored her remark. Dawson said quietly to Caldwell, "You and I need to go on alone from here. Nozzito is only four miles farther, down across the valley. If Corio is still there, I don't want him spooking on us, and get any farther away."

An hour earlier they'd heard an explosion and gunfire echoing in the distance, from the direction of Cedrianno. If they had heard it, they knew there was a good chance Corio had heard it too. "I got you," said Caldwell, already drawing his rifle and laying it across his lap.

Seeing what was going on, Jane stepped her horse closer to Dawson and said, "What? You're going to trust me alone with Tuesday Bonhart?" She looked toward Tuesday with a dark scowl, then back at Dawson. "Ain't you afraid I'll tear her heart out and take a bite out of it, soon as you're gone?"

Tuesday heard her and drew her horse up a few yards back and said to Dawson, "Don't worry about me, Marshal. I've managed to take care of myself in some of the toughest houses west of the Mississippi. Big talk doesn't scare me any." Inside the big wrinkled shirt Shaw had put on her, she'd hidden her derringer within easy reach. She sat calmly returning Jane's harsh stare.

"I don't know how Shaw stands it," Dawson said

sidelong to Caldwell, "but I'm all for leaving this mess, letting him sort it out to suit himself."

"I'm with you," said Caldwell. "But I don't want to see a wounded woman get sat upon by Jane Crowley. She can get mean, especially if it's over some gunslinger she's been moony-eyed over."

"What did I hear you say, Undertaker?" Jane asked. "Don't be bashful. If you've something to say about me, say it to my face."

"Yep, it's time to go," said Dawson. He said to Jane and the other two women, "We're riding into Nozzito. I'm hoping the three of you can stay away from one another until Shaw gets here." He turned his horse and nudged it out along the trail, before any of the women offered any more comment.

Jane and the other two women sat watching until the two lawmen had ridden out of sight. Jane grinned to herself and nudged her horse over closer to Tuesday Bonhart. "Now here we are, all alone," she said.

"Yes, we are," said Tuesday, cool and confident, not giving an inch in spite of her wound.

"Don't fight her, Jane," said Raidy, talking fast, hoping to stop a bloodletting from erupting between the two women. "Shaw is not worth fighting over. He didn't deserve you anyway. He wasn't faithful. I know because he went to bed with me! Tuesday didn't take Shaw from you. He didn't even know her then!"

Jane stopped her horse a few feet from Tuesday with a jolt of realization on her face. Slowly, she turned in the saddle to look at Raidy. "What did you say?"

"I said, Shaw didn't even know her—"

"No," said Jane, "what did you say before that?" She turned her horse quarterwise away from Tuesday, toward Raidy Bowe. "Did you say you went to bed with Shaw? While him and I were still together? You *slept* with him . . . then you *shot* him . . . because you wanted *me*?"

"Yes," said Raidy, "I know it was foolish. But I did it . . . and I'm sorry. Please forgive me. If I had not confessed to it, you would never have known."

"So, confessing it makes it all right?" Jane asked. She shook her head in contemplation.

Listening, Tuesday let her gun hand relax in her lap, still close to the derringer but sensing no need for it now.

Jane looked at Tuesday at length and said, "Don't worry, I'm not going to beat the hell out of you."

"Do I look worried?" Tuesday said coolly.

Jane ignored her words and continued, saying, "You're lucky I don't give a damn about Shaw anymore. Otherwise we'd be hooked together tooth and nail 'til one of us bit the dirt." She slumped in her saddle. After a moment of thought she said, "But ah, hell, we're all the same out here. We have to claw for every damn thing we got here." She turned her horse to the trail. "Come on, Raidy, let's get going. I don't want to have to see his ugly face."

"*Oui*, I'm coming," Raidy said. She moved her horse in too close for comfort, and Jane stepped her mount away a foot. "Damn, give me room to ride, little darling," Jane said. Over her shoulder she said to Tuesday, "You take good care of that gunslinging son of a bitch. . . . Somebody has to, I reckon."

Chapter 24

In Nozzito, Madden Corio knew the first thing he had to do was face the Jordan brothers, Grayson and Tolan, and tell them their brother Bert was dead. He'd done so with his four gunmen drawn close around him, at a hitch rail out in front of the Perro Blanco Cantina. As he'd expected, their first response had been barely controlled rage. But after a few minutes the two calmed down a little.

"Yes," said Corio, "I'm riding Bert's horse, sort of my way of keeping his memory alive." He patted the sweaty horse's head.

"How'd Bert get it?" Grayson asked, studying Corio's eyes closely. Corio stood with the reins to Bert Jordan's horse still in hand. He'd been riding the dead gunman's horse ever since he'd killed him, Tuesday Bonhart having stolen his bay and made her getaway on it. But that was something he didn't want to mention here.

Instead of answering, Corio turned to Max Skinner,

with whom he'd already worked out a story. "You tell them what you saw, Max."

"It was Fast Larry Shaw who killed Bert," Skinner said straight-faced. "I saw him do it. But I was too far away to get there and do anything about it. Luckily, some of Bocanero's rebels made quick work of Shaw. I saw them blow the hell out of him with a French grenade."

But Shaw's death brought the two little consolation. Grayson slammed his fist into his palm. "Damn it, I wish it was us who killed Shaw. I would have done it slow and painfully."

"Bert deserved better," said Tolan, although he wasn't sure what he meant by it. He narrowed his gaze and went on to ask Corio, "One question, Madden. What was Fast Larry Shaw doing riding with you and your men?"

"It's a long story," said Corio. "He rode in with Lowe's wagon drivers. Lowe took him in as a partner. Then Lowe and his young whore got in an argument and she killed Lowe, leaving Shaw in charge." He shook his head and gave a look of regret. "I've got to take responsibility for it. I'm ashamed to say, if I hadn't let Shaw in, poor Bert would still be alive."

Grayson and Tolan looked at each other as if coming to a decision whether or not to hold Corio to blame. Finally, Grayson said, "The way I look at it, Bert, you, me, all of us, we choose this life of ours. We know the risks. So long as Shaw is dead, I reckon we've got no axe to grind."

"Oh, he's dead sure enough," Corio said. "Max saw

it happen. . . . I saw his mangled body afterwards. He barely looked human," he said, throwing in a little more than he and Skinner had planned to.

"Enough said," Tolan declared. He motioned toward the cantina's open door, giving Corio the lead. "Come on in. Let's talk about what you've got lined up."

"The four of you keep an eye on the trails in and out of here," Corio said to his men.

"You got it, boss," said Skinner, reaching out for the reins to Corio's horse.

Corio handed him the reins, gave him a look and said under his breath, "Have these three take turns attending to their horses, and getting themselves something to eat and drink." He looked warily back along the street they'd ridden on; then he turned, stepped onto a low boardwalk and walked into the cantina.

Skinner saw the way Hooks had turned a curious glance toward Corio. He waited until Corio was out of sight, then said, "Don't let it bother you, Hooks. He gets a little overly cautious after a big job."

"Yeah?" said Hooks. "We're not supposed to eat or drink, until it comes our turn? Hell, if I wanted to be treated like this, I'd have joined the army."

"Do like you're told, Hooks," said Skinner. "It's my job to see to it things get done the way *he* wants them done. Don't give me a hard time."

Hooks gave him a harsh stare but let the matter drop. He hitched his horse to the hitch rail beside Brule Kaggan's and Harvey Lemate's.

"You'll get used to it, Hooks," said Kaggan. He and

Lemate gave a short chuckle and walked to the side of the cantina and stood beneath a ragged canvas overhang out of the sun. Skinner walked inside, joining Corio and the Jordans.

A half hour later, outside town, Dawson and Caldwell had ridden at a quick, steady pace down off the high trail and across the valley floor. When they'd reached the far edge of town, they swung around off the wide trail and slipped the rest of the way in on a narrow winding path that ran behind the buildings along the main street. At the corner of an alleyway, they stepped down from their saddles and carefully looked across the street at the five horses standing out in front of the cantina.

"There they are, all five horses," Caldwell said quietly.

"Yep," said Dawson, his Colt held up, his thumb resting over its hammer. "And there's three of the riders standing out front," he added. "Corio must be inside taking it easy, while these men watch his back trail." He glanced both directions along the dirt street, making sure he saw no other gunmen standing around.

"What do you say, Marshal?" Caldwell asked, sliding his rifle from its scabbard and levering a round into its chamber. He stared expectantly at Dawson.

"Let's take them," Dawson replied.

Across the street, Max Skinner walked out of the cantina carrying a tin plate piled high with goat meat and beans. In the same hand as his fork he carried a bottle of mescal. Chewing a mouthful of the greasy meat, he said to the others, "All right, now one of you go get yourself some grub and liquor." He grinned with bulging jaws. "This ain't working out so bad, is it?"

Hooks straightened from against the adobe wall and flipped a cigarette butt away. He looked at Kaggan and Lamate, neither of whom made a move toward the cantina door. "I don't have to be asked twice," he said. But as he started to walk to the cantina door, a shot from Caldwell's rifle lifted him off his feet and slammed him back against the wall where he'd been leaning.

"Look out!" shouted Max Skinner, his plate of food flying from his hand, the bottle of mescal falling to the dirt.

Another rifle shot exploded, clipping Lemate as he made a long dive for the cover of a water trough five yards away.

Skinner got his Colt up and began returning fire as he ran for the front door of the cantina. But two shots from Dawson's Colt hit him, spun him on the spot and sent him stumbling backward through the front door. A third shot pounded into his chest. He flew farther backward inside the cantina. His pistol exploded wildly into the ceiling.

"Damn it to hell!" said Corio, seeing his right-hand man spread-eagle, dead on the floor. He ventured a look out and saw Dawson and Caldwell just as they moved forward and took new cover. "It's them damn lawmen who's been breaking up everything down here! They've got us trapped like rats here!"

"No, they don't," said Grayson, above the sound of

rapid gunfire out on the street. "We hitched our horses out back just in case we needed them there."

"We even brought along a fresh horse for Bert," said Tolan. "Looks like you'll be needing it, though, instead of him."

"Hell then, what are we waiting for?" said Corio, running along with the two brothers in a crouch toward the rear door, his gun drawn and cocked.

Out front, Lemate fired until his Colt was empty. In the dirt a few feet away, Kaggan had fallen dead. "Damn it," Lemate cursed to himself, looking back at Kaggan's bloody body. From the cover of the water trough, he'd heard the pounding of hooves behind the cantina and knew there would be no help coming his way from Corio or the Jordan brothers.

"Skinner? Are you up?" he called out during a lull in the gunfire from the lawmen. But he heard no reply. He searched his gun belt for more bullets but found the belt empty. He let out a sigh of resignation. "To hell with this."

Dawson and Caldwell advanced on the cantina, guns smoking, looking all around for their next target. "Watch the water trough," Dawson said under his breath as the two spread farther apart on the empty dirt street.

No sooner had Dawson said the words than Lemate sprang up, his Colt at arm's length, and let out a loud rebel yell. But as soon as his empty gun leveled toward them, both lawmen fired as one. Their shots lifted him and drove him backward against the adobe building beside the body of Robert Hooks. Lemate slid down, leaving a wide smear of blood behind him. His unloaded Colt fell from his fingertips. He lay staring straight ahead, his eyes wide-open, a dumb, bemused smile frozen forever on his face.

"Curio's getting away," said Dawson to Caldwell, both of them seeing the rise of dust stretching out from the rear of the cantina. The two turned and ran for their horses.

Having left Cedrianno, riding along the high trail in the gun wagon, Shaw heard the gunfire coming from the direction of Nozzito, on the valley floor. By the time he'd reached a spot where he could look out over the valley, the firing had stopped, and three riders had raced across the flatlands and up onto the high trail leading toward him. All that remained was a drifting rise of trail dust.

As Shaw turned away from looking down onto the valley, he saw Tuesday Bonhart riding toward him all alone, her horse at a slow walk. "Fast Larry, are you all right?" she called out to him. She nudged her horse forward with a pained look on her face.

"I'm all right," Shaw called out in reply. "Wait right there for me." He hurried the wagon horses forward with a jiggle of the traces in his hand, and stopped only a few feet from where Tuesday sat slumped in her saddle, her head slightly bowed. "The question is, are *you* doing all right?" he asked.

"Yes, I'm all right," Tuesday said, "just a little tired is all. This saddle is killing my back."

"Here," said Shaw, "this will help some." He stood up, reached out to her and helped her over into the wagon seat beside him. "Where's Jane and Raidy?" he asked. He took her horse's reins, stepped over the wagon seat and walked back and hitched the animal beside his speckled barb.

"They left . . . *together*," Tuesday said in a tired voice, giving Shaw a look as he came back and sat down beside her in the wagon seat.

"You mean . . . ?" He let his words trail.

"I don't mean anything," she said. "Who am I to judge Jane Crowley or anybody else?" She gave a tired smile. "I'm a whore, remember? I used to be anyway," she added.

"Maybe it's time you quit calling yourself that," Shaw said, "since you say you're not going to do it anymore." He put the wagon horses forward on the trail.

"Yeah," she said, "maybe it is time I stopped calling myself a whore." She paused, then weighed her words and asked, "If I could tell you who shot you in the head, would you want to know?"

Shaw considered it. Finally he said, "No, not if it was somebody close to me."

Tuesday knew he meant if it was Jane Crowley, he didn't want to know. "Why is that?" she asked.

"Because if it was somebody close to me, I don't want to go around reminding myself of it all the time," he said.

"I suppose I understand," said Tuesday.

"Besides," said Shaw, deflecting away any thought of who might have shot him, "I could have shot myself for all I know." He shook his head slowly. "That's how wild-eyed drunk I was at the time."

"You could have shot yourself . . . ?" Tuesday asked in a dubious tone. "You don't think about doing something like that, do you?"

"No," Shaw said, "not anymore. But I admit I used to think about it some . . . a few years back." He took a deep breath and let it out. "But I'm past all that now."

"Good," Tuesday said, sounding relieved. She ran her arm through his and snuggled against him. "I'm glad to hear that."

They rode on.

At a spot where the trail turned sharply downward toward the valley and on toward Nozzito, Shaw listened to the sound of horses' hooves drawing closer toward them. He stopped the wagon, untwined his arm from Tuesday's and said in a calm voice, "I want you to do me a favor."

"Sure, Fast Larry," Tuesday said, seeing his demeanor take a solemn turn.

"I want you to take both horses and walk them over off the trail, get them and yourself out of sight, just in case," Shaw said.

"Just in case . . . ?" She stepped down and stood on the trail looking at him, hearing the hooves herself, now that they'd gotten closer. "Are you going to be all right? Should I stay and maybe help?"

Shaw shook his head. "No, Tuesday. Please just do like I asked you. . . ."

Chapter 25

———

Madden Corio and the Jordan brothers, Grayson and Tolan, raced upward along the rocky trail, looking back over their shoulders toward Nozzito. When they came upon the gun wagon sitting sidelong, blocking the narrow trail in front of them, the three had to slide their horses to a halt in order to stop before running into it. "*Shaw!* You lawdog!" Corio shouted in surprise, being the first to see the single figure step around from behind the wagon.

"Hello, Corio." Shaw stood with his feet planted shoulder-width apart. "Surprised to see me?" He wore his battered stovepipe hat at a jaunty angle atop his head, revealing the side of his dirty head bandage. He had pulled back the right lapel of his swallow-tailed coat and hooked it behind the holster of his big Colt.

"What are you doing here *alive*, Shaw?" said Corio. "I thought Sepio Bocanero's men blew you up."

"It wasn't because they didn't try," Shaw said. "But I

got through it." He motioned toward the Gatling gun. "As you can see, I even came out with a souvenir."

"So that was you doing the shooting we heard earlier over at Cedrianno?" Corio said, already trying to think of how to get his hands on the Gatling gun and be ready for the lawmen when they arrived.

"That was me," said Shaw.

"So I guess I shouldn't plan on meeting my men any time soon?"

"That all depends on where you look, Corio," Shaw said.

Catching Shaw's threat, Corio said, "You should have been smarter than to try riding in and taking over Lowe's gang. What was your plan anyway, to take the stolen gun wagons to your lawdog friends?"

"To tell you the truth, Corio," Shaw said, "my head bothered me so bad, I must not have been thinking straight. I should have realized you'd double-cross anybody who got near you." He let his glance cut across the Jordan brothers, then back to Corio. "Is that what got Bert Jordan killed?"

From atop their horses, the Jordan brothers sat watching, listening. "What did you say?" Grayson said to Shaw with a hard stare. "Bert Jordan was our kid brother. Corio said you killed him."

"I recognized both of you," Shaw said, "that's why I said it. The truth is, Corio killed your brother. He killed him because he needed a horse, after his bay got stolen out from under him, by Lowe's woman."

"He's a damn liar!" said Corio. "Lowe's young whore didn't steel my bay. No damn whore ever could!"

"Then where is your bay?" Tolan asked.

"I told you," said Corio, "I'm riding Bert's horse, just to keep Bert in my memor—"

"Yeah, we heard all that," said Tolan, cutting him off. "But where's your bay? I've never seen you without that bay horse somewhere close by."

"Yeah," said Grayson, "so where is it?"

"Here it is," said Tuesday, stepping out onto the trail, the bay right beside her.

Shaw shook his head; he should've known she couldn't stay out of it.

"Remember? I rode off on it before you could feed me to your gunmen?" She posed her words as questions, as if to jog his memory. "You shot me in the back when I made my getaway?" She turned to Grayson Jordan and said, "Hello, Grayson."

"Howdy, Tuesday," said the big gunman. "I had no idea you were Dexter Lowe's gal."

"I wasn't for long," she said. "I had no idea you were Bert Jordan's brother." She nodded at Corio. "I saw his body when we rode back past him on the trail. He was shot in the back, left lying on the ground. His horse was gone." Pointing a finger toward the horse Corio sat upon, she added, "That horse." She let the thought of Bert dying in the dirt fester in the Jordan brothers' minds.

"She's a dirty lying whore!" said Corio.

"I know Tuesday," said Grayson. "She might be a whore, but she's no liar."

Tolan put in, "When we finish killing this lawdog, we're going to cut your heart out and show it to you."

He turned a burning stare to Shaw. "All right, *gunman*, fill your hand—"

Before his words even left his mouth, Shaw's Colt streaked up in a blur of glinting gunmetal. Tolan fell dead from his saddle as Shaw's first shot exploded. Almost as one, the second shot streaked in a blaze of blue-white fire, and Grayson flipped backward over his horse's rump and landed close to his brother.

As the two shots resounded out across the hillsides, Shaw stalled for a moment, his Colt poised and cocked, waiting to see what Tuesday was going to do. He didn't have to wait long.

Corio had swung his gun toward the woman. But Tuesday didn't flinch. The derringer came up, arm's length, as if from out of nowhere.

From twenty feet away the shot made a sharp pop as it fired, and Corio appeared to melt in his saddle. He had managed to draw his gun, but now it dropped, and so did his shoulders. He slumped in his saddle and wobbled back and forth, a strange babbling sound coming from his lips. His horse turned enough for Shaw to see the red gaping hole where his right eye had been. He saw a wide trickle of blood run down Corio's cheek like some sort of terrible teardrop.

Shaw found himself staring, impressed, as Tuesday walked forward, looked up at Corio, then stepped aside as he toppled from his saddle and landed in the dirt at her feet. "Good shot," was all Shaw could think of to say.

"I'm sorry I butted in on things, Fast Larry," Tuesday said. "But this pig shot me. I couldn't let somebody else kill him for me." She reached out with her foot and rolled Corio's face back and forth to make sure he was dead. "I hope you're not angry with me." The derringer seemed to disappear out of sight almost as quickly as she had pulled it.

Shaw shook his head. "No, I'm not," he said. He paused, then said, "So you knew Grayson Jordan too?"

Tuesday thought she caught a tone in Shaw's voice. "I know lots of men, Fast Larry. Is that going to cause us trouble?"

"No," Shaw said, "we both know what trails brought us here." He gave her a thin smile. "You've had your pick of men. . . . I'm honored that you'd have me, Tuesday."

Tuesday returned his smile. Her eyes took on a surprised look of excitement. "Does this mean we're together, Fast Larry?" Before he could even answer, she rushed into his arms in spite of her back wound, and she hugged him tight around his neck, in spite of his head wound.

Dawson and Caldwell, already in hot pursuit of Corio and the Jordans, had heard the sound of gunfire and raced ahead, their guns drawn and ready. But instead of finding trouble awaiting them, they topped a rise in the trail and saw Shaw and Tuesday Bonhart standing in an embrace amid the three bodies on the ground.

"Well . . . isn't this sweet?" Caldwell said to Dawson in a flat tone, slipping his Colt back down into its holster.

Dawson holstered his Colt as well and replied, "One thing you can say about riding with Shaw, there's a surprise around every turn."

Seeing the lawmen approach, Shaw and Tuesday turned, facing them on the trail, each with an arm around the other. When Dawson and Caldwell halted their horses, Shaw said, "I heard the shooting in Nozzito and figured you might stir something my way." He gestured toward the bloody bodies of the Jordan brothers and Madden Corio lying in the dirt.

"Obliged," said Dawson with a touch of his fingers to his hat brim. "How'd it go in Cedrianno?"

"They're all dead." Shaw gave a shrug and nodded toward the Gatling gun. "If I was going to stay in this business, I'd have to get myself one of those. This is perfect country for a gun like that."

"What do you mean if you were going to stay in this business?" Dawson asked. "Don't tell me you're thinking about quitting?"

Shaw gave a tired grin. "Not anymore, I'm not," he said. "I'm all through thinking about it. Now I've done it."

"What are you going to do?" Caldwell asked. He and Dawson watched Shaw walk to the wagon, reach over, lift the Gatling gun from the bed and drop it to the ground. Tuesday walked over, led both their horses back to the wagon and hitched them to the tailgate.

"Whatever we *want* to do," Tuesday said, smiling at the two lawmen as Shaw helped her up onto the wagon seat and climbed up beside her.

"Is that what you say, Shaw?" Dawson asked.

"Yep, it is," Shaw replied. He took a battered badge from his pocket and held it up toward Dawson. "Here, you might need this when you find a replacement."

"There's nobody can replace you, Shaw," said Dawson, shaking his head. "I'm not accepting your badge."

"Either take it or I'll throw it in the dirt," Shaw replied.

"Suit yourself," said Dawson. "I'm not taking it back." He folded his wrists stubbornly across his saddle horn. "You might change your mind someday. What else are you going to do?"

"I told you, Marshal," Tuesday cut in, "whatever we want to do . . . the first thing we think of every day when we open our eyes." She hugged closer to Shaw. "Isn't that right, Fast Larry?"

"That's right," Shaw said, with a slight tip of his tall battered stovepipe hat. "I couldn't have said it better myself."

"I think you might still be a little out of your head, Shaw," Dawson said, sincerely.

"I might be. . . . I probably am," Shaw said, seeming to consider it. "But this feels right." He patted Tuesday's hand lying on his knee. "Sometimes, feeling right is all you get."

Dawson nodded; suddenly he understood.

Shaw smiled down at him as he put the wagon forward. "Adios, *mi amigos.*"

It was the first genuine pleasant smile Dawson had seen on his friend Lawrence Shaw's face for a long time—too long to remember, he told himself.

"Can you at least tell us where you're headed?" Dawson called out as the wagon rolled away.

Shaw looked back over his shoulder; Tuesday turned with him, her head resting over onto his shoulder. "For starters we're headed to France," Shaw said. "We're going to Paris, to visit the Roman Coliseum . . . to walk along the Great Wall."

Dawson chuckled under his breath. He nodded, and called out, "Good luck."

"What do you think of that?" said Caldwell, watching the wagon roll away.

"I think it's good," said Dawson. "He needs a rest after taking a bad wound like that."

"A rest, yes," said Caldwell, "but you heard him. He's quit us."

"Quit us? No, I don't think so," Dawson said. "Notice he didn't throw his badge away?"

"Yes, sure, I noticed, but I don't think it meant anything," said Caldwell. "Do you suppose his head is still foggy? Maybe it's like you said, he's not thinking straight just yet?"

"Yep," said Dawson. "It's hard for him or us, either one, to detect, but you heard the doctor. A head wound like this can affect a man's thinking for the rest of his life."

"So . . ." Caldwell considered it for a moment. "You think he'll be back?"

"He'll be back," Dawson said confidently, gazing off toward the wagon as it rolled over the rise in the trail and sank out of sight.

"What makes you say so?" Caldwell asked.

Dawson looked down at the Gatling gun lying in the dirt. He looked all around at the rough, rugged terrain of the Mexican badlands, then back down at the big gun. Sunlight glinted along its dark iron barrels. "He'll be back. This is *his* kind of country. He can't stay away from it."

Don't miss a single page of action from America's
most exciting Western author, Ralph Cotton.

FIGHTING MEN

Coming from Signet in May 2010

Arizona Territory

Sherman Dahl looked down from atop the high trail at the small cabin standing perched on a rocky turn twenty yards above the braided waters of Panther Creek. He'd observed the cabin and its occupants for the past few minutes, hearing the harsh talk and laughter of drinking men, and a woman's worried voice rising from within the midst of it.

Dahl had already slipped his rifle from its saddle boot and laid it across his lap. But when he heard the woman's voice turn into a plea, followed by a short scream that ended with a resounding slap, he cocked the rifle's hammer and nudged his big chestnut bay forward on a downward winding path through a tangle of bracken and scrub cedar.

"You dirty sons of bitches!" Dahl heard the woman cry out as the cabin door burst open. "I hope you all rot in hell!"

Dahl stopped his horse again and sat still as stone, watching the woman run staggering from the rickety front porch down to the creek's edge, naked, holding a flimsy wadded-up blouse to the middle of her chest. From the open door, he watched Arliss Sattler step out onto the porch, bare chested, a bottle of rye hanging from his fingertips.

"That's right, whore—you wash yourself up some and get back in here," Sattler called out to the woman. "The night ain't even started yet." He laughed heartily; a gold Mexican half-moon ear ornament jiggled on his earlobe.

Dahl stepped the big chestnut bay sideways enough to conceal both the animal and himself from clear view. Yet, even as he did so, quietly, he saw Sattler's face turn up toward him and move back and forth slowly along the shadowy evening trail.

From inside the cabin a drunken gunman named Pete Duvall called out, "Don't let her get away, Arliss. I ain't had my turn at her."

"Don't worry, Pete. She can't get away from here until we let her go," said Sattler as he continued to scan the trail in the grainy evening light.

"What are you looking at up there, Arliss?" asked a gunman named Lou Jecker.

"Nothing to concern you, Lou," said Sattler. "I'm just looking, is all." He spat, ran his hand across his mouth and finally turned his eyes away from the trail where Dahl sat watching, having eased his Winchester stock up against his shoulder in case Sattler spotted him.

"Hell," said Duvall to Jecker, "pay Arliss no mind.

He's been edgy as a damn cat ever since we turned Birksdale on its ear and that rancher's little gal got shot." He eyed Sattler as the bare-chested gunman turned away from them to watch the woman splash cold water all over her and dry herself on the wadded-up blouse. "I think Curly Joe needs to come up with some jobs that require less killing. I'm of a notation that Arliss here doesn't like dirtying his hands with it."

"Don't you concern yourself with what I like or don't like, Pete," Sattler said over his shoulder. "I'll kill anybody that gets in my way, same as any other man in this line of work." He paused, then added, "Killing that little girl was something that never should have happened. It didn't make me a dime richer. Did it you?"

When Sattler's head turned back toward the open door, on the trail above, Dahl took the opportunity to nudge the big bay farther out of sight and down along the trail toward the cabin.

"No," said Duvall. He stood up and walked closer to the open door, stuffing his shirt back into his open trousers. "But Curly Joe likes for us to drop one now and then just to keep folks on their toes. Once word gets around, it shows the next town we ride into that everybody best steer clear and let us alone, else we *will* put somebody in the dirt." He grinned crookedly.

"That's not what it showed me," said Sattler. "What it showed me was that from now on, we can forget about ever giving ourselves up and going to prison. All that's waiting for us is a rope." As soon as he'd spoken, he shouted out to the woman, "Hurry up down there. We're all waiting to get back to it."

"I'm coming—keep your drawers on!" the woman shouted in reply. But as she dipped water in her hand and washed her forearm, she kept her head lowered and searched the rugged, sloping hillside behind the cabin, looking for her best escape route.

"Let Curly Joe hear you talking about giving yourself up and you'll wish somebody would hang you," Jecker said to Sattler.

Sattler turned enough to give Jecker a dark stare and say in a threatening manner, "I never said a damn thing about giving myself up, and I'll burn down any sumbitch who tells Curly Joe that I did."

"We're just talking here," Jecker said, backing away from the matter. He gave a shrug, with a show of his broad, empty hands. "Alls I'm saying is that Curly Joe figures we're in this until they ride us down. There's no giving ourselves up. You should have known that when we joined up."

Sattler let it go. He shook his head and took a long swig of whiskey. When he lowered the bottle and let out a hiss, he wiped his mouth and said, "Killing innocent bystanders is bad business. The whore says that little girl's pa is J. Fenwick Hatton."

"Do you mean James Fenwick Hatton of the Western Pacific Rail Lines?" Jecker asked, his expression turning to one of dread.

"Yep, one and the same," said Sattler. "He also owns one of the biggest cattle operations in this whole territory. His girl was in town shopping with the family's housemaid. Hatton and his wife were off somewhere. But they're back by now, I expect, to bury their daughter—knowing it's Curly Joe's gang who killed her in the street."

"So that means . . ." Duvall let his words trail as he contemplated what Sattler had said.

"It means, this time Curly Joe has gone and killed the wrong innocent bystander," Sattler said, finishing his words for him. "Hatton has a bunch of his men on our trail right now. You can count on it."

"A bunch of men?" Pete Duvall ventured a nervous laugh. "What, you mean a posse of range hands? I believe we can fight our way through them, no trouble at all." He looked around at Jecker and at a silent Chicago gunman named Chester Goines, also known as Big Chicago, for support. Jecker only gave him a worried look. Goines, who had sat quietly listening, continued to do so with a stonelike stare, his black derby hat cocked jauntily on his forehead. Finally he offered, "I wasn't with you on that job, men, so I'm not worried about it."

"But you're with us now," said Jecker. "If somebody comes looking for our blood, you won't run out on us, will you?"

Big Chicago gave him a look. "I've never run out on a pard in my life. I don't care if Hatton or anybody else sends an army of saddle bums and ranch hands. I'll stick."

"If you think a powerful man like J. Fenwick Hatton only has a few saddle bums and ranch hands working for him, you're not long for this earth, Chicago," said Sattler. He turned toward the creek in the evening gloom and called out, "Get on back up here, whore, before I come drag you back by the hair." He looked back and forth along the darkening creek bank. "Where the hell is she?"

"A man like Hatton gets whatever kind of help he's willing to pay for," Jecker put in, looking around at the faces of Duvall and Goines. "In a case like this, his daughter and all, I'd say he'd hire the devil in hell to ride us down, if the devil's for hire."

"Damn it, the whore's gone!" said Sattler. He reached inside the open door, snatched his gun belt from a wall peg and slung it over his bare shoulder. "Come on— help me find her!" Seeing the other three rising too slowly to suit him, he cursed, turned and bounded down off the porch and out across the rocky yard.

A hundred yards from the cabin, the woman heard them coming, running fast. "Oh God!" They were onto her now, she knew, gasping for breath as she pulled herself upward. They would catch her and they would kill her—

"Stop, whore," Arliss Sattler demanded, "or I'll cut your damn throat!"

She clawed and dragged and kicked her way farther up the steep, rocky hillside, making little headway, like someone trying to run in the midst of a bad dream. She wore no shoes and no clothes, save for the wet, flimsy blouse she'd managed to pull over her head on her way. The whiskey, some of which she'd drunk willingly and some of which had been forced upon her, had her struggling to clear her mind.

In what seemed as if only a second later, she heard boots pounding right up behind her through the loose, shifting gravel. "Where do you think you're going, whore?" said Sattler, grabbing her from behind by her blouse.

"Turn me loose," she pleaded drunkenly as the blouse ripped up the back and became a tangle of torn cloth around her neck and under her arm.

Being larger, more powerful, more sober and more able to run across the rocky ground because of his boots, Sattler had overtaken her easily. He held her firmly as the two slid down a few feet through the sharp, loose gravel. "Yeah, I'll turn you loose," he said roughly. He threw her over onto her back and slapped her hard across her face. The world seemed to explode inside her head.

Behind them, halfway across the yard, Jecker called out, "Give it to her right there, Arliss. Damn her deceitful ass."

"Break her damned neck," Duvall shouted drunkenly, the three men stopping only a few feet apart, their guns drawn and cocked.

"Step aside," Jecker called out to Sattler. "I'll put a bullet in her leg—see how she runs then."

"Uh-uh," said Sattler, dragging the woman to her feet. "She agreed to come out here and spend the night. That's what she's getting paid for and that's what she's going to do." He gave her a hard shove down the few remaining feet of rocky hillside and back across the boulder-strewn yard.

"We always get what's coming to us, woman," Jecker said as she staggered past him. He slapped a hard open palm on her bare buttocks.

"I say we all do her right here, right now," said Duvall. He swung an open palm at her behind in the same manner, but missed and almost fell before catching and righting himself.

"No," said Sattler, "get her inside and keep her there." As he spoke he looked around warily at the high ridges above them. "There's something out here that gives me the willies." He raised his Colt from its holster and gave the woman a rough jab forward with the hard steel barrel. But as she staggered toward the cabin, he kept the gun out as if he needed the security of it in hand.

Inside the cabin, Sattler gave the woman another hard shove that sent her tripping to the edge of a low-standing cot topped with a thin, dirty blanket. "Get started, whore," he said coldly.

"Plea-please, Arliss," the woman stammered, gesturing a hand up and down her scratched, scraped and battered body. "Look at me. I'm all dirty. I'm bleeding. Let me get cleaned up some."

"Naw, we already tried that. Remember?" said Sattler. "Now hit that cot and get your heels up," he demanded. Without turning to the others behind him, he said, "Goines, get over here. It's your turn."

But the Chicago gunman neither stepped forward nor replied. Jecker and Duvall both looked back at the wide-open doorway, seeing no sign of Goines, but hearing the sound of hooves pounding away in the growing darkness.

"Where the hell is Big Chicago?" Sattler asked, turning himself toward the waning sound of the hoofbeats.

The three froze in place as the door swung shut with a loud screech. From behind the door a tall figure in a long black riding duster stood against the cabin wall, a Winchester rifle in his left hand. He held it at belly level on the three stunned gunmen. In his right hand he held a black-handled Colt cocked and aimed in the same manner.

"What the . . . ?" said Sattler, his Colt still in his hand. Jecker and Duvall both still held their guns cocked and ready.

"Hey . . . ," Sattler managed to say in a calm, even tone of voice, "I bet you're one of the men Hatton sent to take us down." To Duvall he said, "See, Pete? What'd I just tell you? This is what comes from killing bystanders."

"Yeah," Duvall said, "I expect you were right about that."

Beside Duvall, Jecker took a slow, measured step sideways, noting how the barrel of the stranger's Winchester followed right along with him. "Yeah, but he only sent one man to take us in? That doesn't strike me as too smart on Hatton's part."

"He didn't send me to take you in," Dahl offered softly. He knew that having their guns in their hands would give them confidence, make them think they had an edge. That was all right. He'd anticipated it. He wasn't here to talk them down and capture them. He was here only to kill them—nothing more.

"You sure enough picked a tight place for a fight here," said Sattler, gesturing with his dark eyes about the small, confined cabin. "Like as not, none of us is going to live through this."

"Nothing's perfect," Dahl said in a calm, almost soothing tone.

"This woman will die too," said Jecker, getting worried, looking down the Winchester barrel from only a few feet away. He felt his whiskey wear off quickly.

"Maybe," Dahl said softly. "We'll have to see how it goes."

Duvall started to speak, but before he could form a word, a streak of blue-orange flame exploded from the barrel of the Winchester. There was nothing to talk about, Dahl knew. His bullet lifted Jecker backward and slammed him against the wall above the cot. The woman screamed and tried to roll away as the dead outlaw's blood sprayed her and his body fell limply on top her.

Sattler and Duvall instantly acted as one, their Colts coming up fast and firing. From beneath Jecker's body, the woman saw a streak of fire reach out from Sattler's Colt and seem to explode on the stranger's chest. But the stranger wasn't the least put off. He fired the black-handled Colt twice, thumbing the hammer back for each shot, taking quick but accurate aim as Duvall fanned three wild shots straight at him, kicking up pine splinters on the wall beside his head.

Dahl's first shot hit Sattler in the heart and sent him backward onto the foot of the cot, causing the woman to scream and kick wildly, as two dead men were now on top of her. As the cot broke under the weight, Dahl's second shot, deliberate and well aimed, hit Duval squarely in his forehead as the black outlaw wildly fanned his fourth and final shot, and sprawled dead on the dirt floor.